Caffeine N

Twisted

B.A. MORTON

Fiction aimed at the heart
and the head...

Published by Caffeine Nights Publishing 2015

Copyright © BA Morton 2015

BA Morton has asserted her right under the Copyright, Designs and Patents Act 1998 to be identified as the author of this work.

CONDITIONS OF SALE

All rights reserved. No part of this publication may be reproduced, stored in a retrieval system, or transmitted in any form or by any means, electronic, mechanical, photocopying, scanning, recording or otherwise, without the prior permission of the publisher.

This book has been sold subject to the condition that it shall not, by way of trade or otherwise, be lent, resold, hired out, or otherwise circulated without the publisher's prior consent in any form of binding or cover other than that in which it is published and without a similar condition including this condition being imposed on the subsequent purchaser.

All characters in this publication are fictitious and any resemblance to real persons, living or dead is purely coincidental.

Published in Great Britain by
Caffeine Nights Publishing
4 Eton Close
Walderslade
Chatham
Kent
ME5 9AT

www.caffeine-nights.com
www.caffeinenightsbooks.com

British Library Cataloguing in Publication Data.
A CIP catalogue record for this book is available from the British Library

ISBN: 978-1-910720-26-4

Cover design by
Mark (Wills) Williams

Everything else by
Default, Luck and Accident

Born in the North East of England, B.A.Morton writes across a number of genres including crime, romance, horror and historical fiction. After a twenty year civil service career, she and her family escaped the rat race and relocated to the remote beauty of the Northumberland National Park. She now lives in a cottage built on the remains of a medieval chapel.

A member of the Crime Writer's Association, she is a self confessed crime fiction addict. In 2011, her debut novel "Mrs Jones" a crime thriller set in New York, took second place in the international literary competition, The Yeovil Prize, and launched her writing career.

Website: http://bamorton.weebly.com/

Twisted

B.A. Morton

For Philip

My canny Geordie lad

There was a little girl who had a little curl
Right in the middle of her forehead
And when she was good
She was very good indeed
And when she was bad
She was horrid

Henry Wadsworth Longfellow

One

Today my life is set to change. An opportunity will drop into my lap and I'll grab it with both hands.

I read that in my horoscope so I guess it must true. *Yeah right.* Well, something has to change because my life is one long nightmare. Not the kind where you wake in a cold sweat, but the kind where you'd kill to get out of it.

I'm at that stage now, the killing stage. I've taken things into my own hands. Sick of being the one who waits, who follows, who plays the game – and that's why I'm here where I shouldn't be, doing things I shouldn't be doing.

It's good to be bad ... sometimes. It's even better when you know you're right. And I know I am, though that little voice in my head, the one that whispers sick things in my ear, disagrees. As with most things, *bad* comes in degrees, a one to ten scale, and according to that I'm far worse than everyone thinks but not as bad as I could be. So you see, there's room for improvement whichever way you look at it.

I see her face everywhere these days, even when I shut my eyes. That's not good, but not entirely bad. Motivation, we all need it. Most of us lack it and that's why the world is in the state it's in. In the motivational stakes I'm pleased to say I'm green for go and the rest of the world had better get used to the idea. Looking at her, looking at them, just provides that extra little kick.

The stage is set, the props in place – and if I say so myself, I'm exceptionally good at this. It's good to have a hobby. A vivid imagination and a knack for the creative go a long way. And it proves I'm good at something, despite current opinion. Soon I'll be trending in all the right places for all the wrong reasons. Hashtag psycho.

I run the nylon rope gently through my hands, letting it dangle and brush the wet concrete floor before snapping it tight. The cracking sound bounces back at me from all four walls.

Surround sound, perfect acoustics.

I smirk. The devil's in the detail.

The rope is longer than necessary and stronger than I need but that's good. The voice in my head agrees for once, and that's definitely not good, that's just weird.

I pace the room out, stepping carefully in the dim light to avoid the stains and spillages. Oops, sticky feet, such a messy business. There's a smell down here that has nothing to do with what's contained or restrained, but it adds to the ambience in a wholly appropriate way.

Decay. Good things turned bad. Bad things gone rotten. That pretty much sums me up.

Shit. The camera flash catches me off guard and I drop the rope to shield my eyes. It's set for multiple shots. Clickety-clack. Every picture tells a story. Isn't that the truth? I switch it off, job done for now.

I smile. I can't help it. I'm so close now I can almost taste their horror, their disbelief. Oh my, it's been a long time coming. Hysterical laughter bubbles up from somewhere deep inside and I clamp my lips tight shut to contain it. It wouldn't do to be seen hee-hawing like an idiot, not here anyway. I have a reputation to uphold.

"Shhhh..." I whisper with a finger against my lips. "Not long now."

I turn on the spot slowly. She's still watching me. She's always watching me. Blank eyes, frozen smile, but it doesn't work. The guilt trip, the accusation. She's history. A blank page in someone else's diary. I've started now so I may as well finish.

The others, the controllers, the people in my life who think they're a step ahead, had better watch out, because this time around I'm doing things by *my* rules. They think I'm crazy. They don't know the half of it.

Secret safe, I turn the lock, pocket the key and check my watch, thankful for the illuminated dial as darkness wraps me up and shrouds me from prying eyes. I'm running out of time. Everything is on the clock these days. Tick tock, there and back.

I'm sticking to the plan, crossing things off the list, checking all those boxes with a big fat virtual tick and it's all good, in a deliciously bad way. Methodical, that's me, and there's definitely method in my madness.

I take the stairs with caution, avoiding the rotten treads. Right, left, miss a step. Can't afford to come a cropper, not with so much at stake. And then down the gloomy hall, as graffiti eyes follow my progress. It's cool how they do that when they don't even move. Cool and creepy. I like it. I like this whole place. The way it settles noisily at night with creaks and shudders and groans. It's like a giant sponge, soaking up all the bad stuff and storing it for later. I risk another smile. I can't wait for later.

I slip through the gap in the security shuttering and pull it closed behind me. Now I'm outside, dodging the wino curled in the alley, breathing good air instead of conspiratorial stench and suddenly I'm aware of the rain. It's heavy with the promise of snow, but I'm not thinking of making snow angels, I'm thinking it's a nuisance I could do without.

There's a good reason why there's less crime in winter, it's too bloody cold. I stamp my feet and blow into my cupped hands. I should have worn gloves but it's too late to worry about that now. I shove my hands in my pockets and wait awhile at the end of the alley, torn between the need to get going, to get on with the next stage, but careful not to appear too purposeful to those who might be watching. I've done my share of people-watching lately, a necessary part of the job – know thine enemy – but I don't make a good stalker. Don't have the patience really, all that ticking and tocking, driving me on, counting me down to the time when I press the big red button and the world as I know it says, W*ow!* or W*hat the hell?* or more specifically W*ho* the hell? But I have what I came for and that gives my numb fingers a warm glow.

You see, I have what they want – and in the blackmail trade it's a seller's market.

I want to punch the air and yell out *Yes!* But I don't. Instead, I duck my head and step out into the rain.

Just got to figure out a way to use what I have to get what I want. And believe me, if I get this wrong, if I stuff up on the finer details, then my months of plotting and planning will go out the window and the voice in my head will be shrieking with delight. I can't have that. I'm the boss here, not her, or it, or whoever it is that whispers and teases. Sometimes I need a good push, and hey, *tease* is my middle name. But, now I'm being serious and all that has to stop.

I pull up my hood and keep my eyes down as I sidestep the silent underclass, the unloved, unwanted who scurry to grab the prime spots, to fuel their habits, not their bellies. They're headed for the bright lights, the best doorways, the richest Christmas pickings. I'm headed the other way. It's time to get going, to get back to where I don't belong. I have things to do.

Webs to weave.

Screws to tighten.

Mischief to make.

Two

Miller planned meticulously.

He always did.

It didn't pay to be sloppy when the stakes were high, and today the stakes were colossal. Caught as he was in the no-man's land between knowing what's right and doing what's wrong, he'd done everything he could to minimise risk and maximise success.

The perfect bank – central and yet minutes from the motorway. Big enough to justify the effort and a veritable money-go-round, easy pickings for the right crew – and Miller's team were certainly that.

The perfect time – deposits done, cashiers weary. Streets thronging with shoppers heading for home. Potential witnesses too busy thinking of the gifts they'd just bought to pay any mind to anything else.

The fastest car – procured less than thirty minutes earlier, engine still warm; owner oblivious to its removal.

This was Miller's last outing, and he intended going out with a clichéd bang. But as he reclined in comfort and inhaled the rich fragrance of the BMW's leather interior, he accepted a major flaw in his plan – he hadn't counted on the rain.

It splashed against the windscreen, fat soft drops that hinted of sleet and obscured his view. He watched, momentarily distracted, as the rain increased and the splats joined up, gathering momentum, advancing in ever-increasing sheets down the glass. He turned the ignition and the car hummed gracefully to life. Classical music enveloped him, the wipers swished and the world came back into focus.

The winter evening was drawing in, yet brightly lit shop fronts belied the settling dusk. Miller narrowed his eyes, dazzled by the reflection on the wet glass. Despite his external calm, despite ticking off his checklist and assuring himself he had all eventualities covered, the rain unsettled him. And the fact he was allowing it to disturb him, unsettled him even more. He needed to keep his wits about him one last time. He had to get this job done and then he needed to run, because once this job was over he'd have nowhere left to hide.

He undid the top button of his shirt, loosened his tie and checked his watch. When his mobile rang he allowed himself a wry smile. Dead on time, as he knew it would be. It was all part of the plan – his plan. So why did his unease increase?

"Is it a go?" the voice demanded. Miller expected nothing less. The guy was an associate, not a friend.

Miller considered the rain once more, the inconvenience of it, and then checked his watch again. It was too late to call a halt now.

"Yeah, we're on. You in position?" His adrenalin began to hike. Getting ready for that sports car moment when Jack Miller would go from zero to sixty in less time than it would take the super-fast motor he was sitting in. The feeling was familiar, electricity thrumming deep inside. He liked it, fed greedily on the buzz.

"Of course. Waiting for you. Make sure you deliver."

Miller ended the call, checked his watch again and edged the car into the street. Creeping to the end of the road, he made the slow turn, approaching the waiting taxis. He ignored the line, eased past it and pulled in two cars ahead. As he gripped the gear stick, the passenger and rear door were ripped open and two men fell into the car.

"Go!" The wiry man in front ripped off his Spiderman mask and grinned at Miller. "You won't believe how much we got, Jacky lad." He jabbed at the radio with nicotine-stained fingers. "Bloody hell, what's that shite?" He prodded again, found an alternative channel and pumped up the volume. Miller swallowed a sharp retort. Now wasn't the time to debate musical preferences.

The guy in the back threw a sports bag to the floor and leaned forward between the seats, whooping his satisfaction at a job well done. "Jacky, you pulled it out of the bag again, kidda."

Miller allowed a wry smile. That and a slight inclination of his head the only acknowledgement of his satisfaction. What did they expect? He always pulled it out the bag. That's why he was sitting in the car waiting and they were taking all the risks. He checked the rearview and pulled out into the flow of traffic. The rain had turned to sleet and as he put his foot down, the wipers fought to keep the windscreen clear. He ignored the motorway slip road, choosing instead to head for the river, the dark and deserted dockland roads – and a rendezvous.

"What's up, Jacky?" the guy in the back asked. His mask was pushed up on top of his head, his stubble almost brushing Miller's cheek.

"Change of plan."

"Since when?"

Miller flicked a glance in the rearview and caught his passenger's wild eyes. "There's been a pile-up on the A1, we need to go round."

"Frankie..." the man in front turned with a grimace. "...cool it. Jacky's got it covered."

"Yeah?" Frankie's eyes narrowed to thin slits as his knee jumped in time to the music, banging into the back of the driver's seat. Miller kept his eyes on the road.

The two began a game of sorts between the seats, Frankie and Spiderman, playing the fool. Brothers in arms, a bag full of money and a loaded gun between them. When the wrestling got out of hand, Miller shot them a glance.

"For Christ's sake, settle down. Anyone would think you hadn't done this before."

"Never gone this big before, Jacky."

"What do you mean? I told you what to take – no more – no less." Miller felt a twist in the pit of his stomach. This time around there could be no mistakes. First the rain and now Frankie getting above himself. "I tell you what to do. You do it. That's the way it works, the way it's always worked. It's why you're still young, free and single and not sharing a cell and watching your back in the shower room."

"I'm not your bloody pet dog, Jacky. I saw an opportunity and took it. Just wait till you see what's in the bag. We're set to be the talk of this town. I reckon some major respect is headed our way. No jumped-up hood from south of the river is gonna tell us what we can and can't do any more." Frankie raised his palm and high fived Spiderman.

The bass beat on the radio increased. Spidey hiked the volume until Miller thought the roof would peel right off the car. He inhaled slowly, in through the nose, out through the mouth. He had to keep calm for just a little longer. "You talking about our good friend Otto?"

"Who else?"

"Otto, who owns this town, who owns you, Frankie? You think he's going to take kindly to you running your mouth off – changing the plan? You forgot who pays your wages?"

"Nobody's paying my wages, not you in your Armani suit, not Otto and his heavies, not now. Not with a bag full of cash in my lap."

"You think he'll let you keep it?"

"Damn right," Frankie sneered.

"You think *I'll* let you keep it?" Miller flicked another glance at the mirror and Frankie lost the sneer, pulled out the gun and slammed it against Miller's temple.

Caught off guard, Miller's head snapped back against the headrest. *What the fuck!* He'd left no loose ends, was beyond suspicion; he knew that. It had taken two long, frustrating, years to get to the position he now held within Otto's company; a position of begrudging respect, trusted by Otto and his cohorts. The lads in the car were chancing their arm and flexing their muscles, that's all it was, they knew nothing. Greed had got the better of them and Miller knew all about greed.

"You're a dead man, Frankie," he hissed. Glad that this was the last job and he wouldn't have to listen to Frankie's shit for much longer. Frankie might be a good foot soldier, a decent bag man, but that didn't mean he wasn't expendable. The click reverberated in his ear as Frankie released the safety.

"You reckon, Jacky? You think Otto won't thank us when he hears how we got rid of his rubbish? You figure he won't give us the keys to the bloody city when he sees what we've got and listens to what we have to say. I'd say you're the dead man, Jacky. Dead and fucking buried."

Miller raised an arm to fend off the gun and the car swerved, skidding on the slick road. Cursing, he swung it back around and glimpsed a figure caught in the headlights. Yanking the wheel was instinctive, but it was the rain that turned the manoeuvre from one of avoidance to one that would change his life forever. He floored the brake and the car squealed in protest as it slewed sideways across the road. It hit the kerb, continued on two wheels and rode the side of the nearest building before flipping into the air.

Frankie shot forward between the seats, his propulsion carrying him into Spiderman's outstretched neck, which snapped on impact with a sickening crack but did little to prevent his onward journey through the windscreen. The gun discharged as the car continued to tumble, slamming a bullet into Miller's shoulder before bouncing into the footwell. Miller's arms remained rigid against the wheel as the car reached the pinnacle of its arc and began to fall to earth. As the deafening beat of the in-car sound system provided a grotesque backing track, Miller's head hit the airbag, Frankie hit the ground and the car landed on its roof – slap bang on top of Frankie.

Three

Crazy drivers!

I take a breath as I accept that perhaps today is not the day I end it all under the wheels of a car. But it was close, too close.

Bloody effin' crazy drivers!

I flex my fingers, stretch out my arms, checking cautiously for damage. Head, shoulders, knees and toes, *knees and toes*. I shush the voice, and continue ticking off my list, certain that my desperate leap to safety must have broken something. But I'm whole – for now. Someone up there is evidently on my side, and that's a turn-up for the books. The same can't be said for the occupants of the car.

I stare at it now.

A giant beetle lying crushed on its back, wheels spinning, motor still screeching, and above it all, the thumping, hideous beat. Like the hammers of hell, pounding out. I raise my hands, knuckles grazed and raw and press them over my ears. It makes no difference. The sound is in my head, in the ground beneath my feet, working its way into my bones. Relentless. This must be what it's like to be truly mad. I don't like it. Not one bit. The voice just snorts in my ear, not a proper laugh. It thinks I'm mad already.

Pulling myself up out of the gutter I stand a moment, swaying. I intend to do the right thing. I always *intend* to do the right thing. Sometimes it doesn't work out that way and today is one of those days. The phone is dead. The screen shattered, the casing split. Just as well I sent the pictures. I wasn't going to, not straight away, but the voice in my head nagged on and on and for once I caved and did as I was told.

Two heads are better than one – sometimes.

I hold it to my ear, shake it vigorously *like that'll help* and when it slips through my fingers I let it drop to the ground and finish it off with my heel. Easy come, easy go. Crap phones and bloody stupid drivers. They deserve every damn thing they get. Even as I'm thinking it, I know it's wrong, I'm wrong. I mean, the car is a write-off and the driver...well, it goes without saying. I glance around, hopeful that someone else might appear and take control of the situation, but the street is deserted and feebly lit. No one comes down here. No one but me, but then I'm not like everyone else. I accept the inevitable and reluctantly approach the felled beast. I don't need this. I don't want this. I shouldn't even be here.

One man lies on the ground, half pinned by the crushed car. A cursory glance tells me he's dead. My first dead guy and I don't bat an eye. Oh shit that rhymes, I didn't mean it to, I'm not that weird ... really. God, they're right about me, I'm not right in the head.

Should've taken your meds.

Should've done as you were told.

Could've, should've, the story of my life.

I circle the vehicle slowly, fuelled in equal parts by the desire to be good, the helpful heroine, the saviour of the day, and basic morbid curiosity. Curiosity wins out. A little beat starts to skip in my chest. Anticipation, adrenalin, like the first notes of a bad soundtrack, I try to ignore it. I avoid the shattered glass and lean in a little closer. Another man is crumpled into the darkness of the footwell, his neck at an impossible angle. Okay, two dead guys. The body count is rising and I temper my macabre fascination with sharp breaths in and out, but despite this, my stomach is churning. Crazy drivers perhaps, dead drivers definitely; dead as in mangled and bloody. Have I really just witnessed the end of life – just like that? Wham! Now you're here, now you're not. I want to say *cool* and the word almost tumbles from my open mouth, but I snap it shut when I realise how bad that makes me sound, and I'm not *that* bad. Not yet anyway.

I approach the driver's side. The door is open, twisted by the impact. Deep gouges torn from the tarmac distract me until I can't avoid the inevitable any longer. Soon, people will come, police, do-gooders, and they can't find me here – that's for sure.

Suspended by his seat belt, the driver lies trapped against the crushed roof, his dark hair matted with blood. Unbelievably one hand still grips the wheel, like he's still in control, *yeah right*, the other, slick with yet more blood, hangs limp. There's blood everywhere, more than I've ever seen in one place. My stomach reacts to this information even if my brain doesn't and I swallow the acid taste that burns the back of my throat. His eyes are closed, not tightly as if scrunched up in pain, but softly, his lashes wet against skin that carries the pallor of death. There's something about the scene that holds my attention in a ghoulish way. Time frozen, the '*what if*' scenario. One second either way and he wouldn't be here, covered in blood hanging upside down and I wouldn't be here staring at him like some gawking sideshow freak.

Get a grip, girl, the voice in my head sniggers. Not now, shut up, I'm not listening.

I drag my gaze from the macabre still life, or more apt *still death*, to the rear of the car, checking for passengers, finding none. My eye settles on a sports bag pressed against the back of the driver's seat. It jumps out at me from the dark interior – green, that sickly lime green that sends you dizzy and makes you salivate at the same time. It's a citrus thing, I suppose, but that's not why my mouth is suddenly watering. The impact has burst the zip and it's not sweaty sportswear hanging out. I squint. Try to look closer without getting closer – and I can't quite believe what I see.

Bags – cashier's money bags – lots of them. I can't resist the calculating smile that transforms quickly into one hell of a grin. High five, horoscope. Opportunity has just dropped into my lap.

Right place, right time. Alleluia!

The radio's pounding beat reverberates through the soles of my shoes. I want the noise to stop so I can think, so I can remember who I am and do the right thing, but instead I cast a guilty glance over my shoulder before grabbing the bag.

Shit! It's stuck.

Of course it is. It couldn't be easy. I don't do easy. I do complicated – in a big way. A further tug, but the bag remains fast and now that little inner beat is building into a *look behind you* frenzy. But I don't take heed, because now I've started I have to finish. I want the prize. It's in my stars, for heaven's sake. I deserve it. Bloody crazy driver almost killed me. A bag full of money is the least I deserve. What does he care? He's dead. I'm not. One more quick breath and I reach in past the slumped, blood-soaked body and prove just how bad I am.

The stink of petrol makes me gag. I fumble desperately with shaking fingers but I keep going. *Calm down, keep it real.* My mantra works. A final tug, the strap frees and I'm catapulted back onto the scarred tarmac. It takes me a few seconds to realise that the puddle I've landed in isn't rainwater but rather a growing pool of spilled fuel. Bugger! I realise that I'm part of this now, not just some random onlooker, an accessory to *what* I don't know, but I do know that I need to get out quickly. I scramble to my feet, stumble – stupid shoes – and reach for the dubious stability of twisted metalwork. *Concentrate.* The bag is mine for the taking and I could *really* use that cash. Mischief costs money. Even the voice in my head agrees with me. And then I see it out of the corner of my eye – a tiny spark beneath the rear of the car. Shit! I grab the door with one hand, the bag with the other and pull myself clear.

That was too close. I'm not a cat and I'd like to hang onto my one and only life a little longer. My inner beat is louder than the car radio. It's banging now inside my head, exhilaration adding tinny percussion to the mix. I turn to flee, my grin already wide.

Yes!

Right place, right time, today is turning out just fine – shit, another rhyme – and then wham! I'm stopped dead in my tracks... as a hand slick with blood shoots out and grabs my wrist...

Four

Miller couldn't move.
 Couldn't breathe.
 Seatbelt cutting.
 Lungs bursting.
 Head banging.
 Noise all around.

Suspended in the crushed metal box, darkness filled every void and panic scrabbled wildly inside him. Fear welled up like vomit and he forced it back down. He had to get out. *Get a grip!* He tried to focus, blinked blood away from his eyes, and a blurred image appeared. The grim reaper or an angel of mercy? He didn't care, he just needed out. Adrenalin loaned power to impotent limbs, and reaching out desperately, his fingers tightened around a thin wrist. The owner pulled hard against him but he held on. No way was he letting go.

Beyond his metal prison a spark ignited and the sudden searing light revealed a girl, pulling frantically to be free. Miller raised his other arm. He held the gun with a hand that shook. He held her gaze with desperate eyes.

"H...help me," he wheezed.

She hesitated, eyes sparking between the flames, the gun and the darkness of the street. Miller willed her attention back. The space was shrinking, the oxygen getting thinner, his fear, honed sharp by phobia, sliced at his gut. At that moment he'd have done anything, absolutely anything, to be free, but any deal was saved for later when she reached past him and released the seatbelt. He slumped free, landing in a heap against the dented roof. Curses diluted by relief spewed from his open mouth as his shoulder took the brunt of his weight.

He let go of her wrist, couldn't help it, couldn't hang on, but she didn't run. Instead, she gripped his collar, yanking him roughly as he struggled against the confines of mangled metalwork and buckled steering wheel. Crawling from the crushed space, he collapsed amid the burning petrol. He couldn't think, couldn't co-ordinate his limbs, blood obscured his vision. He fought to breathe as cracked ribs constricted his lungs. He had to move, felt the heat at his back, white hot pain lancing through his shoulder and with the last of his strength he heaved himself up, grabbed his saviour by the throat and pressed the gun to her head.

"Move ... now!"

Disbelief hounded the shock from her face, but he ignored the expression and gripped her tighter, the gun at her temple. *You're a dead man, Jacky!* The car and the girl spun, his vision distorted and he shook his head in a desperate attempt to clear it. *Dead and buried.* His knees buckled and, stumbling blindly, he pulled himself back. *Shit. Breathe, just fucking breathe.* He couldn't fall, knew if he did, if he lost his grip on reality, his grip on the girl, he was dead.

She began to run, and he kept pace, one agonising step after the other. One fist tangled tight in the hair at the nape of her neck, the other dangling loosely at his side, dripping blood, barely able to grip the gun. The hideous sound from the dying car chased them, snapping at their heels and when Miller thought it could get no louder, the flames reached the heart of the car, the fuel tank ignited and the force of the explosion picked them up like rag dolls and swept them across the street.

Gravel stung his cheek. But beneath him there was softness. He began to let go of his tenuous hold on consciousness, to drift. His eyelids drooped, his ragged breathing slowed to shallow. His taut muscles relaxed and gave up the fight and his finger loosened on the trigger. He was almost gone, very nearly at the point of no return, when through the backdrop of roaring flames and popping metal, came the approaching sound of sirens.

Miller jerked awake and, confronted by the young woman lying stunned beneath him, his systems clicked back on. Her eyes flicked open when he raised the gun and rested the barrel between them.

"Can...you...drive?" he rasped each word painfully.

Her pupils dilated, eyes crossing momentarily as she focused on the gun, then drifting back as she swung her gaze to his face. Her chalk white complexion was marred as his blood dripped onto her skin. Her responding shudder rippled through him, preceding her answering nod.

"Good," he grunted as he hauled himself up and dragged her to her feet. "In that case, you're coming with me."

Five

Bloody driver! I can't believe the cheek of him. I save his life and what does he do? He pulls an effing gun on me.

By the time we reach the nearest parked car, the guy is wheezing like a steam train and spitting blood and goodness knows what else. It's pretty gross and that thought sits in my head and cushions me from the voice that's just itching to guffaw at my expense. That's the thing about voices – they're never on your side, bloody spectators, knitting sweaters at the guillotine and cheering as the blade drops. He collapses against the car, almost done in. Just as well because I'm knackered from keeping him upright. But not so jiggered that I haven't enough energy to poke a stick or throw a stone.

I'm crazy. I do crazy things. It's who I am. Can't let the side down, can I?

Crap. Not this car. He can't have this one. It has to stay exactly where it is, where I planned. There's a battered van further down the street, that'll do, that has to do, because no way is he having this one. But he's dead on his feet and going nowhere and the voice is practically choking with the laughter.

Shit.

Okay. Deep breath. Plan B.

I grip the door handle and watch as he slides slowly off the bonnet. Before he hits the ground, I cock my head and smile.

"Keys?"

That pulls him back, mentally and physically and he gives the kind of shudder you'd give if someone woke you by bawling in your ear. He wipes the blood from his face with his sleeve and heaves himself off the bumper. God he's a mess, and as he rounds the car, I take a step back. He's bigger and meaner than me. I'm crazy, but I'm not stupid. He glances at the gun as if he's just remembered it's in his hand and then he raises it and side steps clumsily to maintain his balance.

"Fuck," he wheezes.

Yup, I concur silently. Nothing's easy is it?

I'm yanked roughly to one side. I'm surprised he has the strength and wonder briefly whether I've underestimated him. I get an *uh oh* from the voice, but before I can ponder further, he squeezes the trigger and the window shatters in a confetti of safety glass. I've never heard a gunshot that didn't come gift-wrapped in a TV show or blockbuster movie, but this is for real and it's so close, my ears pop. I flinch, I can't help it, but despite that, I slide a covetous glance at the weapon. Big respect, I could do something with that. Something that would definitely make the others sit up and take note. The voice sniggers and on this occasion I have to agree. There's mischief and there's mayhem. The voice prefers the latter. Okay, I guess the van is out.

Crap.

Just as well I have a Plan C.

He leans past me, reaches inside for the catch and drags the door open. "Get in!"

Another wave of dizziness closes his eyes and I take advantage and wriggle past him into the car. The seat is covered with nuggets of glass and I sweep them away impatiently. I should be running a mile, not sitting here, with his blood on my face, waiting.

Should've, could've ... just like I said.

He keeps the gun on me while he stumbles round the car. I almost laugh out loud. His hand is shaking, his aim a joke, but he thinks he's in control and I let him think it. When he finally falls into the passenger seat, he looks about ready to give up and die. If pain were a colour he'd be pulsing neon red.

"Just drive," he hisses, barely audible. Even the effort of moving his jaw seems to add to his suffering.

I lean in, all innocent. "Sorry, did you say something?"

"Just fucking drive!"

The words are accompanied by a groan like an animal caught in a trap. Despite the fact that he has a gun at my head, I can sympathise. I have a soft spot for dumb animals.

"Oh yeah – how?" I cock one brow smugly. I can afford to be a clever-clogs. He's on his way out, another minute or so and I'll be the one on top sticking a gun in *his* face.

Something shifts in his eyes as if his brain is trying to warn him to watch out, to be on his guard, but he's not listening. He's trying to figure out what I'm saying and I guess by now it sounds like Chinese or double Dutch because it takes a long moment before sluggish comprehension dawns.

"Shhhhit." The word is slurred. His eyes are rolling back in his head. He drags himself back again and I know it'll be the last time – this time around. I can almost feel each laboured breath as if it were my own. Bringing up one booted foot, he kicks at the housing beneath the dash and leans forward, his fingers slippy with blood as he tangles the wires. With a sudden jolt the car kicks into life and he collapses back against the seat. Raising the gun again, he turns to me.

"Drive – Now!"

Now? Well, now that I'm here, slap bang in the middle of *his* mess rather than mine, I'm kind of wondering what to do next and my brain is doing that hopscotch kind of thing, like a fly caught in a web, buzz, buzz, buzz and eff all to show for it. A trillion bright ideas all elbowing their way to the front of the queue, only to discover the shutters are down, *next checkout please*. I can hear the voice telling me what I should do, but that doesn't count.

I mean, he's right next to me with a gun pointed at my chest and my only saving grace is that his aim is slipping. It started at my head and is quickly heading south, which I suppose is an indication of his current state of consciousness. His eyes are closing and I can hear his breathing, it's quick, painful and if I'm honest I'm scared. Not that he'll shoot me, the gun has already slipped to rest on his knee, no, my stomach is twisting at the thought that he might actually die right here in the car next to me and then I'd have to do something about it, about him, and I can't get involved, not in that way, not yet. There's too much other stuff at stake.

I glance across. His eyes are shut tight now. He's out for the count, slumped in his seat, his head against the door and I know I should be doing the right thing. I know it, but I don't do it and that's my problem. That's always been my problem. I'm the proverbial problem child – all grown up. I could drive straight to the hospital and save his life, or straight to the police station and ruin it. Either one would be right, but instead I'm thinking, a bird in the hand or in this case a robber in the hand, must be worth something to someone – but especially to me.

So he's mine for the taking, along with his cash, and as I head back to the funny farm, my mind starts working overtime, calculating how I can turn this to my advantage. Because even if I forget that he held a gun to my head, he did almost run me over, and he did break the phone... *her* phone. So hell, someone's got to pay for that.

I take one hand from the wheel and ease the gun from his slack grip. He doesn't flinch and I take my eyes from the road and chance a quick look. I don't want him dead, not yet anyway. He's grey with pain, but he's breathing. Alive – that works for me.

I smile.

Shit-hot crook he may well be, but I'm in control now and I can guarantee he's never met anyone quite like me.

Six

John Samuels was frustrated. He prided himself on doing a good job. An excellent investigator and a good detective, he might never rise far in the ranks, simply because he lacked the inclination to do so. But he was determined to the point of obsession and tonight he'd been thwarted. For the past eighteen months he'd been one step behind the most successful criminal gang he'd ever come across. Tonight it appeared they'd slipped from his grasp completely and there wasn't a damn thing he could do about it. Justice for Samuels would have seen them serving a twenty stretch in maximum security, not lying dead on the street. He felt undeniably cheated.

"You found anything?"

Samuels turned from surveying the crash scene and greeted his fellow DI with a noncommittal shrug. It was a little early to find anything of value, evidence wise, but that didn't mean he hadn't formed a few opinions. The fire crew was finishing off, hosing down, making the area safe for CSI and Crash Investigators to do their job. He stepped sideways to avoid the tangle of pressure hoses and streams of water and foam snaking down the side of the street.

"Glad you could make it. You're late."

Baker gave a half smile. The odour of cheap booze and cheaper perfume clung to him. Samuels responded with a long-suffering sigh and awaited the latest excuse.

"I had a domestic."

"Blonde or brunette?"

"No, I really had a domestic. Marie left me. Took the kids – left the dog."

Samuels stepped back, unwilling to reveal his impatience and growing disinterest in his partner's marital disharmony. They'd been here many times before. Baker showed up for work when he felt like it, left when he'd had enough, it was little wonder his wife followed the same pattern. The fact he treated his job and his marriage like an inconvenience was something Samuels was sadly used to. The fact he got away with it was something else entirely.

"Oh yeah," he muttered. "What are you going do this time?"

"Sell the dog."

"Be serious."

"She's at her mother's. She'll be back." Baker turned to assess the scene. "So, what do we have?"

"One burned out motor vehicle and two barbecued occupants." Samuels gestured vaguely. The debris was widely scattered. He shielded his mouth with a cotton handkerchief, suppressing a cough. The acrid smell of burned fuel and tyres, along with the underlying tang of cooked flesh, made inhaling uncomfortable, but despite being advised to step back by the fire chief, he was anxious to get on, secure the scene and get out of the rain.

"Barbecue huh, you're making me hungry."

Samuels scowled. "Bloody hell, show some respect for the newly departed."

"You figure only two bodies?"

"Looks like it. They're pretty much cooked. It'll be dentals for ID. The petrol tank blew, so nothing's where it should be and that includes body parts. The guys in white overalls will do a recce, count up the bits, but there's only two as far as I can see."

"The driver?"

"Could be the gentleman under the car," Samuels grimaced. "Well, the majority of him is under the car, the rest is caught on the railings, we might get prints off that bit."

"But you don't think so?"

"There's a partial hand, pretty much burnt, it's hard to say."

"Forget the prints. I mean, do you think that's the driver?"

"No I don't. You know my theory, Martin. This had to be a three-man job. Two in the bank and one in the car."

"You're sure it's them?"

"Pretty sure." He gestured above their heads where an impotent street light hung, glass smashed by the force of the blast. Caught in the shards were the scorched remains of a Spiderman mask.

Baker shoved his hands into his pockets and turned away from the driving rain. "No sign of the money, I suppose?"

Samuels shook his head. "You should have been first on scene if you wanted a freebie. Probably went up in flames anyway. The lab guys will no doubt confirm."

"So, we can assume we're missing a driver and a million quid and everything else is toast?"

"Not quite." Samuels held out a plastic evidence bag containing a mobile phone. The screen was smashed, the battery hanging loose."

Taking the bag, Baker held it up between finger and thumb and turned it slowly. "Where was it found?"

Samuels gestured to the far side of the street. "In the corner, up against the wall; Might not be connected but it's all we've got."

"Witness?"

"Maybe."

"How come they didn't stick around?"

Samuels shrugged. There were many reasons why individuals made themselves scarce when the police were imminent. Conversely, crash scenes tended to pull a crowd, something about the draw of another's misfortune, the macabre fascination with death and the chance to see a body first-hand, but the street was empty, other than the plethora of emergency services.

"Anybody hanging out down here after-dark has got to be up to no good. They probably ran when they heard the sirens."

Baker nodded his agreement. "What do you think?"

Samuels cast a glance past the dazzling arc lights and back along the darkened street. "I figure they did the bank. Driver collects them. He picks up speed, hits something slick – and wham. No more bank robbers."

"Yeah, but what's he doing down here? Why not hit the motorway, head south for London and lose any posse in the big city?"

Samuels shrugged. He was cold and running way past the end of the shift. "Who knows? But if he did get out with the money, which is unlikely given the state of the car and the severity of the blast, he can't have got far. He's got to be injured and he's got to be desperate."

Both men surveyed the route the car had taken before it rode the wall. Baker crossed to the wreckage, weaving his way between smoke blackened fire fighters. Squatting down, he shone his torch into the burnt out interior. The guy who'd roasted inside was still there – what was left of him, contracted into a hideous inhuman shape. Baker rose to his feet and backed away. Shoving his hands back in his pockets, he narrowed his eyes and did a three-sixty degree turn.

"Any blood?"

"Not in the immediate vicinity." Samuels inclined his head toward the overflowing drains. "Likely washed away by now, but forensics will extend the search when it's daylight. See if they can pick up a trail. If there's anything, they'll find it."

Baker nodded and turned his attention to the collection of rundown warehouses that lined the street. Most were deserted, ready for demolition. "Have we searched the surrounding buildings?"

"It's ongoing, but the consensus is either he picked up a ride and is long gone, or he's bleeding out in the gutter."

"No ID from the crime scene? No one come forward yet with a description of the getaway driver? It's the run-up to Christmas. The street outside the bank had to be packed with shoppers. Someone must have seen something."

Samuels shook his head. "Early days. We've got the CCTV to look at from the bank and the street outside, but as for witnesses it's the same as all the other raids. Two armed, masked men hit the bank. They're in and out, no actual violence but plenty of threats..."

"Any sign of the gun?" interrupted Baker.

"Not yet. As I was saying...No one saw them once they left the building, no one saw the car. They do the job and then they disappear. It's well planned and they're well practised."

"Well, someone made a mistake this time."

Samuels pulled up his collar. "This damn weather will be the death of me," he muttered "and it was certainly the death of them."

"You think it's that simple," asked Baker "A skidding car on a wet road?"

"The crash investigators will map out the road and the skid marks, and tell us exactly. But here and now, with what we know, yes I do. I figure they might have been the best bank robbers in the business – hey you can't deny, they've been running circles round us for the past few months. But on this occasion the rain fucked them. It's as simple as that."

****

Baker slid behind the wheel and reached for the seat belt. Glad to be able to slip away quickly. Samuels had it all in hand. He had no intention of spending longer than necessary raking over barbecued remains and getting soaked to the skin while doing it. His wife wouldn't be home till the weekend and he'd a domestic to finish off... A five eight redhead by the name of Colleen.

His phone vibrated as he turned the ignition. He answered it reluctantly.

"Baker?"

The voice was curt, piercing. Baker felt the usual mixture of anticipation and loathing begin to simmer inside. He replied carefully.

"McKenzie."

"What have we got?"

Baker checked the rear view and eased the car away from the cordoned off crash scene. "Not a lot. Our man may have left the scene, he may have the cash. Or he may be dead and the money may have gone up in smoke."

"Lots of maybes. Any leads?"

Baker glanced at the evidence bag on the passenger seat and blinked slowly, suppressing a sly smile as he thought of the shell casing he'd plucked from beneath the smoldering car. It should have been similarly tagged and bagged. Instead it was nestled in his breast pocket "Maybe."

"Explain?"

"He may have taken a hit."

"That would simplify matters."

Baker hesitated "We ... we may have a witness."

"An unnecessary complication. Deal with it."

"In what way?"

"Do what you need to do," snapped McKenzie, "and Baker..."

"Yes?"

"I'm sure I don't need to remind you of the consequences if this situation is not resolved promptly."

Seven

"He's awake."

Micro's thick, nasal voice and pungent halitosis seep into my subconscious, dragging my attention back. I have to stop doing that, daydreaming. Only they're not exactly dreams, more like nightmares. Black voids filled to the brim with nasty stuff trying to climb out. No pink prancing ponies for this whacko. The voice snorts in my ear, *dreams or screams*, like it's all the same, but it's not. There's no waking up from these terrors. They're as much a part of me as the fillings in my teeth and just as painful in the creation.

I shoot a glance at my reluctant white-coated assistant and sigh. Not white, not now, not ever. White implies purity, innocence, Micro and me? we came out of the laundry basket a murky shade of grey. Nevertheless I hope he washes his hands more often than his clothes, but I don't hold my breath. I mean there's grunge and there's grot. Micro misses both targets by a mile and collides in a heap at the centre. He's been sleeping rough again. His carrier bag of treasures is stashed by the door, ready for a quick exit. I'm not tempted to peek. I inhale carefully. In the absence of a deodorant or suitable narcotic, I bite down hard on my lip. That works. I need to concentrate.

He's on the table, my new chum, Mr Bank Robber. Flat on his back, stretched out like he's waiting to be autopsied. That's not so far from the truth, there's enough blood pooling on the floor beneath him to give any self-respecting mortuary a run for its money. I step close, avoid the ooze and pivot on the balls of my feet, all the better to study my catch. He's stirring, not quite conscious but near enough. He tries to twist his head but pain and dizziness put the kibosh on that. He opens bleary eyes instead and I watch, amused, as my lab rat tries to make sense of his surroundings.

"Are you listening?" Micro mutters sourly. "I said he's awake. He's not meant to be."

"So?" I give him my *whatever* shrug. The one I know will rattle his cage. "Do what you have to do." It's hardly rocket science. I'd do it myself if I could but despite appearances to the contrary, Micro is the expert in all pseudo-surgery and under-the-counter pharmaceutical endeavours. I'm tempted though. I'm game for most things. I eye the scalpel clutched in his pudgy paw, employ a large measure of self-discipline and resist the urge to snatch it from him. I applaud myself silently. See? I'm not so bad.

"He should be out of it by now," continues Micro. "He shouldn't be awake. I can't do it when he's conscious." His wheezy, fat laden voice raises an octave, cutting straight through the nasal crap and it's shrill enough to make me wince.

Bugger. I can do without him and his histrionics on top of everything else.

Chummy groans and I can't say I blame him. If someone stood over me with a crazy look and a sharp knife, my heart would be tripping over itself to get out that door. His is doing that and more. I place my palm flat against his chest and his heart almost jumps into my open hand. The beat escalates and I squeeze ever so gently. I can't help myself. If he was a spider he'd be missing a leg by now. But he's not and I have to remember, he's not a pet, or a toy, or a weird exhibit in my hospital of horrors freaky sideshow, he's my 'opportunity' and there's no way he's slipping through my fingers. The voice agrees with my restraint, with a soft chuckle. *Pace yourself. He's going nowhere.*

He's hot, burning up, his shirt's damp with sweat and blood and god knows what. That's not good. I make a mental note to do something about it. Hose him down or strip him off. Either way, I'll wait to see if he survives before I get into the domestics. He tries to struggle but his muscles won't obey, hardly surprising since he's trussed up like a turkey and stuffed to the gills with happy stuff. Or maybe that should be *unhappy* stuff, he's certainly not smiling. He peers at me and struggles to focus, all I can see is confusion, fear, and absolute bewilderment. He's thinking *what the fuck?* If he's able to think at all.

Micro's behind me, creeping this way and that in his creaky plastic soled shoes, edging surreptitiously toward the door. It's an uneven shuffle on account of his gammy leg, but just because he isn't running doesn't mean he doesn't want to. It's obvious he wants out. He's shaking badly, coming down like a broken elevator headed straight for the basement – and if we wait much longer, he won't be good for anything.

I give them both my *who gives a shit* pose, hands on hips. Like I couldn't care less whether Micro stays or Chummy dies.

"Big deal," I shrug. "So he should be sleeping and he's not. Maybe he just needs an extra squeeze of the lemon or maybe you've lost your touch." I smile slyly. I do love to tease. He doesn't want to be here. I don't want him here either. I prefer to work alone, to keep my secrets to myself, but on this occasion I need him. He responds to my manipulation with an indignant snort. Not as hammered as I imagined.

Silly me. That'll teach me to make assumptions.

"Any more and I'll kill the bugger," he grumbles.

Beneath my palm, Chummy's muscles bunch. On a good day I suspect he'd be off the table like a shot with a hand tight at my throat, or the business end of his gun at my head. Fortunately for me it's not a good day for him.

Oh well, we can't all be lucky, can we?

He can hear us though and despite the fact that his brain is probably cabbaged, I guarantee a small part of him is wondering what goodies we've already injected, imagining them hot and slick, coursing through his blood stream. Bad idea, imagination can turn a shitty situation into something far worse. I should know. He begins to shake. Slight tremors begin at his finger tips and wriggle their way up his limbs. His heart rate increases way past the safe zone. Bloody hell, there's two of them at it now, him and Micro, effin' crackheads. I'm the only one in the room with my wits intact and that has to be a first. The voice sniggers. Yeah, I can see the funny side. But I'm not laughing. Drugs and fear – a heady mix that blur the sense of danger while intensifying the threat. He opens his mouth to threaten or plead but nothing comes out.

Oh well, best get on before he bleeds to death.

I shrug at Micro. "Don't be such a tart. You've done far worse than this. Just do it. He'll survive."

"It'll sting," huffs Micro. "He's not going to like it."

Chummy's eyes are drifting shut again. I doubt he'll even feel it. "It'll sting? Oh for heaven's sake, grow a pair. He's tied up. He can't hurt you, even if he wanted to. Just do it. You owe me. Don't forget that."

He wipes grubby hands against his lab coat, like that'll make a difference. I shake my head. "Don't you have gloves?"

"Gloves?"

He makes a move toward his bag and I reach out a hand to stop him. The bag could make it out of here under its own steam if necessary. I know for a fact there's nothing sterile in there.

"Forget it. Just get a move on, will you?"

He angles close to Chummy, eyes bulging, slack jaw working back and forth, like a cow chewing the cud. "You do know who he is," he mutters "who he works for, don't you?"

Now he's the one with the sly smirk. He gives me the look that has my blood boiling and the voice in my head screaming with laughter. The look that says he knows me better than I do, and the annoying thing, is that he probably does. He's privy to things I can only guess at, even if they are buried in the depths of his drug addled brain. I can't have that. This is my show. I make the rules. I count to ten slowly and paste on a not so sweet smile.

"I do now," I reply.

And finally, he gets exactly where I'm coming from and takes a shambling step back.

"And ... and doesn't that tell you something?"

"Of course. It tells me I'm lucky." I grin. False bravado, badly executed. Yup, Micro's not wrong. I've caught me a tiger by the tail, there's no question about that. I just need to make sure when those big sharp teeth come out they aren't bared at me.

"Lucky? Are you mad...?"

"Of course."

"... You'll get yourself killed," he whines, "You'll get me killed. I want nothing to do with it, with him, with you. I'm out of here. You're on your own."

He upends a chair in his haste to leave and the resulting clatter jars Chummy from his stupor. I press my hand down hard against his heaving chest. Not exactly reassuring, more like *stay where you're put, if you know what's good for you*, but either way he's not paying attention to me. He's breathing like a freight train. Bloody hell, the guy is gasping his last and Micro's headed out the effin' door.

"Hey, hang on," I attempt a softer approach. "It'll be cool. Trust me. Nothing bad will happen. You're good at this, you know you are. Just do your stuff and then you can be on your merry way and we'll be quits, friends again, all debts paid off and a few extra quid in your pocket."

He hesitates, the lure of the cash far greater than any perceived danger. The thought of being friends less of a bonus than you'd imagine. I mean, who'd want to be friends with me? *I* don't even want to be friends with me. I'm a bad friend but an even worse enemy – trust me on that. I let him stew for a second or two and that's all it takes for him to see sense, to realise I'm a safer friend than foe, and the door to slam back in its frame.

"And that's it? If I do this, that'll be us finished?" There's hope in his voice and now I feel bad. He knows I'm lying but I play along regardless. The voice tuts disapprovingly and I pretend I can't hear. But of course I can... *nag, nag*... there's no getting away from it.

"Sure. As far as anyone else is aware, I don't even know you," I continue, playing my advantage. "You don't know me. You can walk out of here with one hundred pounds." That gets a response. His bottom lip wobbles into a lopsided smirk. "Yes, you heard right, a hundred quid. That'll buy you a few jelly beans. Get you off the streets for a couple of nights. But ... I hear any whispers, any tittle-tattling, and you know I'll come looking. If I come looking, you know I'll find you. So please, just do yourself a favour, do as I ask and get it over with."

The threat of what I might do if he doesn't play ball erases the smile and he scrunches up his face, pig-like and ugly. He wasn't always like this. Neither was I. Things happen, people change, usually for the worse.

"Two hundred," he demands.

God loves a trier. "One fifty, and that's my final offer."

"You're sick ... you know that don't you?" he splutters.

"And whose fault is that?"

There's a pause, a long silence, broken only by the voice counting down in my ear. *Ten green bottles, nine green bottles* ... Micro responds before any can accidentally fall.

"Fine. It's your game, but don't say I didn't warn you, Babe..."

Babe? Er, No. I don't think so. I bite my tongue and focus on the scalpel.

"You make the rules and you think you'll win, as usual. But this guy..." He shakes his head at me as though I brought the devil home on a first date, "Just don't blame me if you get fucked."

"I won't." Is he crazy? Of course I will – blame him that is, but it's a moot point. No one fucks with me.

Piggy eyes blink shrewdly at me. "Okay. Hold him down. If he moves..."

"He won't move."

I lean all my weight against Chummy's shoulder. My seven stone zilch isn't much compared to him but he's not exactly fighting fit and I have motivation on my side. Even so, I err on the side of caution and hop up on the table with him. Straddling carefully, so I don't get covered in blood and he doesn't open up them peepers and think he just got lucky, I place both palms down and shift all my weight onto his chest, handy for CPR if it comes to that.

Be prepared – a motto to live by – literally.

The voice sniggers softly and I have to agree, I'm certainly no girl guide....although it has to be said, I'm very good with knots.

Anyway, he's going nowhere, unless he takes me with him, but just to be doubly sure, and because I can't resist, I dig my fingers into the hollow above his shoulder blade. He flinches and I intensify my grip as Micro yanks his mouth open and forces cheap whiskey down his throat.

"*Swallow...*" I taunt softly in his ear. He tries to struggle, to twist away, but it's a half-hearted effort, his muscles obviously deaf to the signals screaming from his brain. There isn't a damn thing he can do about it, about us, about the predicament he's in, but it's encouraging to know that he still has a little fight left in him.

My warm breath caresses his cheek gently as the scalpel slices his flesh. And in my head the voice cheers silently.

Round one to me.

Eight

Samuels should have given up and gone home but couldn't shift the feeling that he was missing something crucial and obvious.

Eighteen months' worth of investigations had drawn a blank. Despite hundreds of man-hours expended, he still had nothing concrete to work on. He'd lost count of the number of interviews he'd undertaken and the number of CCTV tapes he'd sat through. He was beginning to wonder whether, in the absence of any arrests, he was the one who'd end up carrying the can for the whole fiasco. There was a definite sense of those around him taking a considered step back while he stood the unwitting victim in the line of judicial fire.

Realistically, there were only a couple of outfits in the city with the intelligence and nerve to carry out such audacious crimes successfully, but despite pressure being applied by Baker, almost to the point of harassment, they'd been unable to loosen a single tongue. Samuels had to conclude that the jobs were being payrolled from outside the region, by a criminal gang far superior to any he'd come across, but he had a natural reluctance to hand over the case after investing so much of his own effort.

He needed to come up with something soon or those above him would step in and take matters into their own hands. What he needed was the driver, and Samuels was convinced he was out there alive – somewhere.

He stood at the office window and gazed out into the night. 11 pm and the station car park should have been relatively peaceful, but tonight it was heaving with reporters and outside broadcast units. *Didn't they have homes to go to?* The latest press release had set them into a renewed frenzy and Samuels suspected it had little to do with actual news and more to do with who could secure the best headline first.

Baker had been missing since his departure from the crash scene, supposedly to follow up leads. Samuels was doubtful that Baker's leads would lead to anywhere but his next conquest, but as always he would be given the benefit of the doubt, albeit reluctantly, as his unconventional policing methods had delivered results in the past and there was always the slim chance that he might uncover something while lurking where he shouldn't.

Samuels gathered up his things, it was time to head home. Maybe a break from the investigation would help him concentrate, or a few hours' sleep might recharge his flagging batteries, but when he pushed his way out of the exit door, any hope that he could slip away quietly was lost as he was immediately assaulted by a barrage of microphones and cameras.

"Detective. Detective, a quick word from you on the latest developments ..." The young woman from a national newspaper jiggled for prime position, thrusting her Dictaphone and ample bosom in his face. Samuels recalled her from an earlier press briefing. The lateness of the hour had not tempered her shrill voice, she was just as annoying and demanding. He hadn't the energy to deflect her. Her peers from the regional press, perhaps in deference to his beleaguered expression or in solidarity against the southern upstart, shouldered her out of the way.

"Have the identities of the deceased been confirmed yet?" asked the guy from the regional TV team, a microphone in his outstretched hand, a cameraman at his side. Samuels ignored him and pushed his way through the crowd.

"Do you have a comment regarding the previous robberies, detective?" The young woman tried again, ducking under the obstructing arm. "They are connected aren't they? What have the police been doing for the last eighteen months? Are they doing anything at all? The taxpayers have a right to know."

Samuels raised a hand to block the flash of the accompanying cameras and shook his head. *What are the police doing?* Sod all, according to the media coverage. Bloody press. If they would all go home instead of taking up residence on police property, perhaps he could get on and investigate instead of wasting time being polite. He drew an exasperated breath.

"As was explained quite clearly at an earlier press briefing, *miss*, any updates will come via the press office. I would ask for your patience in the meantime." He wished for some of Baker's bad manners. Baker would have quelled their insistence with a couple of choice words, but Samuels absorbed his frustration instead and pressed on through the throng towards his car. He fumbled his keys from his pocket, ready for a quick departure.

"The public has right to know if there's a dangerous criminal on the loose." A leather clad reporter sidled close, a familiar face among the sea of many. He caught at Samuels' sleeve as he opened the car door. "Come on, John. Give us something to work with."

"Ralph," Samuels acknowledged him with a quick nod, "Just because you've written shite for *The Gazette* for more years than I've been a copper doesn't mean I owe you any special privileges." Samuels wouldn't have listed Ralph Butters as a friend, but they had, on occasion, shared a pint and information, and more than once their collaboration had proved useful to both parties. This time though, there was very little he could add to the official line.

"Now, now, John," scolded the aged biker halfheartedly, "Just because you're having a rough day, there's no need to scupper mine. A couple of lines, an exclusive, that's all I need, and my editor will put that blasted P45 back in the drawer."

Samuels unlocked the car and slid behind the wheel. The collective newshounds, scenting fresh meat, swung en masse as the rear door to the station opened and two police officers exited. He and Ralph were left in comparative solitude. "Cameron on your case again?" he asked as he started the car.

Ralph shrugged. "New brush...what can I say. The bugger won't stop until he has an office full of southern namby-pambies."

"He doesn't care for the Harley then?"

"Never mind the bike, he's bringing in a ruddy dress code... I mean, come on, me in a suit ....not going to happen is it?"

"I heard he was cosying up to Newcastle's great and good."

"Trying to woo the investors, has big plans apparently."

"Lord save us from big plans," muttered Samuels. "Look, Ralph, if I had anything to say, I'd have said it. You know that. The public have already been warned that our suspect is armed and dangerous. As soon as we have something tangible to report, then I can assure you, the public will be the first to know." He shrugged his apology to the man.

"I'd rather *I* was the first to know. You have my number," Ralph murmured conspiratorially, with a quick glance over his shoulder to ensure the remainder of the pack weren't privy to the exchange.

Samuels smiled wryly. "And you have mine. Now, if you don't mind, I'm away home to my bed. Be sure to let me know if you hear anything before I do."

Nine

Today I went fishing for tuna and hooked myself a shark, and all my little grey cells are tripping over themselves, refiguring and rebooting. My horoscope was definitely on the money.

I watch, fascinated, as Chummy's eyelids flicker. He's dreaming some pain-filled psychotic nightmare and that's all my doing. Well, the psychotic part, there are enough drugs scooting around his system to send him to hell and back and by the look of him he's halfway there already.

Like a fly pinned out on a board, he's spreadeagled on the bed. He was heavier than I imagined, dead weight and all, and by the time I'd heaved him off the table it was all I could do to roll him onto the mattress and catch my breath. Bloody Micro was out the door quicker than a flea on a scabby dog, such a gentleman.

Battered beyond belief, it's a miracle he's still alive, according to Micro, but I take that with a pinch of salt, Micro's obvious attempt to cover his own back in case the knife slipped or Chummy's heart gave out during the operation. *Operation*, I use the term loosely, in truth it was more like the kids' game of the same name and I expected a buzzer to sound every time Micro dug deeper. Fortunately for all concerned, but especially Micro, the patient survived. Micro knows I'm crazy, but he doesn't know how far I'd go, so he keeps on my good side just in case. Anyway, it seems I've bagged myself a man who could teach me a thing or two about unsociable behaviour – and that's why he's trussed up now like a rabid dog. Like I said, I'm crazy but I'm not stupid.

He's photogenic, in a sick way, if you like blood and gore rather than *GQ* poseurs. Maybe this morning, before the crash, he'd have made the front cover, looking cool and dangerous in his designer suit. Now the shirt is bloodied and torn, the jacket in a heap on the floor, the contents of his wallet committed to memory and the only publication he's fit for is the *ten most wanted* poster on the wall at the local nick. His tie is in my pocket, folded all neat and small. Who knows when I might have need of something to tighten around his neck?

The voice likes that. I knew it would.

Great minds ...

The tripod wobbles on the uneven floor but this time I'm ready for the flash ... once bitten and all that, and bingo! One more for the album. He doesn't flicker. I could have some serious fun, but I don't. I'm not that bad ... yet. For once the voice doesn't egg me on. That's a worry. Something's up. But I don't have time to listen to the silence in my head. My mind is full to the brim with other stuff, important stuff.

Now there're two of them – her and him. And they *are* connected. They have to be. Why else would he land in my lap just when I need him? My well-dressed master criminal with seven pints instead of eight.

Blood – thicker than water?

Forget that, but you can't live without it and as he left most of his in the car, Micro hooked him up with some fluids. It's been trickling in, one drip at a time, keeping him hydrated, keeping him alive ... for me ... to play with. Drip-drop, tick-tock. I can't wait for him to wake. The anticipation tickles its way from my stomach right up into my mouth and sneaks its way out in a giggle. Crime doesn't pay, or so they say – shit, another rhyme. Deep breath – start again. Anyway, they're wrong, crime does pay if you're lucky and, despite what Micro might think, today I'm as lucky as hell.

I circle the bed, tiptoeing, catlike, on the wooden boards as if that'll make a difference. I could stamp my feet and scream in his ear but it wouldn't change a thing. The only thing he can hear is his own paranoia. I take a chance and trail my hand experimentally down his bloodstained cheek. His stubble is rough beneath my fingers, his skin hot with fever. He stirs and I step back.

Inside, he's fighting demons.

When he wakes, he'll meet one for real.

Ten

Pain yanked Miller back to the real world in short, sharp jerks. His body was slick with sweat. It coated his face, stinging his grazed cheeks as if someone stood over him rubbing salt in his wounds. He opened reluctant eyes to a yellowing, cracked ceiling. A spider's web of aged plaster drew his bleary gaze to a single bulb hung at its centre. The bulb was out, blackened and useless, what light there was, filtering in from elsewhere. He turned his head slowly, wincing. He felt the pillow, damp against his cheek, flecked with bloodstains and perspiration. Beneath him a lumpy mattress, the sheet sticky with yet more blood, adhered to his skin as he moved.

The room was devoid of the most basic requirements for comfort. Paper peeled from walls stained with damp. Curtains hung haphazardly from an inadequate rail, in a vain attempt to cover a barred window that flashed intermittently with the headlights of traffic rushing close by. The strobing lights speared his eyes and increased the thumping behind his temple. *Is it a go?* The words jarred in his head but his brain refused to supply them with meaning. Close by, a church clock chimed out midnight, and by the time it sounded the last toll, Miller's eyes drifted shut again, any attempt at cognition abandoned.

"Hello, Jack."

The soft, taunting voice lured him back. He re-opened his eyes, and this time his attention was immediately drawn to the only other occupant of the room.

She sat cross legged on a cannibalised car seat. Stuffing protruded through the ripped upholstery and the whole thing appeared at an odd angle, until he realised it wasn't the room skewed by forty-five degrees, but his own equilibrium. He blinked and re-focused his attention on the strange young woman. He recognised her voice from his nightmares but he didn't know her, had never met her and would have remembered if he had.

She watched him thoughtfully, elbows on her knees, chin on her hands, interest flashing in her eyes.

"Jack? That is your name isn't it?" She tilted her head and arched one brow, and he tried very hard to maintain eye contact with her. It wasn't easy. The room was moving like a ship in a storm and his stomach responded accordingly. "I checked your wallet, in case you were someone famous and maybe worth a call. But infamous would be a better description. You're no celebrity are you, Jack? In fact quite the reverse, you're just some dirty bank robber..."

Bank robber?

He shook his head slowly in an attempt to reset the channel. All the while she watched him, her amusement at his confusion escaping between twitching black painted lips. She'd called him *Jack* and that sounded familiar. He rolled the name around a few times, it would have to do for now.

At a disadvantage, laid prone on the bed, he tried to move, to sit up, but one arm was useless, restrained in a makeshift sling, the other tied securely by the wrist to the metal bed head, the rope so tight, the knot so tangled, he could do nothing but stare at it, bewildered.

"What the fuck?"

She shrugged, as if it was the most natural thing in the world to tie up a new acquaintance. "Hedging my bets, Jack," she continued in a sing-song voice, like she was speaking to a child or an idiot. "You're a dangerous criminal, on the *most wanted* list no less, didn't want you going psycho on me, did I?"

Psycho? Maybe she had a point. There was something about being restrained that pushed his dial straight to red. He shifted sideways, an awkward movement that released the tension on the rope at the expense of excruciating pain. He gritted his teeth and kept going, peeling unsteadily away from the sheet and heaving himself upright. A quick glance revealed the primary site of the pain beneath a sodden gauze dressing, strapped inadequately to his shoulder. Bruising radiated out from it like a freshly inked tattoo. Blood, sticky and black, oozed as far as his elbow. He eased himself free of the sling and flexed his arm and hand experimentally.

"Oops, I wouldn't do that if I were you..."

Too late, pain mocked him as he ignored her advice and swung his legs over the side of the bed. Smart-mouthed little bitch, obviously had no idea who she was dealing with.

Small and wiry, she probably wouldn't reach his chin all straightened out, but she had the feral look of a poacher's terrier, bright eyes and a '*go on, I dare you*' attitude. Her blue-bottle hair stood on end, as if she'd just stuck her finger in a live socket. It shimmered in the fractured, on-off light and he squinted at the metallic flicker. Like a hybrid Goth cat-burglar, she presented a theatrical, over the top image which was further enhanced by a plethora of piercings, and so far removed from his reality he could do little else but stare.

She certainly wasn't the type of woman he usually woke up to.

"What happened?"

Her lips merely twitched, and in the absence of a suitable response he glanced around, looking for additional clues, drugs, booze, anything that might help to explain the bizarre situation. His gaze swung from the empty whiskey bottle upended on the floor to the line feeding into the back of his hand and the bag dripping god knows what into his system. He yanked himself free with a grunt. She shook her head reprovingly and tutted her disapproval.

He badly needed a drink, water, coffee anything, just not alcohol, definitely not alcohol, his stomach heaved at the thought. He couldn't believe he'd fallen off the wagon quite so spectacularly. He had a burning need to pee, tried to stand, thought better of it and covered his indecision with a frustrated scowl. "Who are you?"

"That's not important, Jack. Not now, maybe later when we get to know each other a little better."

"Later? Forget later. Just do me a favour, cut the crap and cut the rope. I don't know what the deal is here but I need to leave, and you need to disappear if you don't want to end up in a whole load of trouble."

"Ouch, Jack, there's no need to be so testy. All in good time, I need to be sure you're going to behave."

"Behave?" He tugged at the rope. If it wasn't for the pain, it could almost have been a prank, a set-up, or some weird one night stand gone wrong. He had a sense of being on the clock, of being counted down and he had no answer to that, other than to run – fast. He forced himself to concentrate, to forget the weird stuff and stick to the facts. He was injured. He was in a strange place with an even stranger girl. "There was someone else here, before. I heard someone, a man."

"A man?" She spilled her derision into her hand as if the thought was so funny she couldn't contain her mirth. "That's generous of you," she continued when she recovered her poise. "He's a trier that's for sure, and he may yet live to regret his association with me, but as far as you're concerned, he's history. He won't be back."

Miller shifted uneasily at the flashing image of a scalpel blade. His heart rate hiked and remembered pain added to his load, threatening to tip him back to the oblivion of la-la land. He inhaled carefully, and felt his ribs grind their objection. "Just as well," he muttered "He's dead if he does."

Across from him, on her recycled throne, the queen of the macabre cocked her head and wrinkled her nose. "Tsk tsk," she scolded. "That's not very nice, Jack. Not very nice at all. He was doing you a favour. Tending to your wounds – and let's be honest, Chummy, you do have one or two."

"A doctor?"

"I didn't say that."

"A butcher?"

She smiled. "Getting warmer. Let's just say, Micro's clients don't normally have a pulse."

"Micro?"

"Micro...scope. He's a nerd. What can I say... he bombed out of medical school ... some unpleasantness in the morgue."

"Fuck."

"Something like that."

"Shit."

"Dear me, you are a potty mouth, Jack. Is that all you can do, curse and grumble? Be grateful. I paid your medical bill – well to be precise, you paid your medical bill, I just handled the transaction, but what the heck. Micro's happy, I'm happy, and you should be happy. I just saved your life. I could have dropped you off at A&E... or the local nick. I still could..."

"Why didn't you?"

"Fate. Luck. Whatever. You're my good deed for the day."

"I don't feel so good."

"You don't look so good either." She smirked. "I reckon you'll be seeing snakes and spiders for a little while yet, the perils of unlicensed and unlabelled meds in the hands of untrained medics. Was it two blue and one red twice a day, or one blue and three green thrice a day...? Who knows....who cares...intravenous is far smoother, don't you think? Anyway, don't worry, Jack. Give it a few days and you'll be the dashing, sports car driving, gun-toting villain again."

She'd picked him up and patched him up. He should be thanking her, but the words stuck in his throat, right there alongside villain. He had a dark sense of foreboding deep in his gut. Something important was unravelling as she spoke and he hadn't a clue what it was or how to stop it. The idea that, for once he wasn't totally in control was more disturbing to him than his immediate predicament. He swung another glance around the decrepit room and tried a different tack.

"Where are we?"

She raised one hand and tapped slender fingers thoughtfully at her chin. "Erm ... for now let's just call it the club house. You should be honoured, Jack. It's a very exclusive club, just two members, you and me. Oh and her, but she doesn't count, not really and to be honest, the less said about that the better." She suppressed a giggle with a hand clamped across her mouth. "Oops, sorry about that, Jack," she mumbled through her fingers. "It's definitely not a laughing matter is it? Got to concentrate... con...cen...trate."

"Right ..." She was crazy, if she was real at all, and Miller honestly wasn't sure. He tried to remember the day before or the night before. But there was no *before*... only *now*. He tested the rope again and felt the fibre bite into his skin. The pain was real, there was no getting away from that, and he still needed to pee. In fact his bladder felt fit to burst. He tried to ignore it. "How did I get here?"

"I drove you. Don't you remember? I'm your hostage...figuratively speaking that is."

She leaned toward him and as she did, his stomach took a tumble and he had the craziest urge to lean back out of reach, as if something inside had recognised danger, but his brain couldn't process the image. He didn't understand it. He could have swatted her aside with one hand.

"You put a gun to my head and forced me ... surely you recall that." Her black lips twitched a little more as if she was privy to a huge joke and he was meant to guess the punchline. "You need to remember that bit, Jack, because that's what's going to get you in a whole heap of trouble. Bank robber, kidnapper, two dead guys and a million quid. Tsk, tsk, naughty Jack. You don't do things by halves, do you?"

He glanced at the bag thrown in the corner, at the money spilling out of it. *You're a dead man, Jacky. Dead and buried.* He shuddered, tried very hard to unravel a little more from the tangle in his head – but despite recognising the vivid citrus green, he didn't have the wherewithall to work it out. "I put a gun to *your* head? Right, so how come I'm the one covered in blood, tied to a bed?"

"It's a very long story, Jack and I doubt you'd believe me if I told you." She leaned back on the seat, rocking it awkwardly on its mangled frame. The repeated metallic squawk as the rusted springs collided drew Miller's attention away from her momentarily. He snapped it back when she stilled the seat and continued. "It began for me when I did something I shouldn't and decided I liked it, but I guess it all started for you when I checked my horoscope. Do you believe in all that fate and luck malarkey? I didn't, but I certainly do now. You see, you're my *opportunity*, Jack, and you landed fair and square in my lap."

"Fate and luck? Sure, I believe in luck and I can tell you, your luck will run out if you don't get over here and cut this rope."

"Oh, Jack, I'm so scared," she cooed. "I mean here I am and there you are ... hogtied."

He supposed from her point of view he wasn't in the best position to demand anything. Then again she didn't know him, couldn't possibly know that he could land on his feet, turn the worst situation around and come out on top – usually. Today was a little different, he realised that. "Don't be lulled into a false sense of security, sweetheart. Come on. You've had your fun, untie me."

"Fun? I haven't even started. I saved your neck. You owe me."

"Maybe I do, but I can't deliver on it when I'm tied to a bed. Unless ..." He smiled. It wasn't a nice smile.

"Oh pleeez ... Like I said, you need to promise to behave."

"Scared I might hurt you?"

"Scared you might do something stupid that would mean I would have to hurt you."

He smiled for real then. "Like that's going to happen."

"How do you know it didn't happen already, Jack? Just because you don't remember doesn't mean you weren't yelping and begging me to stop." She dropped her voice to a whisper. "I can hurt you. Believe it."

Miller gave the rope a futile yank. "If you're so scared at what I might do that you had to tie me up, why did you help me in the first place?"

"Hey, get over yourself, Mr Big Shot Bank Robber, I'm not scared of you. I'm just being careful. No point in taking unnecessary risks this early in the game."

"The game?"

"Later, Jack, when we're friends."

He shook his head. "We'll never be friends. So I suggest you cut the rope and head out the door while you have the chance?"

"Is that what you want me to do? Walk out of here and bring back the police?"

Police? "It's what I'd have done in your position."

She arched one brow. "I didn't take you for a squealer, Jack."

Squealer. He could certainly make her squeal, if she would just undo the rope. "If I *did* put a gun to your head, if I'm the big bad monster you're making out, you should have run while you had the chance."

"Monsters come in many forms." She threw him a sly smile. "But to answer your question, I thought about it, Jack. In fact I thought about leaving you to burn."

"Burn?"

"You really don't remember? Some getaway driver you turned out to be. You nearly ran me over. You crashed your car. You killed your mates. You almost burned with them and would have if I hadn't decided to help you out. But hey, save your thanks for later why don't you?"

He peered at her more closely, an attempt to see beyond the Halloween dress-up. Twenties rather than teens, and way too confident for her own good, she obviously had an agenda, a sick and twisted one at that. So did he, he just had to remember the finer details.

"Thanks," he offered begrudgingly.

"You're welcome," she shrugged back at him.

"So why did you help me?"

"I couldn't have you die on me. You have something I want."

"Oh yeah?"

"Oh yeah..."

"So this..." he gestured vaguely to the makeshift dressing and the blood, "... isn't about being a Good Samaritan."

"Not quite."

Miller inclined his head toward the bag laid on the floor beside her, the bag that currently leaked money like a burst cushion. "Why didn't you just take it?"

"Tempting, but that's not what I want."

"Interesting," he muttered sarcastically.

"What's more interesting is the bank robber who couldn't give shit about a million quid."

"Oh I give a shit alright. But don't get carried away. I doubt it's a million."

"You haven't had a chance to count it."

He shrugged. "Take my word for it. You ever inflated an insurance claim? Swore you'd lost diamonds when really they were paste?"

She spread her arms wide. "Oh sure, I do that all the time when I misplace a tiara."

"Yeah, well, bankers are the biggest criminals out."

"You know a lot about bankers and criminals."

"It looks that way doesn't it?" She wasn't the only one playing games and he'd had a lot more practice. "But that's not important, it doesn't matter what I know. What is important is why this has anything to do with a little weirdo like you."

"Hey, now that's just rude. I'll have you know I'm a fully paid-up member of the weird brigade. I have a psych report to prove it. And hey, not so little, Jack." She unfurled herself from the chair and stretched, purposefully, provocatively.

Miller snorted his derision. "Forget it sweetheart. You're not my type. This *dirty bank robber's* not into Gothic revival."

She shot him a look, a mixture of amusement and something else. "Hmmm, emphasis on *dirty*, Jack, you look like something the cat dragged in, or what Micro pulled out the morgue." She wrinkled her nose, "and if I'm being honest you don't smell that sweet either. Petrol, smoke and bodily fluids are so last year." She gestured vaguely in his direction. "I need you clean, fit and ready for action, Jack. The bathroom's down the hall, though I can't guarantee it'll be spider free." She threw him a pair of green, paper-thin surgical scrubs and gave another little twitch of a smile. "Micro left these, a freebie from his last job. I suggest you go clean up and zip up. I'll change your dressing – and then we can get down to business."

"Business? That won't take long. By your own admission, you're my hostage, I'm your captor. You do as I say and we'll both be just fine."

"In your dreams."

He recalled her voice, sly in his ear, her breath soft against his cheek and the pain of the knife at his shoulder. Not dreams, nightmares.

"The rope?" he muttered.

"Your promise?"

"I promise I won't kill you tonight."

"Ditto."

Eleven

The bathroom was a cavernous, utilitarian space with multiple shower heads and a central drain in the stained concrete floor. Miller hesitated at the door, propped unsteadily against the wall, and considered the risks posed to his already dubious health by the cracked tiles and filth, before entering cautiously and scanning the space. The institutional stench of bad drains and caustic bleach battled for supremacy as he tried hard not to inhale. Whatever this place was, it was long since abandoned but the air of dereliction seeped from the darkened corners. He had an overwhelming sense of wrongness that he couldn't shift. He closed his eyes and took a shallow breath. He wasn't easily spooked but chemically-induced paranoia was playing havoc with his imagination. The last thing he wanted was to step inside but the alternative, to leave in the state he was in, covered in blood, would merely draw unwelcome attention and he certainly didn't need that.

"Go on, Jack, don't be shy. I promise I won't look." She stood a few paces behind, gun clasped in both hands, pointed at him like she knew exactly what she was doing, but it was obvious that she didn't. That didn't mean she couldn't shoot him anyway, by mistake, though he doubted that was her intention; if she wanted him dead, she could have simply left him to burn.

"Hey, knock yourself out," he muttered as he shed the remnants of his shirt, unzipped his trousers and finally relieved himself at the urinal. She stepped back into the wide corridor, and lowered the gun.

"No thanks. Once you've seen one ... But I'll be right here, just in case you get any ideas about taking off." She gestured to the expanse of empty hallway behind her. The walls, like that of the room where he'd woken, were damp, but here instead of aged wallpaper, institutional green paint peeled, water dripped at intervals from rusted light fittings and graffiti decorated the length of the corridor. "It's a maze. You'd never find your way out without me. So don't even try."

"What is this place?" he asked. The question, thrown over his shoulder at her, bounced back at him off the tiled walls.

"Can't you guess? It's a house for crazy people. I love it. How about you?"

He shucked out of his trousers and stepped warily into the shower. "I guess not, but then again, I'm not crazy."

"Give it time," she whispered.

He turned the faucet beneath the first shower head and somewhere above, a maze of ceiling mounted pipework began to knock and groan as if he'd just unleashed a beast. *Shit*. He shouldn't have looked up. He began to wobble and placed unsteady hands flat against the cold tile wall. Dipping his head, he hunched his shoulders painfully and waited, suddenly tense, unsure whether she was about to scald him or freeze him. Either was a possibility but regardless he hadn't the energy to move. Tepid water eventually spluttered from the ancient pipes, rust coloured initially, running clearer as the flow became stronger, not unlike what he'd just flushed down the urinal. His kidneys had obviously taken a beating along with the rest of him. He closed his eyes and wondered how she'd managed to provide any water at all in a building that looked set to fall down, but he didn't stress about it, supposing she'd put a knife to the caretaker's throat. It was the least of his problems.

When the chemicals in his system decided to come back out to play and the blood swirling in the blocked drain turned into writhing serpents, he turned off the water and grabbed a grey towel from a rack by the door. A quick glance in the silvered mirror revealed the cause of his confusion. His temple was a mass of bruising, his eyebrow split and taped, one eye almost closed. An angry line of jagged stitches dissected his shoulder. He pulled a face. *Shit*, whatever had happened, he needed to ditch the girl and get out of there fast. If he'd just pulled a million like she said, then it wouldn't be long before someone tried to get it back.

Something nagged at his subconscious as he pulled on the scrubs, a warning of sorts, but he sensed the unease unfurling in his belly had little to do with police armed response units and everything to do with her.

When he came out of the bathroom the little black ghoul was waiting for him, slouched against the doorframe, gun in hand. No chance to explore or escape, not that he felt capable of either. The walk back to the room where he'd woken was enough to confirm that he needed a few more hours before he could think about leaving. He tried to memorise the route, had forgotten it by the time they'd turned the first corner. Too many closed doors, everything looked the same. She nudged him through the only open one, prodding the gun at his bruised kidney.

"Hey," he muttered as he flinched away from the barrel.

"Yup," she replied. "It's turning into one of those days isn't it?" She closed the door behind them, slid the bolt and turned the key. "Just in case you get any ideas," she said as she slipped the key in her pocket and turned; fresh dressings and tape in her hand, a glint in her eye. Little Miz Frankenstein ready to do her worst for the monster.

"The bullet was a devil to get out," she murmured with ill-concealed, macabre fascination as she inspected his shoulder wound, trailing her polished black fingernails over his skin, following the line of stitches. "Such a little thing and such a lot of damage, I'm afraid Micro had to dig deep. It's going to throb...for quite a while."

He flinched. *Bullet?* He didn't remember getting shot. The details were jumbled up along with his concussion. He'd robbed a bank according to her – and as the evidence lay in a bag on the floor, there wasn't much point in denying it. He didn't get the feeling that the picture was entirely wrong, just in need of fine tuning.

She leaned in close, her hair, stiff with gel, brushed his chin as she worked. Tearing off strips of tape with her teeth, she secured the gauze efficiently. She wasn't squeamish and she wasn't fazed by any threat he might pose. That was a mistake, a big mistake, but Miller gave her that one for free. He was far too wrecked to take advantage. He caught a whiff of musky perfume, or maybe she'd been burning incense – or embalming fluid, anything was possible. Either way, he leaned away from her. As if sensing his disinterest she responded by pressing her thumb against the centre of the gauze.

"Jeez...!"

"Oops," she replied with a sly smile. "Did I hurt you, Jack?"

His hand shot out instinctively and he yanked her off, and held her suspended awkwardly by one unbelievably thin wrist. One squeeze and her bone would snap, and that would be it, game over – for her. The temptation was almost too much, but the muscles in his extended arm screamed at him to let go. He hung on and squeezed a little harder.

"Are you crazy? Quit playing your fucking games ... *sweetheart*."

"*Effin'* this *effin'* that, dear me, pick a new word, Jack. Your mother would be ashamed of you. I'm not playing, I can assure you, and please don't call me sweetheart. I'm not sweet and my heart is cold, grey granite. Or so my doctor tells me."

He glared at her, loosened his grip and allowed her to slip from his grasp. He knew he'd hurt her, the angry finger marks encircling her wrist told him that, but he guessed she was holding it in and to be fair, she was doing a pretty good job of it. He wondered what he'd have to do to make her yell. He noted the faint white lines criss-crossing her forearm before she had time to pull down her sleeve, met the defiance in her eyes questioningly and then let it go with a shrug. It was none of his business if the little freak wanted to carve an entire road map on her skin, but it answered his question. She wouldn't yell, ever.

"So, what *is* your name?" he asked as he eased back against the pillow, thankful to be sitting down instead of falling down.

She recovered quickly with a hint of a smile. "Take your pick, what would you like to call me?"

More games. Miller shook his head wearily, reckoned maybe this *was* all a dream and in reality he was sunning himself on a beach somewhere. Or maybe he was dead and already in hell. "A nightmare is what I'd call you."

Black lips and sharp white teeth formed themselves into a grin. *All the better to eat you with.* Miller shuddered, her whole mischief and undead combo unnerved him. Like she was some crazed escapee and somewhere, a man in a white coat had just discovered her padded cell was empty.

"Hey, Jack, show a little gratitude. If it wasn't for me you'd have blown up in the car along with your mates."

The worm turned then in his head, and he heard it, the noise of the incessant music, the explosion. He felt the white hot heat searing his flesh, her hand at his collar pulling him. Saw fragmented images, none of which made any sense. He pulled himself back with a jolt and saw how she narrowed her eyes, studying him. Looking for weakness like a hyena following the herd.

"Mates?"

"Accomplices? Partners in crime? Whatever." She shrugged, reached past him for the remote and flicked on the ancient TV. "Don't take my word for it *Mr Bank Robber* – you're all over the news, check it out yourself."

There was no sound, apart from the soft crackle of static, but he didn't need it. He was headlining. The mangled burned-out wreck of a car flashed on the screen as reporters jostled to get the latest press release from a harassed police official. Up to date news feed, scrolling along the foot, declared him as armed and extremely dangerous. Having pulled off a million pound bank heist, he'd killed his accomplices in a high speed crash and was now at large. Members of the public were being advised not to approach, but to call 999 with any sighting.

"Okay, so I robbed a bank..." It was starting to come back, the wait in the car, the sleet on the screen ... and all the other stuff. Shit! He hadn't robbed the bank, not exactly ... but he had set it up and it wasn't the first time either. "Why didn't you call 999? Why did you patch me up?"

"It's complicated. I'll explain later. Too much detail makes Jack a confused boy."

"According to that I'm armed and extremely dangerous. I could get rid of you just like that." He snapped his fingers and returned his attention to the TV. They were showing pictures of his accomplices, grainy black and white security camera shots, but crucially no image of him – yet. He recognised them, Frankie and Spidey, but only in a distant, guy in the street kind of way. As if it wasn't real. As if he was watching someone else's train wreck of a life play out on TV.

"Armed? Oh of course, silly me. And your gun is, where, exactly?"

When he looked around it was back in her hand. She ran her fingers along the length of the barrel and dropped her gaze to the smattering of dark hair on his belly. Miller shook his head.

"Don't play with that. It's loaded."

She grinned, "Oh, I'm not playing, Jack."

"Yeah? Well don't point it at me."

"Mmm, perhaps you're right. One bullet hole is enough to be going on with. Two would just be greedy. A bullet saved is ... a bullet saved. Who knows when we might need it?"

"*We?* There is no *we*."

"I disagree."

"That figures. Look, why don't you go find someone else to torture?" he muttered. "Or, better still top up the pain relief and leave me to die in peace."

She laid the gun to one side and reached for a small nylon backpack. "Are you still hurting, Jack?" She pulled out a box of super strength, probably illegal, mind altering capsules. She dangled them in front of him. "Micro left these. How pain-free do you want to be?"

He eyed her and considered the risk of allowing his faculties to be compromised to an even greater degree than they already were. Decided that in her presence he'd do well to keep his wits about him. He had stuff to do, important stuff that wouldn't wait. But he wasn't a fool and he couldn't do much at all feeling the way he did.

"Just enough to take the edge off."

"Tough guy, huh?"

"When I need to be."

"Good," she replied as she pulled a bottle of water from the bag. She twisted the cap, dropped one capsule into his palm and passed him the water. "A tough guy is exactly what I want, and for what I have in mind, you'll definitely need to be chemical free." She grinned. "Enjoy it while you can, Jack, tomorrow you start earning your keep."

Twelve

I can't quite believe my luck. A million quid, or even half a million, is nothing compared to him. That banged up, shot up, dirty bank robber is my ticket to freedom whether he likes it or not. But it won't be easy, I mean let's face it, on the one to ten badness scale, I'd say he's a few steps ahead of me. Big bad bank robber versus little ole' me. But then I'm crazy and that has to count for something.

He's sleeping now, reluctantly, drugged to the eyeballs on Micro's happy pills. He wanted to leave, had important bank robber stuff to do, but I couldn't have that, not after all the effort I'd put in, saving his neck and all. And anyway, he wouldn't have made it to the end of the road. Chummy's not looking quite as chipper as I need him to be. So for now he stays. Safe and sound where the police can't find him, 'til I'm ready for the next step and he's ready for me.

I have to be quick. So much to do. Busy, buzzy bee. There and back, down the stairs, down the ladder into the dark, check in on her, tighten the rope, set the camera and all that malarkey, and now him as well. I had it all planned down to the last full stop, but now everything is different and I need to adapt. Just as well I'm flexible. *Believe it.* The voice sniggers and I'm not entirely sure whose side it's on now. I don't trust it and I don't trust him. Why should I? He's a criminal on the run, with a gun. Oh shit, another rhyme. I have to stop doing that. It's creeping me out.

Down here in the bowels of the building, in my secret place, there's no sound except for my own breathing, and her of course, but lately she's been keeping her own counsel. That's good. It makes things easier, more clinical. To begin with I was on my own, then the voice joined in and it got a little messy. In my head that is. The room is messy too, her stuff – all over. The shoes, the clothes, the plastic, processed must-haves that make her what she is. They're all in a heap, waiting for me to up the ante, waiting for the next stage of the game. I step carefully around the central chair, checking the light, checking her. If the bulb goes I'm knackered, I don't like the dark and it doesn't like me, but I can live with the constant flickering. It's how I feel, off and on. Tonight I'm more 'on' than ever and I know it's all down to him. Jack. He's my ace card, my real life clockwork soldier. All I need do is put a key in his back and wind him up, and I do so love to wind things up. But I have a few little domestics to get out of the way first.

I pull the tape from my pocket and secure the latest images. I'm almost done, so close now. The second wall is almost complete. She's watching me as usual. Her fear is almost tangible, my anticipation, like acid drops, sharp on my tongue. I can't say I blame her accusatory stare. She's not long for this world and she knows it. Me, I'd be kicking and screaming to the last, but she doesn't. She just watches me, more fool her. Perhaps if she showed a little mettle I might not be here now doing what I'm doing and she wouldn't be here now, suffering the consequences.

Oh well, who knows? Perhaps the police will save her, or her daddy will buy her freedom, or maybe I'll keep her all to myself, forever, just in case. They think they're good, but I know I'm better, I've had lots of time to practise, and now I have Chummy on my side. So what the heck, let's get this show on the road.

I stand back to admire my work.

Brilliant, but brutal, whispers the voice.

Can't say fairer than that.

Thirteen

Samuels propped himself up against the corner of the desk and watched Baker through the open doorway. He was exhausted. They were eighteen hours into the crash investigation and he still hadn't managed to catch more than a couple of hours' break, let alone a crook, yet Baker had strolled in this morning like he hadn't a care in the world. Suit pressed, hair trimmed, smug smile in situ. Someone needed to have a word with him, a strong word – and if he didn't do it, personnel surely should. He took a sip of coffee and bided his time, not entirely convinced that Baker would take any notice of what he had to say. His thoughts were interrupted as DCI Davies, slipped unobtrusively into the room and took a seat behind the desk.

Davies looked like he'd had even less sleep. Pallid skin complemented his grey hair, and the way he sagged as he dropped into the seat suggested he carried the weight of the entire unit on his shoulders. Samuels suspected he probably did, and more. This case had run on endlessly, maintaining a high profile among news agencies throughout. The crash had merely ignited the frenzy. The press was on their back, the banking demi-gods were kicking off, funding was almost exhausted and despite having two of the gang laid out in the morgue they were no nearer to an arrest, let alone recovering the stolen cash. To date, almost ten million had been taken from four different branches of the same bank and questions were being asked in high places about police ineptitude and the general state of lawlessness that seemed prevalent in city. The fact that many more millions had been lost via bankers' bonuses and irregular accounting seemed to have been glossed over. Samuels suspected the full weight of the promo vehicle had been unleashed to ensure any blame for the sorry state of the economy was laid squarely on the shoulders of the criminal fraternity, and by default, the beleaguered police, rather than the unscrupulous pin-striped fat-cats. Davies was catching it from further up the food chain and it was only to be expected that he would dump his frustration on those beneath him. As if preparing to do just that, he straightened his tie, shuffled his papers and then fixed Samuels with a weary frown.

"Morning, John. You look as bad as I feel. Where's your other half?"

Samuels gestured to the outer office. "Baker? On his way, sir."

"On his way? He's always on his bloody way. I tell you, John, I'm not in the mood for his antics this morning. This ruddy case is headlining – and mark my words, it's going to get a whole lot worse. The press are buzzing like flies on hot shite and I'm sick to death of swatting them. There are various barmy theories circulating among those who believe they know more than those paid to fight crime, so we need to stay focused on what we have so far and not allow ourselves to get sidetracked by the ruddy cavalcade encamped in the car park..." He broke off and turned as Baker slid in, wearing a sheepish expression and shrugging an insincere apology. Davies scowled.

"Glad you could join us, DI Baker. Do you have a problem that you'd like to share?"

"Sir?"

"Or, heaven forbid, some information vital to the case?"

"Uh?"

"How else can you explain your poxy time management?"

Baker glanced at his watch. "Sorry, sir. I was following up on some leads. Forgot the time. It won't happen again."

Davies grunted his acceptance of the lame excuse and Samuels swallowed his annoyance. Of course it would happen again.

"Make sure it doesn't, Baker. I don't have time to sit on my hands and wait while you finish your latte or lemon tea or whatever piss comes out of the vending machine these days, and I have even less time to chase around after you." He turned his attention back to Samuels. "So, John what have you got? Please tell me it's something worth repeating. I have a press briefing scheduled this morning and I'd really like to report some progress and save the department from another roasting."

"There have been some developments overnight, sir. Not entirely conclusive but encouraging."

"There has?" Baker edged forward.

Samuels shot him a look. If Baker had been in attendance instead of chasing women, he would have known exactly what had transpired, but it wasn't his job to bury his colleague in front of the boss. Baker was perfectly capable of doing that all by himself.

Samuels pulled up a chair, dropped a thin file on the desk and took out an A4 colour print. "Main development overnight, it looks like we may finally have an ID on our driver." He paused as both Davies and Baker leaned in to get a better view. "Jack Miller, white, male, twenty-nine. He's a bit of dark horse. Served a couple of years for assault and then dropped off the radar. I doubt he's been squeaky clean since, so we need to know what he's been up to for the last couple of years and who he's been up to it with. Maybe he just copped for this last job, but I've always fancied the same man for them all."

Davies nodded. "You've made no secret of the fact, John and it sounds reasonable to me. If he is our driver and we can collar him for all four jobs, then I don't need to tell you how relieved the guys upstairs will be. We nab him and we follow his lead back to who we think is behind the set-up. We're talking big money here and big kudos for us if we nail them all."

Samuels studied the image for a moment or two, undeniably intrigued by the man who'd evaded capture for the past eighteen months. It was a typical police mug shot, with an arrest number tagged beneath. Miller was unshaven and had the usual hooded look of a captured man. The blackened eye and split lip suggested that he'd resisted arrest. But Samuels didn't get the impression that he was looking at a common thug. There was intelligence in the eyes, a cockiness that had probably earned him a good hiding at the hands of the arresting officers. Now Samuels had a picture of his opponent he felt re-energised to crack the case. He narrowed his eyes and studied the image a little harder. There was something nagging and he wasn't sure what it was.

"How did we get the ID so quickly?" asked Baker sceptically and Samuels was instantly pulled back to the conversation as

Baker continued. "There was nothing at the scene, the car was toast and any forensics washed away by the fire crew."

Samuels nodded. "I don't expect forensics to come up with anything useable for a day or two yet, but sometimes things just work in our favour. We've had news bulletins going out hourly since 8pm last night. The crash attracted a fair bit of interest, some of it legitimate, some of it less so. We managed to get a halfway decent CCTV image from the latest bank, one of the robbers got greedy, jacked a customer on the way out, right in front of a camera. Can you believe that? A million quid in the bag and he rolls some guy in the queue. We got the image out on the 10pm slot and an anonymous call came in from a member of the public just after midnight. They put names on the two deceased and we're confirming with dentals as we speak. They also suggested our man Miller as a possible associate."

"Anonymous, so not yet verified?"

Samuels glowered at Baker. "No, not verified, but given the circumstances I think it's a good call. He fits the profile."

"Along with a good proportion of the criminal fraternity, Male, white, late twenties, priors for assault and, let me guess, car theft...?"

Samuels exhaled slowly. Baker's evening mustn't have gone as well as expected, perhaps his wife had shown up after all. Either way, it appeared he was determined to sour the morning's milk. Samuels was just as determined to prevent him. "Do you have a better option, Martin? Maybe from one of those leads you were following up that delayed you this morning?"

Baker scowled right back at him. "I'm just playing devil's advocate, offering another opinion, John. Anonymous tip-offs, crank calls, bloody waste of everyone's time. I just don't want you headed down the wrong road, that's all."

"So, that's a no to any further leads from your end then?" countered Samuels.

"Ladies!" Davies swung an irritated glance between the two. "Have we released any details yet, John? I want this bugger's face on every broadsheet, on every news feed in the land. If he thinks he can hightail it with ten million and leave us looking stupid he's got another think coming."

"Not yet, sir, I wanted to run it by you first. Obviously at this early stage details are currently hazy, and as DI Baker has rightly pointed out we need to keep an open mind, but I have men working on it as we speak. They're gathering everything there is to know about Miller. His current associates; where he lives, where he works. If he is our man, then we'll have his shoe size and what he had for breakfast by the end of the day. If he's not, then we'll have him eliminated from our enquiries."

"Of course it could all be a load of tosh, some aggrieved cellmate, looking to settle a score," added Baker, "and even if Miller is our guy, he's likely lying dead in a gutter somewhere. You saw the state of the car."

Davies shook his head dismissively at Baker. "Good work, John. Pull out the bugger's record. Speak to the original arresting officer if you need to. Get his details out there as a 'person of interest' if nothing else. I want this bleeder caught before the banks lose any more money and I lose any more sleep." He paused and zeroed back in on Baker. "And since you're so keen to debunk the ID, you can start by getting out there on the street, checking every ruddy gutter and see if you can't find me a body."

Samuels shoved his hands deep in his pockets, studied the polish on his shoes at some length, and when he was sure he could meet Baker's eye without smirking, he raised his head. "Let me know how you get on, Martin."

Baker scowled, pulled himself out of the chair and headed for the door. "I'd best get on with it, then."

"Good idea, DI Baker," barked Davies, "I'll expect your detailed report by the end of the day, but before you head out to the badlands, there's another case that you both need to be aware of, that's just waiting to slip into the vacant front page slot when the gutter press tire of bleedin' bank robbers."

He leaned forward over the desk and took over the computer. Samuels edged in to get a better view of the screen. "I'm sensing you're underplaying this."

"You're not wrong, John, relations between the department and the press are bad enough but this is where things start to get sticky. If this is as serious as I believe, we can't afford to drop the ball. This is just a heads-up at the moment, but I've a feeling in my water that it's going to end badly for all concerned."

On cue, Davies brought up a press image for an upmarket magazine taken at the premiere of a newly released film. A young woman clung to the arm of an older man. Blonde haired, suntanned, stick thin and balancing on dangerously high heels, her head was slightly bowed as she pressed a kiss on the head of a Chihuahua dog nestled under her arm. Both girl and dog were in matching outfits; the dog by far the more modestly dressed. The camera had caught her escort gazing at her cleavage, while the young woman glanced through lowered lashes at a younger man to her right.

"She looks familiar," said Baker, his attention on the cleavage rather than the face.

"She should," replied Davies. "That's Jasmine O'Hanlon...." He turned to Samuels. "John, I wouldn't normally be piling crap cases on you but you've had dealings with Robert O'Hanlon in the past haven't you?"

"The judge?"

"Retired now, but yes, Judge O'Hanlon."

"Only in passing. I was involved in a couple of court cases that he presided over."

"Didn't you head up the investigation into witness intimidation on the Taylor trial?"

"Yes." He shot a glance at Baker, who was itching to leave, presumably to get back to whatever he'd been doing before being called to the office. He doubted trawling the docklands was high on his wish list, but nevertheless, he seemed anxious to be on his way. Perhaps mention of the Taylor case had brought him out in a sweat. As Samuels recalled, it wasn't Baker's finest hour and had almost resulted in his suspension. "Baker and I handled that one. It must be two or three years ago now. I can't say I've come across him since. He's a bit of an arse, to be honest, sir."

"Pompous git," interjected Baker and both Samuels and Davies scowled their response.

"Yes well, regardless of what you might think of him, John, he thinks highly of you. So much so, he's asked specifically for your involvement in this potentially high profile, headlining case."

"Another one? They seem to be stacking up."

"You know how it goes, John. Never rains but it pours. I need you to get over to O'Hanlon's, get a statement. Find out what, if anything, is going on. Could be nothing to do with the fact that daddy was a hanging judge, but I'm not going to bet the farm on it."

"I'm sorry, sir, but you've lost me, what *is* going on?"

Davies blinked his confusion. "Apologies, John, lot on my mind, not enough sleep. I should have made it clear at the outset. O'Hanlon's daughter didn't come home last night."

"Oh." Samuels returned his attention to the image on the screen. The shot was not entirely complimentary. He made a mental note; perhaps not the best photo to release to the press if it turned out Jasmine's absence was something other than voluntary. Realistically though, one night away was hardly cause for concern. "Are we sure she hasn't just stayed with friends? Or spent the night with a boyfriend?"

"It's a possibility, John, but..."

"Boyfriend?" Baker interrupted with a snort, "Isn't she engaged to that bloody arse wipe who plays for the premier league? Or was that last week?"

Davies glowered at him. "As I was saying, John. It's very likely that her absence from daddy's breakfast table is quite legitimate, but her father believes otherwise and we have to consider the possibility that during the course of her partying, she may have fallen foul of something or someone. Just check it out. Speak to O'Hanlon in the first instance and see what you think."

"And Miller?" Samuels couldn't hide his frustration. The last thing he wanted was to go chasing after a girl who was likely off on her next jolly, when he was within a hair's breadth of bagging his most-wanted.

"DI Baker can take the reins on that for a few hours. If the laddo is face down in a gutter as Baker seems to think, then all well and good. If not, then we're running two cases until we locate Jasmine O'Hanlon."

"That's a tall order," said Samuels as he gathered up Miller's file.

"You don't need to tell me. I've had funding slashed to the point where overtime is a dirty word. I tell you, we'll be raiding the ruddy swear jar for pennies before the end of the week. Get your team to do the donkey work, John. I need you at the front end."

Samuels shrugged, he wasn't sure why he was suddenly detective of the month but with a young woman possibly at risk he wasn't about to argue.

"Did you meet her when you dealt with the Taylor case?" asked Davies.

Samuels shook his head. "Jasmine? No, I think she might have been away at university or finishing school or wherever rich kids pretend to study, we're talking two, three years ago. She would have been what? Twenty? Twenty-one?"

"Any initial thoughts?"

"Nothing helpful, sir." He avoided Baker's eye and gestured to the computer screen. "I'm afraid the image pretty much says it all. Rich, spoilt, daddy's girl who likes to party. I think she spends a lot of her time in London, socialising, or so the paparazzi would have us believe. In fact, that's probably where she is now. She's had a few high profile engagements, an equal number of high profile bust-ups. The meat and potatoes of the gossip columns." He smiled, "Not that I indulge in those kinds of publications, you understand, sir, but my teenage daughters seem to find the antics of the rich and famous entertaining."

"What about Mrs O'Hanlon?"

"Yes, I did meet her. Nice enough, not Jasmine's mother though. Argentinian I believe, didn't speak a lot of English. I think she's wife number three or four. O'Hanlon's a bit of a goat as I recall."

"Significant?"

"I doubt it."

"Well, get over there, John. He's expecting you. With any luck, Jasmine will be home by the time you arrive." Davies turned to Baker. "Are you still here, DI Baker? The gutter waits for no man. I want Miller, preferably with a bag full of cash and a full confession, but if a body is all you can find me I suppose that'll have to do."

Baker smiled. "I'll see what I can do, guv."

Fourteen

She woke him next morning with breakfast, Costa coffee in a cardboard beaker and a hot bacon sandwich, dripping with fat. If the bullet didn't kill him, the cholesterol surely would. While Miller had lost another six hours to the dragon, she'd been out and about in broad daylight dressed like she'd just shimmied down someone's drainpipe. As long as she hadn't been followed and the coffee was hot and strong he supposed he could live with that.

She'd been shopping, or more likely shop*lifting*, either way he was grateful for the clean clothes, which turned out a pretty good fit, but when she tossed him a fresh T-shirt with a graphic on the front resembling a do-it-yourself autopsy, he confirmed his opinion of her. The girl was a nut job.

He still felt like shit, wasn't quite sure how he'd got through the past few hours. Figured he had a way to go on the getting worse scale before things were likely to get any better. His shoulder ached deep inside like the worst kind of toothache, but the white hot stabbing pain and the screams that haunted his sleep had subsided. He eyed her suspiciously, wondering if she'd spent the night sticking hot needles in the wound just for fun and whether the screams belonged to another unlucky victim or were in fact his own.

He'd had some time to think. In the early hours when the traffic had slowed to intermittent and the flashing lights dulled. Between his determination to stay clear headed and his reliance on narcotics, he'd had a brief lucid moment when the world as he knew it had come crashing down on his head in glorious Technicolor. It wasn't pretty, didn't make a lot of sense, but had given him the feeling that he was central to something far bigger than he was currently aware. The details had faded but the feeling was still there, deep in the pit of his stomach. Like a rat trying to gnaw its way out.

The bank job he couldn't recall, the crash was merely a blur. According to the TV he'd killed two mates, but he felt nothing. No remorse, no sense of loss, and he was sure he would, or should, if indeed they were brothers in arms. As the drugs almost reclaimed him, his thoughts had settled on the girl. The freaky little ghoul who by all accounts had saved his life in order to get her kicks by playing mind games with him. She'd had no trouble getting to sleep, curled in the chair like a contented cat, claws retracted. He'd watched her purr as dawn crept into the room, bathing the drab interior in frigid light. Even wounded, he could easily have overpowered her. But why bother? Let her play her games; let her run around in crazy circles while he licked his wounds and made his plans. Making plans was something he was undeniably good at, *usually*. And while he apparently had something she wanted, he held the upper hand, even if she didn't quite realise it.

She held up her hand with one digit extended. "How many fingers do you see, Jack?"

"One," he grunted in reply.

She grinned at him. "Okay, ready to roll."

"I thought you were meant to be my hostage." He took a gulp of coffee, felt it hitting all the right spots, switching him back on, one nerve ending at a time. "How come you weren't swept up by an armed response unit as soon as you stepped out the door?"

"I adopted a cunning disguise." She dangled a pair of overlarge sunglasses between finger and thumb and gave him an *I know something you don't know* smile.

"Yeah, I would never have guessed it was you." He wolfed down the bacon sandwich and looked hungrily at hers. Rat aside, his belly was churning, he needed food to counteract the drugs – and while his shoulder was giving him all kinds of hell, he definitely needed those.

"Mmm, I should probably explain about the whole hostage situation." She took a bite, wiped tomato sauce from her lips with the back of her hand and forestalled him with a raised palm while she took her time chewing.

"Situation?" He wasn't sure which was more distracting, the food or the feeling she was about to throw him yet another spiked ball. He tensed in anticipation.

"Best laid plans and all that...You see, as luck or fate would have it, someone far more interesting than me has been snatched, and what do you know? ... oh dear... you're in the frame."

"Cut the crap."

She smiled. "Yes I know. It's hard to believe anyone could be more interesting than me, but that's life."

"I said cut the crap." It seemed she couldn't help herself. Yesterday she'd had the upper hand and he was the first to admit her superiority, but today was a different story. He was fed, dressed and able to walk in a straight enough line and count fingers, even if he was partially fuelled on illegal substances. Nowhere near one hundred percent but rational enough to know that he had to hit the road and get as far away from her and the police as he could. "Look, as soon as this coffee is done, I'm gone. You can stay here and play at being a hostage or a psycho for as long as you want ... I can tie *you* to the bedpost this time if you'd like, but me? I'm out of here."

She shrugged him off like it was all a load of blah, took another bite and made him wait while she swallowed. "It's not crap. Some media doll has disappeared."

"Yeah. Sure." He pulled himself off the bed and crossed to the window. Twitching the sagging curtains aside, he scanned the rundown vista. A collection of half-derelict buildings, pretty much deserted, apart from stray dogs and feral cats, was all that was out there, but the noise from the motorway flyover was ever-present, rattling the glass in the badly fitted frames. In the distance across the corrugated rooftops, a church spire seemed isolated and out of place. He tried to work out where he was from the available points of reference but his internal sat-nav was pretty much knackered.

"Why would I be in the frame? You're not making any sense. Why would they link a bank job to a kidnapping?"

She looked up from her breakfast, licked the grease from her fingers and responded. "Well they haven't yet – put two and two together that is. But they will. Just give them time. Despite what you criminal masterminds think, the police are quite adept at working things out ... eventually."

"Huh?" He was the first to admit his concussion was becoming a liability, but this time his confusion had nothing to do with his injuries. "I don't get it?"

"Well there's a surprise. It's quite simple. You twoc'd the wrong car, Jack."

"What?"

"In your desperate, *Tarantino-esque*, fleeing the scene delirium, you stole the wrong car, or the right car, depending on your point of view." She shrugged. "I tried to tell you. But you were having none of it, playing the tough guy, gun at my head. You didn't just land in the shit, Jack. You lay down and rolled right in it. You need to use a little more of this." She tapped at her head as amusement leaked colour into her pale cheeks.

Miller let the curtain swing back and turned to face her, not quite sure he'd heard correctly. But was certain he had when he caught the smug look on her face. If she thought the situation was funny, it was a pretty good bet that it wasn't. He leaned carefully back against the windowsill and supported his bad arm with his good. "Whose car?"

"Don't you remember, Jack?"

"Do I look like I remember?"

"Sorry, that's right. You were a little preoccupied, lots of swearing, very little sense. Mmm, I guess nothing changes, eh? Let me remind you. Little sports number, ice blue metallic paint, matching powder blue interior. Ring any bells? Well, I say blue, but that's the thing. It's more like slaughterhouse red now. You see that's what happens when you bleed all over the upholstery...Oops!"

Miller grimaced. "I said whose car, not what car?"

"And here's me thinking a getaway driver would be interested in the make and model numbers. Oh well, live and learn. Personalised number plates – JAZ 1 – come on, Jack, think!"

Miller shook his head. He hadn't a clue who she meant. "I'm supposed to deduce something from that?"

"Jeez, Jack. What do bank robbers do all day? Sew swag bags and count bullets? Don't you read the newspapers, listen to the society gossip, who's hot and who's not? No? You've never lived, Jack. It's a weird and wonderful world out there and you think I'm crazy? Jazz O'Hanlon, serial girlfriend, celebrity whore, judge's daughter. You certainly know how to pick them."

O'Hanlon. Miller's face twisted. The knot in the pit of his stomach tightened. "I jacked her *car*, not her."

"So you say, but who's going to believe you? You have to admit," she stifled a giggle, "it's a bit of a cock-up, Jack. You're going down for the whole shebang and you don't even know who the girl is. Things couldn't get any worse, or better. Have you ever wished you'd just turned off the alarm and stayed in bed?"

"I know who she is," he hissed. "Who wouldn't? She's slapped all over the bloody twitter-sphere and tabloid press on a regular basis. This guy, that guy, this party, that party, like anyone gives a fuck. It doesn't mean I had anything to do with her disappearance." He paused, suddenly unsure, recalling the screams from his muddled nightmares. "Did I?"

"No, Jack, rest easy, the car was empty when we got there. Not a trace of the delightful Jazz, other than her perfume." She wrinkled her nose. "I'm the only girl you threatened with a gun, but I'm afraid crazy hostages like me don't make the best alibis do they? I mean, *'Yer Honour, Mr Bank Robber 'ere couldn't have kidnapped that poor tart because he was far too busy snatching me'* Mmm, I don't think that one is going to win over the jury, is it?"

"You think this is funny?"

"Well, you have to admit..."

"And in the meantime while you're having a bloody good giggle, my blood's all over her car."

"'Fraid so, and that's not all."

"Go on." He dipped his head, massaged his temple.

"You shot out the window with your gun." She waved it at him for additional emphasis. "I expect you left the shell in there somewhere too. Dear me, I hope she's insured."

"Shit." He shook his head, couldn't believe his bad luck. First the crash, now this. He drew in a long breath. Maybe a little oxygen might dilute the chemicals and help him think straight. Sure, he'd heard of the girl, but it was her father, big bad Bob O'Hanlon who was currently causing his gut to react. "Where's the car?"

"Not where's the girl?" She snorted her disapproval. "Right, so not a gentleman then, eh?"

"I couldn't give a fuck about the girl. I know I don't have her, that's good enough for me."

"Mmm, not good enough for the police though. When they start processing that DNA, they're going to get all excited and you're going to be hotter than you already are." She took a sip from her coffee. "Perhaps I should clarify hot. I mean in the criminal sense, not the *flippin' heck, get your ruddy kit off now* sense." Her lips twitched slyly, "Just so we're clear on that."

"Clear as a bell."

"Anyway, as I was saying, that's around the time when you're going to realise how lucky you were to bump in to me."

"Luck? Luck doesn't come into it. It's simple. We just need to torch the car."

"Oh."

"Oh, what?"

"Oh, that might be difficult."

"Why?" Everything was bloody difficult. He rolled his neck to ease the sudden tension in it. She was right. He should have stayed in bed. "Where did you leave it?"

"Not far."

"Okay, that's cool. We just need to get rid of it. Drive it out to the sticks, dump it and torch it."

"Like I said, that might be a problem, Jack."

"Huh?"

"Erm, I think the police just found it. I heard the commotion when I came back with breakfast. You know, beep, beep, reversing buzzers, flashing blue lights, lots of excited plods with tape measures and notebooks. It'll be on the back of the low-loader, gift wrapped in tarpaulin and headed back to CSI base camp by now. Just like I said – hot stuff. Are your ears burning, Jack? or maybe your neck? I imagine the noose is tightening as we speak."

"Are you fucking kidding me? We're sitting here yapping and all the while the police are outside?" He stepped toward her but she didn't flicker, didn't bat an eye. Didn't show the slightest concern that she was two feet away from a dangerous felon who was about ready to cut through her weird crap and show her what *dangerous* actually meant. Okay, so she was the one holding the gun, but she still should be scared, if she had any sense, and he was way past wondering why she wasn't.

She dismissed his ire with a wave of her hand. "Chill out, Jack. I'm not that stupid. It's a couple of streets away, police tape and all. No one comes out this far, there's nothing here, nothing worth visiting or searching. This old place may as well not exist for all the attention the police will give it. The site's all locked up, patrolled by security guards. No one can get in or out. It's certainly not top of the list for an escaped felon with a cool million in his back pocket and a body over his shoulder. Anyway, stop complaining, you should be pleased. All this extra publicity will do wonders for your street cred."

"Street cred? Are you crazy?"

"Sure, Jack. Better to be hung for a sheep as a lamb, or in this case *a wolf as a sheep* and you're definitely the big bad wolf in this story. They'll be in a real spin about the missing judge's daughter and they'll all be in a knot about you. Just think what'll happen when they tie the two of you together."

Miller figured the coffee hit had gone to his head or she'd spiked it on the way in. He raised his hand to stop her. "Hang on, back up, you're not making any sense. You said they'd just towed the car. If that's the case, they haven't had time to do any analyses. If the police haven't made the connection yet, how have you?"

She smirked. "Because I'm one step ahead, always, and you need to remember that, Jack."

"What do you know?"

"I know how to get you off the hook."

"I didn't do anything. I don't need your help. I can get myself off the hook."

"It's a very sharp hook, Jack. But what the heck, you're right, you didn't do anything, you're an innocent man. Only, that's not quite right is it? Big bad bank robber, poor little rich girl. The press will crucify you. The police will supply the cross. And whoever is waiting for all that money you're holding onto is going to bang in the nails. But hey, it's your call. You want to bluff your way out of this? You go for it, Jack. The way I see it, and for what it's worth, the only way you can wriggle out of this is if Mizz Jazzicles turns up safe and well. It's not likely is it? I mean, whichever sicko has her, took her for a reason, right?" She smiled slyly. "She's probably dead already."

He was backed into a corner and he didn't like it. He liked it even less that a scrap of a girl he could fettle with one hand was doing the backing – and enjoying every minute of it. "So," he muttered, "come on then, what do you suggest? That's what you want isn't it, for me to play along?"

"Well, now that you ask, we could try and find her first, dead or alive. Beat the police at their own game. That would be cool, hunt the victim. Hand her back, or get rid of the body, I'm easy either way. There might even be a reward." She threw a glance at the bag in the corner. "Not that you need any more dosh." She leaned a little closer and her lips began to twitch, as if she was filled to the brim with bubbles of laughter and the laws of physics had taken control. "Of course if you want me to help you, you need to help me – and that brings us right back around to why you're here and why I'm here and why the world is round...tra la la la." She began to hum – out of tune. And he stared at her, bewildered. Mad. She was bloody barking mad.

"You know where she is, don't you? You know where the little tart is and you're playing some kind of twisted game."

"Maybe I do, maybe I don't. Maybe you'll never find out."

"Hang on," he shook his head, confusion lifting. He could see it clearly now – too clearly. "That guy, the guy with the knife, what did you call him? Shit." He shook his head, tried to remember, "Micro? that was it, fucking Micro. He took her, didn't he? That's what you're saying? That you've both been playing some sick little game, and like a loaded dice, I just rolled onto the board." She'd raised the bar, way past weirdo, sicko little freak and heading right on up to psycho.

She smiled. "Roll up, roll up. Place your bets, gents..."

"I'm right aren't I?"

"Hey, believe what you want."

He tapped his head, "You have problems sweetheart, big problems, and I don't mean me."

She tutted. "Oh, Jack, you don't know the half of it. My problems make your problems look like assets. Never mind. Not to worry. Do you believe in the stars and all that crazy horoscope stuff?"

He flexed his arm, testing his resilience to the pain. He needed something to take his mind off the temptation to shut her up once and for all. "What in Christ's name are you talking about now?"

"Karma, Jack. That's what I'm talking about. I was all set to go it alone, I mean hey, what's new, but then you dropped into my lap, just like my horoscope said – and well, what better way to make sure we understand each other. To make sure you do as you're told and behave. And with your reputation, Jack, I need to be very sure you'll do what I want, not what you want."

"My reputation?"

"Sure, Jack, now don't go all coy on me. Otto Braun's right hand man, quite the Mr Fixit by all accounts. You're known for getting the job done whatever the cost and for getting exactly what you want. I don't want you thinking you're going to be taking control of our little venture, edging me out."

Otto? Oh shit! It was all coming back, a great tsunami of stuff, bad stuff, dangerous stuff, rolling right up the foreshore and headed straight for him. And Jazz O'Hanlon, Hanging O'Hanlon's only child, was the perfect storm thrown right at the centre of it all. Fuck! He could actually feel his heart banging away in his chest, like someone had added a few extra beats just for fun. He took a long, slow breath.

"You know a hell of a lot about a guy you never met before. A guy whose wallet you had to check in order to ID."

"What can I say? You have your planners and you have your opportunists. And then once in a while someone happens along whose pretty good at both. I see an opportunity, Jack, and I take it, and when it's secure in the palm of my hand I set about the planning."

Miller snorted. "You think you've got me in the palm of your hand?"

She smiled, a smug smile that he itched to wipe off her face. If she wasn't holding the gun he'd have done exactly that. "I know I have," she replied. "You do as I say, I make things happen, Jazz goes free and you can walk out of here with your cash. I'll even drive you to the airport, or the ferry terminal or wherever bank robbers go when they need to lie low."

"And if I don't?"

"Then I make another call and the boys in blue will be down here, weapons drawn, bodybag at the ready. It's nothing personal, Jack. I'm sure you're a very nice robber, as far as robbers go, but you know, you really can't have your wicked way with an A-lister and hope to get away with it. People don't like that kind of behaviour, it makes them nervous."

"Nothing personal? That makes everything cool then doesn't it? But what's to stop me snapping your scrawny little neck and taking off?" He leaned in close, his face right next to hers, his angry breath hot against her cheek. "Does that make *you* nervous?"

She cocked her head, twitched her lips and assessed him shrewdly. "Nervous? Nope, but then I'm not like everyone else – am I? And yes, I suppose you could finish me off with a punch, or a hand at my throat, or even a bullet, but then there'd be no one to call off the game, no one to fix Jazz's breakfast and I'm not sure how long she'd last without her *five a day smoothie*...her being so skinny and all, so...go figure."

"You think you've got it all sewn up, don't you?"

"Pretty much," she replied sweetly.

"Well you're wrong. There's a flaw in your twisted little plan. You see, I couldn't give a shit about you or her."

She shrugged her reply as if she couldn't give a shit either.

"No, but you care about him. The guy who put you away, don't you? It's written all over your face, Jack."

And she was right about that. Hanging fucking O'Hanlon.

"Where is she?"

"You really think I'd tell you?"

"I really think you should."

She grinned. "Good one. No chance."

"I could make you tell me."

She waggled the gun at him. "No you couldn't."

The pause that followed lengthened into a frustrated silence as Miller tried to second guess her. He couldn't, because for the life of him he couldn't work out what on earth the connection was between the little Goth weirdo with the gun and a high court judge. The daughter, Jazz, was an incidental, a means to an end, and he was beginning to realise that he probably was too. The difference being that he was definitely the wild card in this bizarre game. He had a history with O'Hanlon that eclipsed anything the crazy girl could possibly conceive.

"Okay. Where's my phone?" He reached out his hand and waited.

She stood, slipped her hand into the pocket of her skinny black jeans, and made a big deal of wiggling her behind before pulling out the mobile and throwing it to him with a grin.

"You've a load of missed calls, Jack. People wondering where you are. People who care whether you're alive or dead, that's nice, isn't it?"

He gave a sour smile. She could wiggle all she liked. "You called anyone from this phone?"

"I might have done. I might not. Time will tell. The police could be outside right now polishing up their weapons and trading shootout stories."

"With any luck you'll get caught in the crossfire." He glanced up at her "Are you really that stupid?"

"Not entirely. You need to have someplace for them to contact you, you know, develop a rapport. Come on, Jack, you've seen it on TV I'm sure. Shit hot police negotiator talks bad ass felon into handing over innocent hostage. It'll be great. Like I said before, street cred!" She grinned again, like she just couldn't keep her amusement to herself.

"So you did call someone?"

"Maybe just a little call." She held her finger and thumb, a fraction apart. "Just to open lines of communication. I mean, you couldn't do it, could you? You can thank me later."

"Who did you call?"

"Who do you think?"

"What did you say?"

"Save me from the big bad robber – or words to that effect. I may have exaggerated a little. Added a few sound effects, heavy breathing, the odd squeal. I mean where's the harm in a little improvisation? Necessity is the mother of all invention."

"Thanks."

"You're welcome."

"Okay, say I believe you, which I don't, but just for the sake of argument, say I believe that you could organise and execute the disappearance of a high profile figure, who is probably never alone, and would never stray anywhere near your warped little world. Say you and your good buddy Egor could lure her into this rat infested wasteland, manhandle her, kicking and screaming from her Barbie car, what then? What's the deal? Why her? Why anybody?"

"Why? Because I'm a nut job, and it's about time people started to take me seriously. Why her? Because of him. Why him? Because he has something of mine and I want it back...back...back." She banged sharply at her forehead with the heel of her hand as if the record in her head was scratched and she was trying to re-set the needle. "So..." she continued when she was back on track, "Why do you rob banks?"

"Because I'm good at it." He watched her carefully, the way her eyes re-focused and her lips whispered silent thoughts, and he wondered, not for the first time, whether he wasn't the only one in the room who would fail a drug screen.

"That's good to know," she sighed.

He shrugged off the weirdness and scanned down the list of missed calls. Bloody Otto, wondering about his million quid. Only it wasn't a million as the media had stated. It was barely half that. He could tell just by looking at the bag. Someone was trying to pull a fast one. Frankie? The phone beeped a low battery warning and he cursed under his breath. The charger was back at his flat. The police were probably there too.

"Do you have a phone?"

She shrugged. "I had hers...I broke it when you almost ran me over."

Another fleeting image flashed painfully in his head. Rain on the windshield, the skidding car, the girl in the lights. The gun at his temple...Frankie! Fucking Frankie had changed the plan, what else had he done? He shook his head, as if that might rattle everything back into place. Something was seriously wrong and it had bugger all to do with the hole in his shoulder. "Be thankful it was just your phone," he muttered, "It could have been your neck."

She grinned back at him. "Why, Jack, do I detect a note of remorse? Would you prefer it if I'd had the life crushed out of me?"

"There's time yet."

"Promises, promises."

He shot her another glance, wondered, how much she knew and whether he should simply wring the truth out of her "Don't push it, Spook, you've no idea what I'm capable of."

"Spook..." She sounded the word out, whispered it seductively. "I like it...and so appropriate, Jack. By the time we're done, I'll be haunting your every waking moment." She reached out a pale hand "Hi, I'm Spook, pleased to meet you."

"Did you hear what I said? Quit playing games, you've no idea what I might do."

"Oh, but I do, Jack. I know exactly what you're capable of, your strengths and weaknesses, your little eccentricities, your likes and dislikes – and that's why you're the perfect man for the job."

He shook his head, weary already with her mind games, but now resigned to hearing her out. Getting it over with, so he could get out and get on with his life. "My biggest fan eh? You know, Spook, there's something weird, and if I'm honest, kind of kinky, about hero worship."

"Kinky? Oh I wouldn't call it that, Jack. It's more along the lines of *know thine enemy* or *keep your friends close but your enemies closer.*"

"I'm not your enemy – yet."

"No, but you're going to help me smite them, in biblical fashion."

"Why? I'd have thought you more than capable of smiting and spiting all by yourself?"

She narrowed her eyes, opened her mouth to reply and he recognised the effort it took for her to hang onto the words.

"Not quite." She replied and for once there wasn't a trace of smugness coating her words.

He knew then, suddenly and categorically, that whoever she was, it would be a mistake to underestimate her. She'd hauled him out of a burning car, she'd turned the tables, she had his gun, his cash, a body in the trunk, and she wanted even more.

There had to be a bloody good reason. "Okay, let's hear it. What's this job that's so important you've got some rich man's plaything hidden away somewhere as insurance."

"Are you concerned for her, Jack? Does the thought of a defenceless, frightened young woman prick at your conscience?"

"The thought of serving time for something I didn't do concerns me more."

"Hang on to that thought, Jack."

"The job?" he repeated "I've only so much patience, and even less time. You string this out much longer and I'll put a bullet in your clever little head and take my chances."

"Okay, okay." She returned to the car seat, settling her small frame into its embrace, feet tucked beneath her as if preparing to tell a story. "It's quite simple really...I want you to steal something."

He cocked his head and looked at her. "I just robbed a bank. You want money, take it. I'm sure you and Otto can sort it out later...Just make him an offer he can't refuse."

"I don't want the money."

"Then what do you want?"

"Something far more valuable."

"What?"

"Later."

He drained the last of the coffee, crumpled the carton and aimed for the bin. He was done with her games. The carton hit the side of the bin and ricocheted across the room. She sent him a sly grin.

"Hope you're a better shot with a gun."

"Believe it, Spook." He reached for the sports bag, pulled out a bundle of notes in a cashier's wrap and threw them at her. "Make yourself useful. Go and get me a couple of pay-as-you-go mobiles, a decent shirt – I'm not a fucking hippy – and food, anything, I could eat a scabby horse."

"That'll be the drugs."

"Very likely. When you come back we'll discuss what you want me to do – and whether I'm going to do it." He glanced up and caught her eye. "Stay clear of where you left the car."

"Why?"

"Why? Do I need to spell it out? I thought you were some kind of mini master criminal. You keep making mistakes." He shook his head. "You make too many, don't expect me to pick up the pieces. Bunny girl Jazz will go hungry and I'll be long gone."

She scowled, black brows knotted, black lips in an almost pout. Pulling herself out of the chair, she drew herself up to her full height and jabbed a black tipped fingernail at his chest. "Hey, don't you forget, Jack, I'm calling the shots here."

"Sure you are, crazy girl." He cocked his head and sent her a sly smile of his own. "Now you run along like a good little ghoul, while I get busy with the dirty bank robber stuff."

Fifteen

He gave her twenty minutes, which he reckoned was long enough to get far enough away. Then he pulled himself off the bed, swallowed a pill, pocketed the remainder and drained the rest of the water. Despite the attempt at rehydration, he was still shaky on his feet, but couldn't afford to hang around. It was time to move, before the police came a calling or Spook returned to finish the game.

He scanned the room with a calculating eye. There was far too much evidence to erase. The blood-stained sheets, the mess in the shower. His DNA was everywhere and he couldn't do a thing about it. He checked the number of shells left in the clip before stuffing the gun in the waistband of his trousers. She'd got complacent, turned her back on him – big mistake. He'd slipped the gun right out of her bag as she undid the bolts prior to leaving. He couldn't take the risk that she'd use it just for kicks, he had enough shit linked to his name without taking the blame for any random shooting she undertook. Unaware that she'd lost her advantage, she'd given him that kooky smile as she left, like she had it all sussed and he had nothing better to do but sit and wait. He'd heard her laughter as she re-locked the door and headed out to play. Another mistake. He could pick his way through any lock with his eyes closed.

When the door was open he picked up the sports bag, pulled out a bundle of notes and tossed them onto the mattress. He owed her that, at least. If it weren't for her and her freaky games, he'd have been well on his way to hell.

She'd left her sunglasses on the side table. Cheap black frames, smudged plastic lenses, not exactly Gucci. He frowned as he slipped them on. As a device to draw attention away from the obvious battering he'd taken to his face, he figured they would work – but as a disguise, *cunning* or not, they fell short. If the police had identified him, his picture would be all over the news and the last thing he wanted was to be recognised ... particularly by the wrong side, whoever they may be.

He let himself out of the room, checked right and left in case the crazy girl was lurking in the shadows with a sharp knife, but the wide corridor was empty, the silence punctuated only by the leaky pipes from the bathroom to his right. He headed left, for no other reason than, *keep left*, was a sensible option for any getaway driver. He bypassed a service lift and kept going. He'd no desire to find himself trapped inside if the power went down, and by the way the lights flickered on and off it was a fairly good bet. When he reached the nearest stairwell, he realised he'd been inadvertently following a blue line painted on the floor directing all and sundry to radiology and he finally understood where he was – the decommissioned infirmary.

Empty for a number of years, developers had finally gained permission to demolish the rambling fire damaged Victorian edifice and construct the kind of chic apartments that would do better in an equally chic locale. Miller doubted whether those who could afford the rents would necessarily choose to live cheek by jowl with the detritus of an inner city brown-field industrial site and the endless noise and pollution of the motorway. Apparently he wasn't the only one who shared those concerns. It seemed that work on the site had been temporarily halted due to planning wrangles, red tape and a last-ditch attempt by heritage anoraks to save the building's architectural assets. With Christmas just around the corner, the contractors had locked up the site and gone home. But not so securely that a little ghoul couldn't gain access and a bank robber couldn't escape.

Miller took the stairs slowly, one hand anchoring him to the safety of the banister as each downward step threatened his equilibrium and each footfall echoed in the empty shell. If there was anyone else in the building, then he'd just announced his presence. He paused on the ground floor and listened. Somewhere far off, a door slammed, caught by the wind perhaps, he couldn't be sure, but there were no accompanying footsteps to prove otherwise.

Stepping into the wide reception area, he negotiated the piles of builders' equipment stacked haphazardly in the centre of the space. The internal stripping out of any valuable materials had begun, ahead of the final demolition. The walls were back to bare brick and huge sheets of polished mahogany panels were stacked on pallets ready for removal. Miller didn't need to try the main exit doors to know that they were barred from the outside. Spook obviously had another way in and out of the building, there was no way she could have dragged him from the stolen car, up three flights of stairs and through a maze of corridors, unless she'd had help. He thought again of the guy with the knife, freak-show's sidekick, and his stomach recoiled at the remembered pungency... and fear. He didn't do fear. He did ruthless, committed, and determined to the point of obsession. People feared *him*. And the thought that a half pint girl with blue hair and black talons had reduced him to a gibbering wreck, albeit with the aid of some nasty narcotics, was enough to give him indigestion.

He turned slowly on the spot and gathered his poise, the place was vast and he had neither the time nor energy to rake about in dusty side wards or darkened corridors looking for Spook's secret rat-run. Instead he picked up a wrench with his good arm, tested the weight, and when satisfied it was up to the job, he knocked out the glass in the nearest window.

Once outside, he stood bent double, recovering from the ill-advised scramble over the windowsill and the six-foot drop to the ground beneath. His shoulder screamed and his ribs joined in, but he resisted the lure of a chemical top up. He needed to think straight and keep on thinking straight. He wheezed a much needed breath instead, while overhead, his attention was caught by the mid-morning traffic on the flyover.

A recent extension to the motorway system, it almost clipped the roof of the building and was probably one of the reasons the infirmary had finally closed down. Relocated to a quieter spot or simply squeezed out by NHS cuts? Miller wasn't sure and didn't care. He focused on the traffic, it was heavier going into town rather than out and as he needed to find out what the hell was going on, there was only one direction to choose. He turned for the town centre and started walking.

Within two blocks he was questioning his decision to leave his bed. His shoulder throbbed and his ribs reminded him at every step that they'd taken a beating on his behalf. He pulled up the collar of his bloodied jacket and stuffed his hands in the pockets. The T-shirt alone was no protection against the wintry showers, but Armani or not, a bullet holed jacket was a liability he should probably have left behind. He needed to get off the street and out of the weather. What he needed was a car. He was a planner after all, just a little slow off the starting blocks this morning.

Within four blocks he'd swapped the industrial landscape for a fledgling business park and was back in control. He'd acquired himself a new set of wheels, from someone who should have known better than to park it out of sight. A sporty little boy racer, Ferrari red with a real growl under the bonnet. It didn't deserve to be left unattended. If he didn't take it, some low life would have its alloys by the end of the day. He sank gratefully into the upholstery, fingered the dash reverently and sorted his priorities, heater first, music second. When he'd driven far enough from where he'd taken the car, he parked up and pulled out his phone and prayed the battery would hold out. It was time to check in.

He scrolled his contacts and despite his concussion, one in particular stood out – Harry. Harry who? He was sure he should know, but when he tried all he got for his trouble was the busy tone and didn't have time or battery life to wait. As soon as he disconnected the call, the phone sprang to life, vibrating angrily in his hand as if frustrated at being contained. He checked the number. Otto. He couldn't put it off any longer.

"Jacky?" A man's voice, low and throaty, whispered down the line. A cadence of surprise, revealing the caller's belief the call would remain unanswered.

"Yeah." Miller pulled at his fragmented memory. The voice was familiar but he couldn't place a name. "Who wants to know?"

"Who wants to know? Who wants to fucking know? Are you messing with me?"

It wasn't Otto, he was sure about that. The voice lacked the grit that would by necessity fuel any crime lord big enough to bankroll the type of jobs he'd been involved in. He checked in the mirror, swivelled round as best he could in the low-slung sports seat, but his cursory scan of the street revealed no threat to his position, no tactical response unit lurking in the shadows. He might be currently off the radar but he knew it wouldn't last long.

"Just being careful."

"Careful? Bit late for that. What happened?"

"You don't want to know."

"I think I do."

"Put it this way, I hit a few obstacles."

"No shit. The boss isn't happy. That wasn't part of the plan. You need to get yourself down here pretty damn quick."

Sure he could do that, if he knew where *down here* was, but he had a certain reluctance to admit he was missing crucial parts of the bigger picture. "How about somewhere a little less obvious?" he suggested.

A car cruised by and Miller watched as it slowed, ready to take a left turn adjacent to where he sat. The occupants didn't look his way, were engaged in conversation, nevertheless his hand hovered over the gun at his waist and his adrenalin began to pump. Ordinarily he wasn't this jumpy. He was used to being in control. The car made the turn and Miller exhaled slowly and returned his attention to the call.

A long pause was followed by muffled background conversation, some obvious discord that spilled onto the open line in the form of a string of expletives. Miller got the idea that when told to jump, that's exactly what he was expected to do. Seeing as he was in no fit state to jump anywhere, and had a natural aversion to being *told* anything, he held his tongue, tapping a beat on the steering wheel as he counted how many curses could be strung together in one sentence without the words losing meaning. He got to eight.

"Somewhere less obvious? Get real, Jacky," came the eventual reply. "The Scally, thirty minutes and if you're dragging a tail, you'd better have it docked by the time you get here."

"Sure," replied Miller. He knew The Scally in the same way he knew how to breathe. No amount of head injury could erase that. He scowled, tried to push the memories a little further, but it was still a jumble.

"Oh, and Jacky."

"Yeah?"

"Don't forget the bag."

He ended the call. He'd hung about long enough. It was probably wise to make a move before the police currently combing the area where Spook had dumped the car decided to sniff about closer to home. He checked the rearview mirror, half expected to see his ghoulish black shadow creeping up on him, but the street was empty. Smiling, he turned the ignition and the car responded with a throaty growl. Spook would have to up her game, if she planned on keeping up with him.

Sixteen

He thinks I'm barmy. He's not alone in that. Anyway I'll play along. It's a good game and sometimes no matter how much your head is telling you to hang onto the leash, you just have to let that puppy run. He's running now, but not away, never away, not Jack. I know his type. He's curious, about me, about all the other stuff he can't remember and his curiosity will bring him bouncing right back... eventually.

He warned me off...oops...red rag and all that. So I had to be sure. And that's why I'm down here watching the plod, checking the players, rating their form, discreetly of course, perched on the wall like a great black crow. They're buzzing all over her car doing whatever it is they do. The boys in blue, stopping anyone who looks vaguely sober, shooing away the idly curious. Guys in white coveralls taking their photos, logging the evidence. Oh dear, poor Jack. We're back to the green bottles again and there's no way he can stop them from falling. Unless he does as I want – of course.

Micro is there, in the shadows. I see him and I know he sees me by the way he shuffles back out of sight. I run my finger quickety-quick across my throat and he gets the message. He knows what happens to tittle-tattles.

I'm not sure about him, Ginger-nut, the guy in the suit, phone at his ear, ordering everyone about. What is it with suits? Got to hand it to Jack, at least he can pull it off, has a bit of urban style. But this guy...nope. Smug smile, smug swagger, pleased with himself. That won't last. I'll make sure of it.

He looks straight at me and I look straight back. Dare him to join the dots and see the bigger picture. Of course he doesn't, because his mind is elsewhere, thinking of the points he's just scored, or the woman he's just screwed. *Uh oh* the voice whispers *big mistake.*

I raise one hand and make the shape of a gun. It should be real, but it's not. Tsk tsk, naughty Jack. Once a thief, always a thief. I scrunch up one eye, nice and tight and check my aim, left a bit, right a bit, bingo! Dead centre between Ginger's piggy eyes and then I hold my breath and squeeze that trigger... *bang you're dead.* But he doesn't fall. He just shakes his head. Noooooo... the rhymes are back and there's a sly giggle in my left ear. "Shut up!" I shout at the top of my voice. I'm not listening, not now, I'm far too busy. But the voice doesn't care that I'm on surveillance, and the copper in the suit looks at me like I've lost the plot, which of course I haven't, or I'm playing a game, which of course I am...and so is he – he just doesn't know it yet. *Tag, you're it!*

Taking sides? the voice whispers, sly and mean. I shrug. So, what do I care? I'm in charge, I'm picking my team, one soldier at a time and this plod in a suit just chose his side, which, of course, isn't mine. Dirty dog, sniffing around like he's the man, the one in control. I need to keep my eye on him.

But not now. Now I have far more interesting stuff to do. Got to keep the dice rolling.

I shimmy to the end of the wall, my crow feet dangling. It's a long drop, but what the heck, no problem for me. I have feline genes. I pick my landing spot between a dumped PC monitor and a roll of wet carpet. Fly tippers. Any old place, any old time, let's hope there's not a body rolled up in the Axminster – I can't be sharing the spotlight with some other psycho.

I look up when he barks at me, the dog in the suit, and he's heading my way, a slow saunter, hands in his pockets, like he has all the time in the world and he assumes I do too. Oh well, so much for a quick exit. I just can't resist an opportunity for mischief and a few more minutes won't kill me, though I can't say the same for him.

I read somewhere that you can drown in two inches of water. I stare at the puddle in front of his feet. Maybe? Maybe not? Maybe later. I remain on my perch, pull myself to my feet and consolidate my position, looking down on him.

"DI Baker," he announces with a self-important flourish as he thrusts his ID in my general direction. Could have been a supermarket loyalty card or a library ticket for all the chance he gives me to check it. Nice. Professional. I get the feeling he'd rather be elsewhere doing something else. Wouldn't we all? Though I doubt we share the same interests. The voice sniggers and this time I try to resist. I can behave when the circumstances dictate, but I don't always choose to. The voice eggs me on regardless, so I do my *wobbling on the high beam* balancing act, arms outstretched, feigning a case of vertigo. Ginger-nut takes a step back, with a *what the fuck?* expression on his face, obviously not so keen to catch me if I fall.

"This vehicle..." he gestures to the car being hoisted onto the flatbed truck, "did you happen to see who parked it?" He shouts at me as if I'm deaf or stupid or both. I wonder if he shouts at everyone. I wonder if anyone listens.

I shake my head in reply and wobble a little more, right there on the top of the wall where the bricks meet in a point and little nuggets of iron protrude. At one time there would have been railings on top of the brick. But now just the nuggets remain. I step over them slowly, concentrating on my feet rather than the detective. Hey this is cool in a *double dog dare you* kind of way. I should do it more often. Take it up, run away with the circus and join a high wire act. *Roll up, roll up and see the amazing Spook and her death-defying balancing act.* Death-defying? The voice loves that. Anyway, I have a good head for heights and I have no intention of falling. I'm also annoying Ginger-nut big time. It's almost worth the risk of taking a tumble just to wind him up. A few shards of weathered brick shear off beneath my feet and he steps back even further to avoid the brick dust and old lime mortar.

"Were you around here last night?" He brushes a few specks from his lapel and glowers at me.

I shake my head again. I've no real urge to speak to him when he's shouting at me. So I move backwards, which I have to admit is tricky what with all that crossing of feet and flailing of arms and whatnot. His jaw tightens. Temper, temper, that's not very nice. DI Baker obviously believes he's due a tad more respect from the general public and isn't impressed in the slightest that I can stand on one leg at such a perilous height.

"Do you want to get down off the wall so we can talk?" he asks, but what he means is 'get down you effin' weirdo or I'll arrest you for trespass or obstruction or any damn thing I like.'

I smirk and that seems to do the trick. After all, it's not what you say, it's the space between the words that really count and smirking is basically *'eff off'* in the universal language of clever shite.

He gives a quick glance over his shoulder to make sure the boys in blue are busy with their notebooks and then reaches up to catch my ankle. Has it in his head to yank me off my perch, perhaps. *Uh oh, another big mistake.*

"Hey!" I exclaim as loudly as I can and all the white coats and blue uniforms turn to see what the fuss is all about. They're thinking *bloody hell she's going to fall and that great lump's just standing there.* There's a collective held breath that seems to roll towards us, gathering momentum until it catches Ginger-nut on the back of the neck and knocks some sense into him. Tsk-tsk, detective, you really shouldn't mess with a messer.

I raise one hand and give him the opportunity to count my fingers, but he's not nearly as good at maths as my new pal Jack. I get a muttered "get your fucking arse down here before I...." but before he can detail his favoured form of police brutality I twist around and drop to the ground on the other side of the wall. I hear him cursing as I head on down the alley, something about crack-heads and wasters. He won't follow; I'm far too weird, the lane's far too messy, clean suit and all, more fool him. I'm laughing out loud and the voice joins in. For once I don't mind, two's company after all.

Seventeen

Judge O'Hanlon's house was straight off the cover of *Homes and Gardens*. A desirable residence if ever there was one. Samuels was impressed. He'd visited once before, on a case, and just because his wages didn't stretch that far didn't mean he couldn't appreciate the finer things in life. The Georgian pile came with its own stables, private lake and a view to die for. Samuels did a mental reckoning, a prime site in the Tyne Valley, commuting distance from Newcastle, and an international airport on the doorstep, but not so close that you'd be shaken out of bed by jet engines at four in the morning. All in all a pretty penny – and a possible motive if Jasmine's disappearance was in fact the result of some foul play. Added to that the fact that daddy had come up against some of the biggest rogues and toughest nuts in the North East during the course of his career and Samuels was beginning to have doubts that party loving Jasmine was just enjoying a sleepover at a friend's house. He was an optimistic man, but from experience he knew that, more often than not, his gut was way ahead of his brain when it came to solving crime.

He pulled his car alongside the three already parked on the gravel drive and sat a moment, gathering his thoughts. If he were being honest, he didn't want to be there. The feeling of being sidetracked from the case that had overtaken his life for the past eighteen months was frustrating. The idea that Baker had been left to trample all over Miller, his main suspect, rankled even more. What on earth was the boss thinking about, pulling him out even for a short time and giving Baker free rein? Baker wouldn't do as thorough a job, he never did, and Samuels was growing increasingly weary at mopping up and covering up for Baker's shortcomings. He held tightly to the hope that the skill and dedication of the men he'd left to dig into Miller's background would suffice until he could get back to the station.

O'Hanlon was waiting impatiently at the top of the stone entrance steps, pacing back and forth with an awkward, lopsided gait, supported by a walking stick. He snorted his annoyance, as if he expected Samuels should have flashed a blue light to get there sooner. He made a show of checking his watch to illustrate his point before steering Samuels through an impressive formal reception hallway to a panelled study at the rear of the house. Samuels gravitated with some relief to the fireplace where a roaring fire beckoned. Somehow he doubted O'Hanlon had been responsible for chopping logs and carrying coal, which meant he employed staff to do the ancillary tasks, and that meant additional people to interview. He groaned inwardly. He could feel Miller slipping away from him and felt bad that he was allowing his own frustration to interfere in such a sensitive case.

"It's a cold one this morning, sir," he offered as he warmed his hands. "Snow on the way, so the forecasters are warning." He gestured vaguely through the French doors to the vast grounds beyond. "I'll bet you get a good covering here."

O'Hanlon agreed with a tight smile. "Nothing a decent four-wheel drive can't handle."

"Mmm, I suppose you're used to the vagaries of the weather and have all the necessary kit to cope with it. That must make life easier?" He thought of his own home and the steep drive he had to dig out by hand to get his car out of the garage when it snowed. "How long have you lived here, sir? It's a beautiful spot."

"Many, many years, Detective Samuels, but as you know I didn't ask you here to discuss the property market or the wonderful Tyne Valley vistas. I'm sure DCI Davies will have relayed my concerns to you. I ... I seem to have mislaid my daughter." He faltered with nervous laughter and Samuels glimpsed a chink in his high court judge veneer as he continued. "Although she's confident, capable and socially adept, I'm nevertheless increasingly worried about Jasmine and her whereabouts. It's not like her to absent herself without leaving a note or a message."

"Yes, of course, Mr O'Hanlon. I'm sorry. And here's me jabbering on and on. DCI Davies briefed me earlier this morning. He suggested your level of concern warranted our highest priority."

O'Hanlon smiled. "I would hope that any missing person would warrant such attention, detective." He lowered himself heavily into a seat behind his desk, balancing his stick carefully against the furniture, and gestured Samuels toward an empty chair. Samuels declined with a shake of the head, much preferring to saunter the room at his leisure, a useful device of distraction when interviewing suspects and witnesses, though O'Hanlon, as a worried parent, was neither.

"Of course, sir, but ordinarily we would wait a little longer before escalating procedures. I'm sure you're aware, as an adult, Jasmine is entitled to absent herself at will – and although her lack of contact is worrying, there may be a simple explanation for that."

"I fully understand, DI Samuels, but I can't stress highly enough that this is a genuine case for concern. I can assure you Jasmine has not run off to Gretna Green with her latest beau, nor has she packed a case and taken off for Rio. She has disappeared, detective. Plain and simple." He drew a breath before continuing. "As *you're* no doubt aware, young women go missing the length and breadth of the country on a regular basis. Sadly, some are never heard of again, much to the distress of their families, while a small number are finally discovered floating in canals or dumped at the side of the road. I know this, detective. So don't try to protect me from the grim realities or pull the wool over my eyes. I have presided over cases and made judgement on the perpetrators of such evil crimes. I know what can happen. I sincerely hope that in this case it hasn't."

"I appreciate your concern, sir. Of course you're worried..."

"Worried? My daughter hasn't been seen since yesterday morning when she left to attend an appointment. There has been no word from her. No phone calls or messages. It's completely out of character, detective, so yes, I'm extremely worried."

Samuels pulled out his notebook and suppressed a sigh. A familiar twist in the pit of his stomach, put him instantly on alert. O'Hanlon suspected foul play and Samuels wondered whether he had a particular reason for his suspicions, or whether he had simply been privy to too many horrors to consider anything else.

All the same, a morning appointment changed his own preconceptions. So Jasmine hadn't stayed out partying after all. "What kind of appointment, Mr O'Hanlon?"

O'Hanlon stared at him, a little distracted, as if his mind was elsewhere, caught in a nightmare trawling country lanes and river banks for his daughter's body. Understandable enough, thought Samuels, considering the circumstances, but not helpful. "The appointment, sir?" he prompted gently.

"Good grief, man," snapped O'Hanlon "I've no idea. Hair, nails, something of that ilk. She doesn't share the minutiae of her life with her father and I confess to having little interest in it." He paused, took a deep breath and a moment to control his emotions. "I'm sorry, that's very wrong, I realise that now. I should know where she spends her time, shouldn't I?"

"She's a grown woman, sir. I doubt she'd expect you to be privy to her social calendar." Samuels thought of his own girls. At fifteen and seventeen, they would think it strange indeed if he were to suddenly show an interest in their beauty regimes, and yet, like O'Hanlon, he retained a need to know where they were even if it wasn't cool to do so.

"I see. Perhaps one of your household would know where she planned to go yesterday. The name of the salon or shops she frequented. Your wife maybe?"

"My wife is out of the country, visiting family. Her mother is very ill. I did intend to accompany her but something came up. Something I couldn't postpone. I could phone her." He glanced at his watch again, "Oh, time differences..." He was rambling, Samuels recognised his indecision.

"Not to worry, sir. Maybe Jasmine's friends could fill in the blanks?"

"Perhaps, though most are in London."

Samuels doubted that he even knew who they were and suspected he was currently regretting his lack of interest in his daughter's life. "Nevertheless I'll need their names and contact details if you have them. We need to clarify who saw or spoke to her last and when and where that was. Does Jasmine have a current boyfriend, sir?"

O'Hanlon, grimaced. "She does. In fact today she should be confirming arrangements for her engagement party."

Samuels looked up from his notes. "Is that the footballer? I believe I read something about that recently."

"Footballer? Good lord, no. Ned Gillespie is the son of an associate of mine. He works in the city. Import and Export. A good career, a well-placed individual. An excellent match for Jasmine. Don't believe everything you read in the glossies, DI Samuels."

Samuels cast his eye casually around the room. There were many photographs of O'Hanlon, some of his current wife and lots of Jasmine. Baby photos, school uniform shots, the obligatory gymkhana, pretty pony, cute kid shots and a few more formal pictures of Jasmine with her father and current step mother at various events. Nothing unusual or of real interest, no different to family photos the world over, perhaps with the exception of the ponies, which certainly weren't of the pit or beach variety, a subtle reminder that Jasmine came from a wealthy background. The few later photos showed the Jasmine he was more used to seeing in the press, smiling, posing, phone in her hand, suitor on her arm. She was an attractive, photogenic young woman and as such, attracted a lot of attention. There was always the possibility that yesterday she'd attracted the wrong sort.

"Do you mind if I borrow this one, sir?" He asked as he carefully removed one framed picture from the polished surface of a glazed bookcase. It was less controversial than the image he'd viewed at the station, more girl next door than scheming socialite.

"Not at all, if you think it'll help." O'Hanlon reached out with a trembling hand for the picture. Samuels looked away to save the man's embarrassment at his own debilitation. He certainly wasn't the man Samuels remembered from his previous encounters. He wondered whether ill health had influenced the judge's decision to retire from the bench, or whether his current malaise was a direct result of Jasmine's disappearance. "Please," continued O'Hanlon "allow me to remove it from the frame. It'll be easier to carry that way."

"I see she likes to sail." Samuels commented as he studied a shot of Jasmine at the prow of a yacht. The Caribbean or Mediterranean perhaps, somewhere with crystal blue water and plenty of sunshine, definitely not the North Sea, that was for sure. O'Hanlon followed his gaze and snorted.

"At twenty-one, she was engaged to a shipping magnate's son. Her love of the sea lasted about as long as her love for him. At twenty-two, an American rock star took her fancy, at twenty-three, an Icelandic crime writer... I suspect he wrote in English." He paused, "Let me explain, detective. Jasmine loves life but she is high maintenance. Always has been. Don't get me wrong, Jasmine is a sweet, beautiful girl but she is indulged, my fault entirely. She was ill as a child, she's still not strong, despite appearances, hence my concern over her disappearance."

Samuels nodded. "Has she ever gone missing before?"

"No."

"Has she had any problems, at home, at work..." he glanced up, "does she work?"

O'Hanlon shrugged. "She doesn't need to."

"Right. So what does she do with herself all day? When she's not at the salon or popping down to London to meet with ..." he checked his notes, "Ned?" He tried to maintain a non-judgemental tone, but he knew he'd failed when he earned a raised brow from O'Hanlon.

"She reads, she enjoys art, music, visits the galleries, the fashion shows ..."

"She didn't fancy going into law like her father, then?"

O'Hanlon shook his head. "No." was his short reply, and Samuels reckoned that was the end of that topic.

"Has she always lived at home, sir?" Privately he thought it strange that a twenty-four year old of obvious means would choose the restraints of an overbearing, overprotective father rather than the freedom of a London apartment. He had supportive parents, but he'd still left home at the first opportunity.

O'Hanlon sighed as if he was becoming increasingly irritated by Samuels' questions. "We have properties in London and Rome. Jasmine splits her time between them. She returns to Northumberland for a traditional Christmas."

"I see." There had been no signs of the fast-approaching holiday as he'd passed through the hallway. No Christmas tree at the foot of the stairs or holly wreath on the door. "Okay, any problems that you're aware of? Spats with girlfriends, trouble from ex-boyfriends?" There had been a few *ex boyfriends*, he wasn't so sure about girlfriends, but either way he was starting to build a picture of a girl with more money than sense and more acquaintances than true friends.

"Detective, all I know is that she left here at approximately 11am yesterday. It's now almost twenty-four hours and I've heard nothing, absolutely nothing."

"Have you spoken to Ned?"

O'Hanlon frowned. "No not yet. I didn't want to worry him until I was sure."

Worry him? or alert him to the fact that dear little Jasmine might have given him the heave-ho, just like the yachtsman, the footballer and all those in between? Samuels sensed reluctance in O'Hanlon to tell him the full story, despite his concern for his only child.

"Sure of what, sir?"

"Sure that there is something to worry about, detective."

"I will need to contact him myself, sir. You do understand that, don't you? He may have information. Jasmine may have told him of her plans. She might actually be with him now. Have you tried to contact her?"

"I've called her phone repeatedly. Left messages for her to call back. At first the calls went straight to voice mail. Now the line is dead."

"Mr O'Hanlon, you've had occasion to lock horns in the past with many in the criminal fraternity. Do you suspect that your career on the bench may have some bearing on Jasmine's disappearance?"

"I'm not sure I know what you mean."

Samuels thought he'd made himself very clear. He tried again. "Simply put. Do you have any enemies? Anyone who would take pleasure from seeing you distressed or would benefit from taking your daughter from you?"

"Detective, I think that's highly unlikely. Yes, I've no doubt there are convicted criminals who would like nothing better than to see me squirm, but I've been retired for almost two years now and Jasmine has remained untouched by my judicial decisions for twenty-four years. Why now, when I have no further influence, would someone think to use her as leverage or indeed as a stick to beat me with?"

Samuels shrugged, why indeed?

"I'd like to take a look at Jasmine's room if I may. Perhaps you'd accompany me. You might notice if anything's missing, clothes, a suitcase, that kind of thing."

"There's nothing missing, detective. I've already checked."

"Well perhaps we can check together. Something may jog your memory."

O'Hanlon struggled to his feet and reached for his stick. "Yes of course, if you think it will help."

Jasmine's room overlooked the lake at the rear of the house. It was spacious, well-appointed and exactly what Samuels expected to see. A walk-in wardrobe full of designer labels, enough shoes to keep a small country shod and a dressing table overflowing with make-up, creams and perfumes. If there was anything out of place, it didn't jump out at him. He ran his hand idly over the various cosmetics and turned to O'Hanlon, who hovered by the open door.

"Perhaps you could get those numbers for me, sir. Jasmine's, Ned's and anyone else you think could be useful, while I finish up here. We may be able to locate Jasmine through her mobile phone, or at least get an idea of where and when it was last used."

"Now?"

"If you don't mind."

"Of course," muttered O'Hanlon.

Samuels sensed O'Hanlon's reluctance to leave him alone in the room. He waited until he had gone before pulling out his phone and using the camera to take some random shots that might provide him with more insight when he had time to look at them properly. Ideally back at the station, when O'Hanlon wasn't breathing down his neck. He focused on Jasmine's cluttered dressing table. He hoped that, like the contents of a ladies handbag, it might offer up some additional clues. Stuck to the mirror was a photo, presumably of Ned, with a lipstick kiss at the corner and a biro line scored through the image from corner to corner. Hmmm, perhaps Daddy's opinion of an ideal choice of suitor was not wholly shared by Jasmine. Samuels made a note to speak to Ned sooner rather than later.

Adjacent to the photo was an invitation to the opening of a new gallery in London. The examples of conceptual art illustrating the card didn't interest Samuels in the slightest, but the date on the invite did. Christmas Eve. Samuels had to assume that Jasmine intended to accept the invitation and attend.

Beneath the invitation, stuck to the mirror with Christmas adhesive tape, was an appointment card for a city centre salon. Bingo! He jotted down the details and when he'd done, he pocketed his notebook and followed O'Hanlon downstairs.

"You know, Mr O'Hanlon, in the majority of cases like this, the missing person turns up safe and well and there's a perfectly logical reason for their absence. I'm sure the same will apply here and you have nothing to worry about."

"I do hope you're correct, detective."

Samuels nodded, turned to leave and then paused on the threshold to slip a card with his contact details from his wallet. "If Jasmine does get in touch or if you're contacted by anyone else regarding your daughter, please let me know immediately."

"Of course."

"Just one last thing," added Samuels as he reached the bottom step and pulled his car keys from his pocket. "Can I ask why you sent for me?"

O'Hanlon regarded him in silence for a moment or two before replying. "I recalled the professional way you carried out your duties when we last had occasion to meet. I continue to hear good things about you, Samuels. You're a good, honest, reliable officer and I know that you'll do your utmost to find Jasmine."

"I'd like to think we're all, honest and reliable, sir?"

O'Hanlon smiled grimly. "I wish that were true, detective, but after twenty years on the bench I know that's not the case."

Eighteen

"Samuels, Baker, my office now!" Davies' voice bellowed through the incident room. Samuels had barely shrugged out of his coat. He glanced across at Baker, who had followed him into the station. There was no mistaking his smug expression. He wondered what had transpired in his absence and his stomach churned with irritation. That would just put the icing on the cake, and the end to an exhausting twenty-four hours, if Baker had managed to scoop up Miller while he was busy cataloguing the many failed romances of Jasmine O'Hanlon. Not that he wanted Miller to evade capture, but if he was going to be apprehended, Samuels naturally wanted to be the one slipping on the cuffs.

"What's up, sir?" he asked as he hovered in the doorway. For once Baker had beaten him to it and was in there and already seated.

Davies grimaced "What's up? I'll tell you what's up, John, ruddy tabloid vultures. Someone should take a shotgun to the lot of them."

"Huh?"

"Shut the door, John and take a seat before I have a bloody coronary."

"Why, what's happened? Have we got Miller?"

"Not yet, but he just rode his way up to number one on our most wanted list, closely followed by that imbecile of a muckraker Cameron, at *The Gazette*."

"I'm not with you, sir."

"No, I don't expect you are, John. You've spent the morning out in the sticks hobnobbing with the landed gentry while all of us poor buggers have been shaking this case until it seems every bleedin' crime on the books has dropped out."

"You were the one who sent me out there, sir." Samuels reminded his boss.

"Yes, well, that's as maybe. In a nutshell, while you were away all the ruddy mice came out to play. That'll teach me to delegate. I should have pulled on my green wellies and gone to see O'Hanlon myself." He turned abruptly to Baker. "Did you bring coffee in with you?"

"Er, no, sir. I just got back when you called."

"Right well ... I suppose it'll have to wait." He turned back to Samuels, the colour infusing his cheeks a clear indication of just how rattled he was. Perhaps it was just as well he wasn't adding caffeine to the mix, considered Samuels, but nevertheless his disquiet was catching and Samuels wished he would just get on with it. "We received another photo, John, a whole ruddy gallery in fact. In addition, that piss-pot Cameron received a phone call and DI Baker didn't find a body in the gutter, though I'm sure we all wish he had. He found a car instead."

Baker smiled smugly.

"A good morning all round, then, though I'm not sure I understand what all the fuss is about. I've only been away a couple of hours."

"All the fuss! I'll give you bloody fuss, John. As if I'm not getting enough grief over the bank robberies, that tosser Miller has a spade in his hand and is digging my ruddy grave."

"Sorry, I don't get it, "said Samuels. "What has this to do with our man?"

"Just sit down, John. I'm getting to it." He scooped up a sheaf of photocopies, which he laid face down on the desk and then took a long calming breath. When it seemed to Samuels that he'd forgotten what he was about to say, he smiled and continued. "Okay, first things first, how did you get on with O'Hanlon?"

Samuels shrugged. "Difficult to say. He's worried about his daughter. I get the impression he has a specific reason why he's worried, but he's playing things close to his chest for some reason."

"Any leads?"

"Same old stuff. I have the salon she visited yesterday morning. The boyfriend in London, that's about it. No known arguments, no fallings out. I haven't had a chance to pursue anything, sir. I just got through the door."

Davies nodded. "You may well be right in your initial impression, John. In fact I think it's a good bet that O'Hanlon does know more than he's letting on. That man has rubbed shoulders with almost as many scroats as we have and the majority of them are behind bars because of him. He no doubt rubbed a few of them up the wrong way when he donned his wig and gown and I suspect there'll be more than a few languishing at Her Majesty's pleasure and wishing bad things on the judge who put them there."

"I expect you're right, sir, though he certainly didn't bite when nudged in that direction. In fact he was quite dismissive of the theory."

"Yes, well I reckon he'll bite your bloody hand off now. These images were received this morning, John. The techies tell me they may have encountered some delivery problem due to the size of the file. They were brought to my attention less than an hour ago. The delay may well be significant. Time will tell."

Samuels glanced at Baker. It was obvious by his sudden interest that this was fresh news to him too. Somehow that made up for the fact that he'd borne the initial brunt of Davies' frustration.

"They are disturbing," continued Davies as picked up the papers and crossed to the wall-mounted white board. He fastened the topmost image to the board with a magnet and stood back. "Very disturbing."

The first image was indistinct. Davies looked on as Samuels and Baker struggled to work out exactly what they were looking at. Wet grey concrete and a curled length of blue nylon rope, illuminated by a camera flash. It wouldn't have looked out of place on the stark wall of an upmarket gallery, one of those obtuse images that everyone raved about simply because of the name of the creator. Only this wasn't a work of art, it was the first page in a chilling story board. The shot was angled down toward the floor, so there was nothing else in the picture. No clue as to the surroundings or whether the image had been taken indoors or out.

"Huh?" Baker echoed Samuels' own confusion as they both edged closer and cocked their heads this way and that in an effort to make sense of the picture. Davies repositioned it on whiteboard to make room for the second image.

Picture two was taken from more or less the same position but a little higher from the ground, as if the photographer had simply raised the camera height. The shot captured the four legs of a wooden chair – and a pair of feet encased in bright red stiletto shoes. The patent leather was badly scuffed as if the shoe, and by default the wearer, had been dragged over a rough surface. One of the ridiculously high heels was snapped. Slender ankles were tightly bound to the chair legs with the nylon rope.

"Shit, that's all we bloody need." Samuels leaned away as realisation dawned. No wonder the boss was in a flap. Davies raised a palm to forestall any questions and proceeded to pin up the subsequent images.

The young woman's legs were bound again at the knees, her tanned thighs bare. Shot by shot the camera meandered its way up her torso. She was clothed, but barely decent. Short skirt, tighter top, dressed for summer in St Tropez, not winter in the north of England. Her skin was covered in fine goose pimples. The camera lens had picked up every tiny detail.

Her head was downcast, chin on her chest, a tangle of long blonde hair shielding her face. Her arms, presumably tied at the wrists, were suspended above her head, out of shot, but her shoulders were pulled into what must have been a painful position, particularly if she'd been restrained in that position for any length of time.

The final shot caught her looking directly into the camera lens through flash-glazed blue eyes. Hair swept roughly aside to reveal teared mascara, smudged lipstick and a filthy rag stuffed into her mouth. On a handwritten sign strung around her neck were two words, *For Sale*.

"Bloody hell!" muttered Samuels. "Have these images been verified? Is that definitely her – Jasmine?"

Davies placed the original image from the day before next to it. Although the difference between the happy go-lucky girl on the arm of a billionaire and the wretched young woman tied to a chair was startling, it was obvious they were both images of the same girl.

Samuels shook his head. "I don't get it, sir. You said Miller had just moved up a notch. I don't get the connection?"

Davies resumed his seat at the desk. "The mobile phone you lifted from the crash scene was registered to Jasmine."

"She must have witnessed the crash. Wrong place. Wrong time?" suggested Baker.

"Not necessarily." Samuels traced the images absently with his hand as if that might help him understand what had happened. "The phone was there. It doesn't mean she was there at the time of the crash and it doesn't tie her to our man. We're looking at two entirely separate incidents. I don't see why you're connecting them."

Davies sighed as if the connection was obvious and Samuels was missing some glaring point. "The phone was used to send the images, John."

"It still doesn't link her to Miller. It just doesn't make sense. There's nothing in his profile to suggest anything as serious as this." Samuels gestured to the images on the board.

"He robbed a string of banks, John. I'd say that was pretty serious. He's a career criminal."

"Yes, sir, but this is something entirely different. We all know that." He pointed to the last image, "This is all about power. He's a bank robber, not a psycho."

"How do we know what he is?" added Baker. "He just killed two of his muckas, who knows how crazy he is? That arrest sheet was what, three years old? You said it yourself, where's he been since, what's he been doing?"

Samuels ignored Baker and stared at the images, as if they might summon up the answer. He directed his next question to Davies. "No, sir, hang on, you said the images were sent yesterday. What time yesterday?"

"We can't be sure when they were taken, but they were sent at 4:37pm."

Samuels pulled out his notebook and sifted through the pages looking for the required details. "The bank was hit at 4:30pm. Officers arrived on scene at the crash at 4:57pm. There's no way that Miller could have been in two places at the same time."

"You seem keen to offer him an alibi, John."

"I'm not. I just can't get this to work, logistically."

Baker shrugged. "Unless he was sending the images when he crashed the car, you know, distracted, not watching where he was going."

Samuels shook his head. "That just doesn't work for me. Sorry."

"John, there's more."

"What?" Samuels frowned at Davies.

"Like I said, we received the images via the phone that was found at the crash scene. Jasmine's phone. The person who has Jasmine sent those images. I think we can all agree on that. You're quite right, John. There's nothing to suggest from that evidence that our man Miller has any connection, other than bad timing and bad driving. However..." he turned to Baker. "While trawling the gutters for the elusive Mr Miller, DI Baker here came up trumps. He found the missing girl's car. Over to you, Baker."

"Abandoned, driver's window shot out, interior covered in blood." Baker paused for effect.

"I suppose that changes things," muttered Samuels.

"Indeed it does, John. It turns a bad situation into a disaster."

"Her blood?"

"That was my first thought, but after seeing those pictures I'd say it's unlikely," said Baker. "The images don't show any injuries that would generate that much blood. The car was covered. Main concentration found on the front passenger seat, but traces on the bonnet and front bumper."

"Perhaps she hit him?"

"Perhaps, but doubtful."

"Any witnesses?"

"No. The car was dumped down by the brown-field regeneration zone. When our guys showed up it attracted a bit of interest, enticed the low-lifes out of the gutter. A few kids nicking lead off factory roofs, a couple of winos, a weirdo Goth, you know how it is, your typical scrap yard junkies. No one saw anything, no one heard anything."

"So again, I have to ask, why Miller?"

Baker slid a sly smile into his detective of the year performance and Samuels bit back a sharp reaction. "Because although we haven't got any DNA results yet, we have got a number of bloodstained fingerprints lifted from the interior which match Miller's. He shot out the window, he hotwired the car. I don't think there's any doubt about that."

Davies pushed back his seat and got to his feet. "Thank you, DI Baker. Good work. So now we know for sure Miller is injured, and badly, if the amount of blood is any indication. An injured animal is at its most dangerous, detectives. I'm sure you both realise that. We need officers checking the hospitals, pharmacies ... any reported break-ins. If he seeks medical help, I want to know about it."

"It's being done as we speak, sir," confirmed Baker. Samuels bristled at his smug tone but wasn't quite sure what to say in response. He still couldn't make sense of the sequence of events.

"So we have Miller in her car. I'm sorry but that still doesn't put him with her."

"John, bloody hell what more do you want? The guy is a nutter. Robs the bank, probably high on something, crashes the car, grabs the girl. Does it matter how he did it?"

"It matters to me. We're meant to investigate, not jump to conclusions."

"You're absolutely right, John." Davies shot a warning glance at Baker, "But perhaps this final piece in the puzzle will convince you that Miller is our man, both for the bank and the kidnapping."

"Go on."

"At approx 6am this morning. Cameron, the idiot editor of *The Gazette*, was woken by a phone call. Despite his state, having been out on the piss with members of the council 'til the early hours, he reports the caller was female and in a high state of distress. She identified herself simply as Jazz. She claimed she was being held at gunpoint and forced to make the call by Miller. I have his transcript of the call here." He pulled out a sheet of paper and offered it to Samuels.

"He didn't record it?" Samuels scanned the brief summary. It didn't make for pleasant reading. The young woman was obviously terrified. The sentences were garbled, many unfinished.

"Like I said, an idiot, a hung-over idiot at that, but let's be honest here, John, who does record their telephone calls other than telesales companies and the emergency services?"

"So how do we know it wasn't some crank call from some bird he stood up at the councillors' Christmas party?"

"We had his phone records checked. The call came from a mobile phone registered to Jack Miller."

There wasn't much that Samuels could say to that. He crossed to the window and watched as sleet battered the glass.

"Okay," he admitted begrudgingly. "So basically, you're saying he robbed the bank, crashed the car, bumped into the girl and snatched her?"

"That's how it's looking."

"And the images?"

"Could be the techies got it wrong and it was 4:37am rather than pm."

"Since when did we alter the facts to fit?"

Davies exhaled his exasperation loudly. "If you have a better explanation, John. I'd love to hear it. In the meantime, we need to squeeze O'Hanlon a little harder to see if there's a connection between him and Miller that we've missed."

Samuels nodded. "Was there any demand in the telephone call?"

"Not that Cameron can recall."

"So why make the call?"

"He's just letting us know that he means business. I expect he'll call again."

"Any idea where she's being held?"

"No, but we do have Miller's phone number and the address registered to it, and the next time he uses it we can try for an exact location."

"Do we really think he's that stupid?"

"We can hope, but as we have his number we can pre-empt that call."

Davies turned away from Baker and addressed Samuels directly.

"I know we've had bulletins on all major channels since news of the crash broke but now we up the ante. We need to get Miller's face out there and we need to get Jasmine O'Hanlon's out there too. I have a press conference in..." he checked his watch, "...twenty minutes, and I'll be sticking with *concern growing for missing twenty-four year old socialite.*"

"Are you going to connect the cases?"

Davies smiled. "I'm going to plant the suggestion by denying the connection. Let's rattle Miller's cage in the hope that Jazz will fall out of her own accord. But let's not play our hand too soon. She's a vulnerable innocent in all this and we can't let our burning desire to catch Miller jeopardise her safety."

"Vulnerable?"

Davies glared at Baker. "You saw the pictures. Whoever has her is disturbed and if that *is* Miller then, I must assume that he is also. So yes, of course she's vulnerable."

"Sure," Baker raised his hands in apology "That's not what I meant."

"What *do* you mean?"

"I mean, get a look at her...she's a stunner but has she anything between her ears, is she going to keep her wits about her or play right into his hands?"

"What are you saying?"

Baker shrugged. "I'm saying we need armed response on standby, if we get this loser in our sights, we need to take him out. No questions. The longer he has her, the more damage he'll do. He's done the bank, got away with the money and now he's got himself some pretty tasty dessert."

Samuels glanced at Davies, keen to catch his reaction. Baker's usual chauvinistic comments were misplaced, but he was correct. They couldn't afford to take chances. But a shoot to kill was unwise while there was any possibility that he was holding a hostage.

Davies inclined his head briefly. "No need to get all gung-ho, DI Baker, let's hope it doesn't come to that. As I said I'm meeting the press shortly and I'll feed them as little as possible, though I'm sure Cameron will be difficult to gag unless I promise him an exclusive. We shall see. Let me have an update as soon as you have one." He paused to study the men closely. "I can't stress enough, the need to wrap this up quickly and successfully, gentleman."

Davies shuffled up the papers from his desk, a good indication that the meeting was over. "We need to know everything about what Jasmine did yesterday. Who she met, what she bought... we may have our theories, but yes, John, we also need evidence that will carry this case all the way to court and beyond." He shot a quick glance at Baker before returning his attention to Samuels. "And while we're about it, I'd quite like to know what she was doing down by the docks after dark. If it transpires she was doing anything daddy wouldn't like, then we keep a lid on it."

Samuels agreed with his boss. He had an idea that cover girl Jazz, with her pet Chihuahua and string of eligible suitors, was not the innocent little girl daddy assumed.

"And let's not forget we have two enquiries running here," continued Davies. "Make sure someone goes back over the CCTV... yes I know we've been over them till we're sick of the sight of them, but we're missing something. Look at the new tapes. See if they provide anything additional. Go over the witness statements from the bank. Miller planned these robberies. He got clean away three times out of four. It was only the rain that jinxed him this time...someone must be helping him. Maybe that someone is inside the bank? Cashier; cleaner; bloke who waters the plants? Go back over everything." He pointed a stubby finger at Baker. "I want you both over at Miller's flat, turn the place upside down. Let's see what makes this laddo tick."

Baker smiled. "Sure thing, guv. I'm on it. If there's anything in that flat, I'll find it."

"Good. And John, if he makes contact I want you on the other end of the line. If anyone is going to talk sense into the ruddy tosser, I'd put my money on you."

Samuels watched as Baker headed straight to the coffee machine. Baker might well be correct in his assumption that the only way to stop Miller was with a bullet. But the thought of him evading prison, even by virtue of a marksman's shot, rankled. He wanted him caught, not killed. He wanted to look him in the eye and ask him how he'd robbed four banks and got away with it.

****

Baker took his coffee, mumbled a throwaway comment about needing a quick cigarette, then bypassed his desk and headed for the privacy of the car park. He sheltered in the doorway and pulled out his phone, safe from the escalating weather and any prying eyes or ears. McKenzie picked up at the third ring.

"We have a problem."

"We do?"

Baker cast a quick glance over his shoulder. "The witness is high profile. Miller's name is out."

"That's two problems."

"Yeah, well, like I said; problems. He has a hostage, Jazz O'Hanlon, the judge's daughter."

"So I hear."

"You do? So...this changes things surely?"

"Not at all, it merely adds a challenge. I'm sure you'll think of something. What about Miller, do you have a plan?"

Baker twisted his face, sure he had a plan; it involved keeping as far away as possible from the self-righteous Samuels. "He's a psycho, we're on shoot first; ask questions later."

"Good make sure you aim well. In the meantime Baker, you're on the graveyard shift."

"Huh?"

"Bury everything...including Miller."

Nineteen

Miller parked in the alley adjacent to the bar, nosing the car alongside overflowing bins and general crap. It stood out but there was nothing he could do about that. Elsewhere, the car shouted money. Parked here, it screamed drugs. He reached for the bag stuffed in the passenger footwell, lifted out a few bundles and tucked them under the seat. He figured, on balance, he was due some disability pay. He stepped from the car and adjusted his shoulder with a well concealed wince, before giving the guy propping up the side entrance the look that said quite clearly *don't fuck with the car*. Despite the fact it might yet prove to be his downfall, he was protective already. He gave it a lingering look. It was one hell of a motor. Shame he'd have to dump it by the end of the day.

Unwilling to force his way past the goon, with a shoulder that should have stayed in bed, he eased gently by instead. The man watched him. Miller was aware of the glare at his back and felt the need to make a stand, even though he wasn't quite sure what he was standing up to. He paused in the confines of the narrow corridor and turned.

"You got a problem, mate?"

The guy shrugged his massive frame. "I don't, but hey, can't say the same about you, Jacky boy. You fucked up big time. Your run of luck just ran out. Otto is not a happy man."

Okay, so he appeared to be well known, which kind of left him on the back foot, seeing as how he couldn't recall much at all. But reading between the lines, he got the feeling he wasn't usually in such deep shit. In fact, he figured with the kind of reputation Spook had alluded to, maybe he could pull this back around. He just needed to keep his wits about him.

The bar was gloomy, deliberately so. Most of the clientele, having suffered the glare of police line-ups, were unwilling to promote themselves under bright lights, indoors or out. So they congregated in The Scally, where deals were done and small fortunes made and lost all under the cover of semi darkness. Miller pocketed the glasses. He felt immediately at home and wasn't sure whether that was something he should be feeling good about. Having a natural gravitas to the seedy side of the street wasn't ordinarily something to be proud of.

"Is Otto around?" he asked after a cursory inspection revealed plenty of guys he wouldn't want to turn his back on, but no obvious candidate for the role of crime kingpin.

The barman considered him for a moment. Took in his battered appearance with a hint of a smirk and gestured to the stairs at the back of the room. "He's waiting for you. As you know, Jacky, the big man doesn't like to be kept waiting."

Stairs...there just had to be stairs. He ignored the pain in his shoulder and drew in a breath. The sooner he got this done, the sooner he could go curl up in a corner and die. He climbed them cautiously; stepping over a couple who it seemed couldn't wait to get home. He shook his head when he realised they weren't wrapped around each other getting acquainted. They were actually stoned and had probably been there since the previous night. He avoided a stain that in the dim light could easily be mistaken for blood but was more likely urine and revised his initial impression. The place was rank. Even worse than the dump he'd just come from. He kept his hands by his sides, unwilling to snag a discarded needle in the gloom.

He was met at the top by a man, as wide as he was tall, who gestured for him to raise his arms, a drill which relieved him of his gun, after a none-too-gentle patting down. His shoulder shrieked its protest at being manhandled and his mind strayed to the meds in his pocket. He should have popped one before he'd tackled the stairs, but figured when dealing with a man who didn't like to be kept waiting, he'd most likely need his chemical-free wits about him more than he needed his shoulder.

"Jacky." Otto was seated behind a desk with his back to the window. The desk was small, or Otto was huge. Either way, the light coming in from behind made him look like some kind of cartoon caricature, all steroids and glistening skin. Miller squinted, which he figured he was meant to do and what the whole set up was about.

"Otto," he replied. He wasn't offered a seat, so he stood, concentrating on the pain in his shoulder, using the regular beat of each throb to focus his mind.

Otto's suit would have been surprisingly smart had it been the correct size. As it was, the pin stripes were distorted in line with his various bulges and his tie was slightly askew. Miller figured Otto had got out of bed on the wrong side and he was the most likely cause.

"You had me worried, Jacky. No contact, no word except what they're saying all over the news. Here I am, thinking you must be dead. Or worse, you'd gone into business for yourself and taken my money with you." He cocked his head and studied Miller through piggy eyes deep set into his paunchy face.

The slightly feminine voice was at odds with his appearance and it threw Miller momentarily. It was there in the foggy recesses of his misbehaving memory, just out of reach, but definitely there. The picture was gradually coming together. He just needed it to get in focus, sooner rather than later.

"I had some issues," he muttered. "I came as soon as I was able." *Able*, he conceded, was perhaps an exaggeration.

"What happened, Jacky?"

Miller sighed. "Rain, Otto. That's what happened."

"And your two compadres?"

"What can I say, they fucking drowned."

"Must have been a helluva downpour?"

"You could say."

"You brought my money?"

Miller dropped the bag at his feet and nodded.

Otto's gaze followed the bag. "Is it all there?"

Miller shrugged. "More or less. I had some expenses. I couldn't exactly roll into A&E. I had to pay through the nose."

"They're saying you lifted a million. How much have you brought me?"

Miller thought of the money he'd left for the freaky girl and the two hundred grand he'd stashed in the car. "Banks exaggerate, you know that. It's all down to insurance. They're bigger crooks than we are." He held his nerve. Wasn't entirely sure whether staring Otto down was his usual tack, or the right thing to do under the circumstances, but was reluctant to show weakness by turning away.

Otto narrowed his eyes and stared straight back.

"And the police, how come they have you bang to rights? You managed to slide through clean as a whistle before. How did they get your name? Are you getting sloppy, Jacky?"

"So it's out there already?" Miller knew it wouldn't take the police long, but had hoped for a little longer to settle some old scores and get clean away.

"You, Frankie and Spidey, all over the news. Here I am enjoying my breakfast, watching bleedin' *Lorraine* on the telly and up you pop in all your glory. Not a pretty sight I can tell you. Someone has been making their gob go, Jacky, and we need to stop the rot before it leads right back here."

Miller knew exactly how they'd identified him and it had nothing to do with being sloppy. He thought of Spook. He should have put a bullet in her head while he had the chance. "Maybe you need to look closer to home, Otto." He gave a sideways glance at the guys slouched in the doorway. "Maybe someone doesn't care for the way I do things."

Otto studied him some more.

"Someone like Frankie, eh?"

"I told you, Frankie's dead."

"Convenient."

"For whom?"

"Frankie's been making his mouth go, Jacky. Not a happy soldier by all accounts."

Miller shrugged. "Frankie always was a gobshite."

"Maybe. But he's not talking now is he?"

Despite a twisting gut, Miller stood his ground, shifting his weight unobtrusively to ease the pain radiating from his shoulder. *You're a dead man, Jacky. Dead and fucking buried.* He tried to shake the words out of his head. Just what had that tosser Frankie said?

Otto narrowed his eyes slyly. "So, just an unfortunate accident that knocks out the little scroat with the big gob and leaves you with the cash?"

"Leaves *you* with the cash, Otto. Not me. But yeah, that's about it. Very unfortunate. I'm gutted."

"And shot?"

"Yeah, fucking Frankie – again – playing the fool. These things happen."

Otto nodded as if getting shot for all the wrong reasons was an everyday occurrence. "Does it hurt, Jacky?"

Miller shrugged. "What do you think?"

"Well it serves you fucking right!" Otto pounded a fist so hard on the desk top that a porcelain statue of Elvis bounced straight off and smashed on the floor. Miller sidestepped to avoid the dismembered king's head. The guys at the door stepped back, as if they fully expected Otto to pull out a gun and finish off what Frankie started. Instead, he leaned forward as far as the desk and his girth would allow. "My nose is telling me something isn't right here. Now it could be my allergies..." he swept an accusing look at the henchman, "anyone got a cat under their coat? No, I didn't think so. So, Jacky, that leaves me with an itchy snout and no fucking gobshite to scratch it. Like I said, very bleedin' convenient."

Miller spread his arms wide and risked an irritated sigh. "I crashed the car. I was lucky, the guys weren't. That's it, Otto. Nothing more to tell."

Otto snorted. "Oh, but there is, Jacky. You've missed out the best bit. When were you going to tell me about the girl?"

Miller looked at the ceiling, counted the cobwebs hanging from the light fittings and played for time. Which bloody girl? He thought again of Spook. There was probably a file an inch thick on that one. Shrinks could write an entire thesis based solely on her and dine out on the proceeds. But of course that wasn't who Otto meant. The identity of his *victim* must also be common knowledge and by the look of glee on Otto's face he reckoned it probably wasn't wise to admit he didn't actually have her.

"There's not a lot to tell," he hedged. "She got in my way, I moved her aside."

Otto smiled. "Jacky, you are one cool customer. Jazz O'Hanlon – that girl has got to be worth at least ten times what's in the bag... maybe more with the right handling." He rubbed his hands together in Fagan-esque anticipation.

Miller felt his *couldn't give a fuck* façade begin to crumble. He could almost hear the cell doors clanging shut and the jangle of keys being thrown away. He made a concerted effort to straighten up. "Really?"

Relaxing back in his seat, Otto steepled his fingers and narrowed his eyes. "You know, Jacky, I accept you're one slick bank robber, can't fault your planning or your delivery – except maybe this one time, and we'll get to the bottom of that later, you can be sure of that. You've netted me a pretty penny these last few months, always know where to get it, how to get it, in, out, no problems whatsoever. In fact, after my dear old mother, I'd have put you next on my Christmas card list. But, Jacky lad, now I'm disappointed. I never took you for what they're saying on the news."

"What are they saying on the news...?"

Otto shook his head theatrically and raised one brow. "Now I know she's a looker an' all and probably very tempting to a young hot-blooded lad such as yourself, but they reckon you aren't the nicest of kidnappers. That sewer rat Cameron at *The Gazette* says the judge's darling daughter has been – how shall I put it – compromised in a way unbecoming in a gentleman."

"Huh?"

"'You been messing with the merchandise, Jacky?"

Miller grimaced. So this was Spook's idea of improvisation. He'd hoped she was just messing about in her crazy way, spinning him a line, but obviously not. "Who said I was a gentleman?" he grunted.

Otto laughed; a badly executed attempt at a guffaw that came out as high pitched giggle. Miller looked away and caught the henchmen out the corner of his eye as they shuffled with embarrassment.

"That's why I like you, Jacky, always the comedian. But joking aside, this is business. Where is she, lad? You know we're in this together, share and share alike. You work for me and I carry the can for all your misdemeanours."

"Don't worry, Otto, she's cool. I have her tucked away in a safe place." So safe, he hadn't a clue where it was.

"I need more than that, Jacky. In fact I need the girl." He grinned slyly. "You're wrecked, lad. Just look at you. Let me pick up the pieces and maybe, just maybe, I'll forget about the cock-up at the bank and the unfortunate demise of your cohorts. Hand her over and head on down to the beach, Jacky. I hear the Costas calling your name."

Sure he could do that. He could hand over the hostage he didn't have, if the hostage he'd just ditched hadn't pulled a fast one on him. He gestured to the money bag. "I kept my end of the bargain. Any additional perks are mine."

Otto sighed deeply. "Now, Jacky, you know that's not how things work. You've been with me long enough to know that you don't walk away unless I say you can. And I'm saying you can't. I'm saying you'll stay where you're fucking put, until I tell you otherwise."

Miller straightened up, cast an eye about the room and figured his chances of making it out and down the stairs in one piece were slim to say the least. Otto watched him shrewdly.

"Jacky, I figure you've had a bump on the head, gone and got yourself shot an' all, so I'm going to forgive the fact you cost me two good men. I'm even going to overlook the fact that you might have forgotten your manners and gotten a little frisky in the young lady's presence. But don't go thinking I'm getting soft. You work for me. I want that girl and since you don't want to give her up just yet, you may as well work the deal out with McKenzie."

"McKenzie?"

Otto spread his podgy hands wide and shook his head. "Jeez, Jacky, take a pill, do something, anything, but don't stand there and tell me that you don't know who McKenzie is. You've been feeding him for the last eighteen months..."

The dominoes lined up in Miller's head began to topple, building speed exponentially, until the room swam before him and he had to sidestep to maintain his balance.

"Hey, Jacky?"

He felt a rough tug on his arm and he swung around with a curse as pain jolted him back.

Otto was staring at him, the goons were staring at him and Miller stared straight back. They had every right to look at him like he was some freak show idiot. What the fuck had he got himself caught up in?

"Jacky, you need a doctor? You've gone a funny colour."

He swallowed. He couldn't even begin to fathom it out, but he could stall. At the very least he could do that, until his natural ability for planning kicked in.

"I just took a bullet in the shoulder, Otto. I need to lay low for a few days."

"You haven't got days, Jacky. You've got the law on one side, you've got me on the other and somewhere in the middle you have McKenzie. We all want the same thing. Now, if you don't want to end up with a few more bullet holes, I suggest you quit being a soft shite and get out there and bring me that sweet little package, Jazz O'Hanlon."

Miller smiled sourly. It wasn't as if he wouldn't like to oblige. If he had the girl he would have thrown her in the ring and let them all fight over her. But unfortunately if he wanted off the hook, he had to come up with the goods – and to do that, he needed to find Spook.

Twenty

He was down the stairs and practically out the door. Gun returned, self-esteem almost intact, when a commotion at the bar drew his attention. Through the gloom he could see someone had pulled a knife and was currently looking down the barrel of the barman's sawn-off.

Otto, lumbering down the stairs in Miller's wake, stumbled over the recumbent couple and broke his fall on Miller's retreating back. The resulting heavy hand on his shoulder caused Miller to yell out with pain. All eyes turned from the incident at the bar to the spectacle of Otto, practically upended. Smirks were quickly stifled as Otto covered his less than dignified entrance with a scowl.

"What the fuck?" He shoved Miller aside and zeroed in on the standoff at the bar. "What's going on? Since when did we let the fucking undead in here?" Miller didn't have to look. He knew exactly who Otto referred to. He swung his gaze all the same, and there she was – his ruddy shadow – the ghoul with the knife.

"She was sniffing around outside," said the barman. "I sent her packing, next thing she's trying to roll a punter. Seemed a little too interested in what's going on down here."

Otto stepped closer, angling his head for a better look. Miller glanced from one to the other. If she had any sense she'd be taking a step back, but instead she squared herself up, stuck out her chin and glared straight back at Otto.

"You got a problem, sugar?" asked Otto. He tapped at his head like he'd already worked out she wasn't quite on the same wavelength as the rest of the population. "You know where you are? You know who you're messing with?"

Spook's lips twitched in that amused way of hers and Miller waited. Despite the fact that his mind was still half-set jelly, he knew for a fact Otto wouldn't find her funny at all. She dropped her gaze and shook her head dismissively at the badly fitted suit. Lowering the hand with the knife, she proceeded to circle Otto slowly, tutting under her breath. Otto looked on, bewildered. The elephant and the mouse. Only this little mouse wasn't about to get trodden on. As she rounded Otto's oversized rear she flicked a glance at Miller and winked.

The little bride of Frankenstein was going to get herself killed and although it was probably long overdue and he'd every reason to want to see the back of her, Miller couldn't let that happen – yet.

Otto, finally jarred out of his stupor, reached out his oversized mauler as she strayed too close, grabbed Spook by the throat and shook her. Miller tensed, torn between the desire to punch the air and cheer Otto on and the need to intervene.

"What are you, some kind of freak? Think you can come in here and play your bleedin' kooky games?" She hung from his hand like a painted marionette, offering no resistance whatsoever. Miller, the only one party to her peculiar behaviour, guessed that everything she did was choreographed – and her broken little bird act was no exception. He sensed her amusement, it fizzled out from her like electricity, so much so, he was surprised Otto wasn't lit up like a Christmas tree. Apparently oblivious, to the ticking bomb in his hand, Otto turned to the barman and with very little effort sent her sprawling across the floor towards him. "Get rid of her. We don't need any additional attention. We've got enough of that, thanks to Jacky boy here."

"What do you want me to do with her?" The guy pulled her to her feet, knocked the knife from her hand and placed the twin barrels of the shotgun at her head. He gave her a sidelong glance, maybe considering what *he* might like to do with her. She gave him a similar one back and Miller reckoned if push came to shove, Spook would likely come out on top. She was a fraction of the man's size, but where cunning was concerned she was way out in front. All the same, he couldn't take the risk of her meeting her match before she'd delivered up his hostage.

"Fuck her, kill her...do what you like. Just make sure when you're done her body doesn't lead the police back here. They're going to be all over this place like a bloody rash by the end of the day and I don't want the stink of the recently deceased to catch their snouts."

It seemed Otto's day wasn't getting any better and neither was his temper, and it sounded to Miller like his cue. He sighed, stepped forward reluctantly and raised his own weapon.

"She's with me." The words were forced out and he knew, as the last syllable hit the room, that he would live to regret them. The barman shifted his aim and Miller heard at least half a dozen weapons being similarly cocked behind him. Over by the dart board, a thug in knock-off designer gear brandished an upturned beer bottle. A Newcastle standoff – half a dozen shooters and a bottle of Brown Ale, things couldn't really get any worse.

"Huh?" One word from Otto, but it kind of summed up Miller's own take on the whole situation.

"I told her to wait outside." He shrugged. "She's not housebroken yet."

Otto looked from one to the other. "Jacky, you've got me worried. You've been mixing with the wrong sort."

Miller gave a sour smile in response. "What can I say, I have exotic tastes." In his peripheral vision he caught Spook's amusement. He didn't share it.

"Exotic, I can appreciate, but downright weird is, well, just weird. You need a break, Jacky, far away from here, with a willowy blonde on your arm." He shrugged at the barman. "Let her go, Benny."

Benny dropped her reluctantly. Miller figured Benny had a secret fancy for the exotic and wasn't entirely pleased at having the opportunity snatched out from under his nose. Spook landed, catlike, retrieved her knife from the bar room floor and wagged a scolding finger at her captor. His aggressive step towards her was immediately matched by Miller. Checkmate. His fingers tightened around the gun. His shoulder screamed its protest as he held his arm outstretched. This was madness. He couldn't believe he was standing up against Otto's heavies for a weirdo who got her kicks with a sharp blade. She'd tied him to a bed, tortured him, filled him with so many drugs he still wasn't sure which way was up, but without her he was totally fucked and he knew it.

Spook sashayed innocently through the testosterone atmosphere, dropped her thick black lashes at Otto and fitted herself snugly beneath Miller's arm.

She hadn't said a single word and yet she had every guy and every gun in the room hanging on her every move. Something had to give and Miller decided it had better be him. His shoulder couldn't take any more. He exhaled slowly, lowered his weapon and sensed the same being replicated behind him. There was only Benny left, looking aggrieved. As luck would have it, Otto stepped in to save the day.

"Put it away, Benny, and think yourself lucky. A girl like that...you'd likely catch something *exotic* and your missus would have your hide." He turned to Miller, his eyes revealing he wasn't totally convinced at what had just gone down but had more important things to think about. "Are you still here, Jacky?" He tapped at his watch and shook his head. "Time's ticking on and you know what you have to do. I suggest you jump to it."

Miller bundled Spook along the narrow corridor, bouncing his way off the stacked crates of counterfeit booze and cigarettes lining the walls. For once, the pain in his shoulder wasn't the uppermost thing on his mind.

"Have you got a death wish?" he hissed in her ear, his hand tight at the back of her neck. He wanted to shake the attitude out of her. Maybe he would, when she'd served her purpose.

"Haven't we all?"

"You're crazy. Fucking crazy."

"You shouldn't have dumped me, Jack."

"Dumped you? Sweetheart when I dump you, you'll know about it. You'll be in the river with a bag of ready-mix tied to your ankle."

"Don't call me sweetheart," she scolded softly.

"I'll call you any damn thing I like. You nearly got me killed in there..." He braced himself with a hand on her back as she stumbled headlong into the exit; an armour plated door that already bore the scars of a few failed assaults. The fact that the bullet holes and bloodstains were on the inside bore testament to the ferocity of The Scally's usual bar room brawls. The doorman who should have been manning it had abandoned his post to catch the entertainment in the bar. Miller wished he'd stuck around. He'd a mind to take out his frustration on someone his own size.

He gave the outward-opening door a hefty kick and barrelled out of it, dragging Spook by the collar, but she was quickly discarded when the sudden daylight, in stark contrast to the dingy bar interior, had him reaching to shield his eyes instead. "Shit," he muttered as he fumbled for the sunglasses stuffed in the neck of his T-shirt. "Come on, we haven't got all day." He shoved her from behind, the gun, still in his hand, pressed hard into the small of her back and she grumbled her response. "Those buggers in there won't stand around forever. They'll be out here any minute gawking like bloody sightseers, wondering what the hell I'm doing with the likes of you and laying bets..." he stopped dead in his tracks, his words petering out.

A patrol car blocked the end of the alley. Two police officers were circling his car, checking details via their radios. There was a sound of static and the reversing horn of a tow truck.

Shit!

He grabbed a handful of Spook's collar and hurriedly stepped back, but the spring-loaded door had locked shut behind them. With no doorman inside to release the catch, there was nowhere for them to go. Miller slipped the gun into his jeans and adjusted his T-shirt to cover the stock. As the nearest officer raised his head at the commotion, Spook turned, slipped a hand around the back of Miller's neck and rose on tiptoe to meet him.

"Come on, Jack," she breathed against his mouth, "show 'em what you've got." She angled her mouth, pressed hard against him and he tasted his own blood as her teeth caught his lip.

He shot a glance past her. The officer was watching with mild interest, his attention swaying between them and the car. Miller took a breath, swung her round and pushed her up against the barred door. "Make like your enjoying this," he hissed as he closed the gap.

She kissed him again, made it last and slid her hands beneath his T-shirt, raking her nails against his skin. "What makes you think I'm not?"

He winced as her nails dug deeper into his back, her fingers squeezing hard against battered ribs, giving him little option but to press closer. "We have our wires crossed, sweetheart. I'm sure you're absolutely enjoying this little game, but the police will be expecting something a little less..."

"Exotic? Remember, Jack, I'm not properly housebroken. Is this what you mean?"

She smoothed her palms down, and slipped her tongue into his mouth. She tasted of aniseed. When he found his own hands straying and his mouth following hers, he pulled himself back with a jolt and scrubbed her taste from his lips with the back of his hand.

"Get a room, mate," called the police officer as he climbed back into his car. "Or we'll book you both."

Miller nodded, mumbling his acquiescence, but he didn't step away from her until he heard the sound of the tow truck pulling away. The police followed it out of the alley in first gear, dodging the slalom of refuse and wheelie bins. He watched until the tail lights disappeared, then he turned back and scowled his irritation. Her black lip gloss was smudged, her mask of chalk-like makeup slightly askew, but the look on her face was of the self-satisfied cat that got the cream.

"So, Jack, how was that for you?"

"I'm a man. You put your hand in my pants and your tongue in my mouth and I'm gonna respond. Don't go thinking I actually like you." He shifted his gaze to the space where the car had been parked. "You just cost me two hundred grand."

Her lips twitched. "Jack, have a little faith?" She unhooked her black nylon bag from her shoulder and tossed it to him. "What do you think I was doing, sniffing around out here? I spotted the plod. I retrieved the cash. You can thank me later."

He had to admit, reluctantly albeit, that she was good. She'd perfected the art of being one step ahead. He didn't know how she did it but for once he was glad of it – and it certainly made sense to keep her on side until he got what he wanted.

"How did you know I was here?"

She tapped at her nose. "Need to know, Jack."

"Never mind *need to know*. What we need are wheels."

"Tra-la," she announced with a flourish and a dangling of car keys.

"What did you get?"

She pointed a polished black finger nail toward the end of the alley, where a beat-up Transit van sat unobtrusively alongside the crap. It didn't scream money or drugs.

For a moment he was stuck for words. He thought of the car that had just been towed and shrugged away the injustice. He only hoped they wouldn't need to make a quick getaway. "Where'd you get it?"

"A long stay car park. It should be good for a week or so."

Scrap yard more like. He cast a critical eye over it, kicked at the tyres before slipping into the driver's seat.

"I've seen better..."

"I don't doubt it, Mr Getaway Driver, but this one should see our job out without attracting unwanted attention."

"*Our* job?"

"Sure. Get with it. We're a team now. What are you waiting for?" She turned in her seat, slotted her seat belt into place and grinned at him. "Hit the road, Jack ..."

Twenty One

"Where are we going?" asked Spook.

"Where's Jazz?" countered Miller as he bounced the van along the cobbled alley and out onto the main road, nipping into the flow of traffic as the lights at the junction ahead changed in his favour.

"I asked first."

He shot her a quick glance before checking his mirror and changing lanes. "My flat, I need to get a change of clothes, pick up a few things."

"The police will be all over it."

"Thanks to you."

She shrugged her disinterest. "You don't have time for that. We have a deal."

"Do we?"

"Sure we do. The girl in exchange for your expertise. It won't take you long."

"I need to see the girl first."

She shook her head. "No way. Do you think I'm stupid?"

"You have to give me something ...."

She grinned, "What, like a finger?"

"Fuck, no!" He slammed on the brakes and leaned on the horn as a motorcyclist cut in front of him.

"A lock of her hair? A note to her daddy written in blood?"

"Be serious."

"I am."

"Seriously crazy."

"Yes well, we all do crazy things on occasion. I mean just look at you, Mr Bank Robber, you're hardly squeaky clean are you?"

He turned to look at her. She had her crossed feet braced on the dashboard, her arms folded loosely in her lap, like she hadn't a care in the world. "Yeah, but at least I'm not a nut job."

He slowed the van and cruised down the length of a terrace of tall Victorian houses. Student lets and subdivided flats and bedsits dominated the street. The whole area was transient, the population refreshed with every new university intake. One building stood out from the rest, its future infamy assured simply by the number of police cars parked outside on the double yellows. An officer stood sentry at the smashed front door while white-clad scene of crime officers exited with plastic bags. Bags full of his stuff. Shit. He ducked his head as he passed, thankful for the anonymity of the battered van. Maybe Spook wasn't so crazy after all.

The road was heavily marked with parking restrictions. Miller took a left turn and crossed a few similar streets before pulling up behind an Indian takeaway and switching off the engine. He sat for a moment staring out through the grimy windshield, taking stock while Spook sat and played with the stud in her tongue, click-clacking it against her teeth. He hadn't noticed it until earlier when she'd shoved both it and her tongue in his mouth. He shuddered the memory away. Another mistake to add to the many.

"Okay, here's where we deal," he said, turning in his seat to look at her. "I want some evidence of Jazz that proves to me that you have her and she's still alive. When you've done that, we can talk about what you want me to do for you. If you can't or won't provide that assurance, then you can get out of the van and keep walking. I'll head the other way and you can do whatever you want with your house guest. I'll be so far away with my two hundred grand, the police will never find me and you can go steal whatever it is that's so important to you, all by your lonesome. Get it?"

She shrugged her bottom off the seat, wriggled her hand into her back pocket and pulled out a phone. She took a moment to skim through various menus and when she found what she was looking for she held it out in front of his face.

"Will that do?"

The photo was of Jazz, or at least Miller had to assume that was the case, as despite all the images plastered in the media to date, he'd never seen the cover girl bound hand and foot. The chair she was tied to was laid on its side on a wet floor as if someone had kicked it, or she had overbalanced it herself, in her struggle to be free. Her eyes were closed. Her blonde hair adhered to her face.

"Did you know a person can drown in two inches of water?"

"What ...?" He looked from the picture to her and back again. He had underestimated her.

"I said, did you know a person can drown ..."

"I heard you the first time."

"Right, well I'm just pointing out that the room in which she's being held has a tendency to flood. So probably best all round if there's less chat and more action ... don't you think?"

"Is she alive?"

"Of course – for now, hence the need for speed, Jack."

Miller stared at her blankly as numerous scenarios helter-skeltered through his head. In each one she ended up grinning and he ended up in the shite. "I thought you didn't have a phone."

"You thought wrong."

"You're mad."

"I think we already established that. But don't worry. I'm on the genius side of lunacy. When I kill, I do it with style. So, do we have a deal?"

Miller looked again at the image on the phone. If the girl died he'd be going down for ever, or Otto would save the taxpayer's money and put him six feet under. But strangely, what was even more disturbing was the realisation that if the girl died he couldn't live with himself, knowing he could have prevented it. The under-the-counter drugs had obviously addled his brain, or perhaps he was still concussed, or maybe, just maybe he wasn't quite the monster he thought he was. "Okay," he sighed, "What do you want me to do?"

"The judge has something I want. I was going to exchange his daughter for it, but the way I see it you can get it for me and we can deal on the girl later."

"We?"

"I'm sure you know someone who's in the market for a slightly-soiled cover girl ... for a price."

"I'm sure I do. What's your connection to the judge?"

"It's not important."

"It might be."

"Believe me, it isn't. He has something of mine. I want it back. It's that simple."

"So ask him?"

She exhaled forcefully and pinned him with an exasperated look. "Get real, Jack."

Okay maybe she was right. But he doubted it was simple. What could a high court judge be hanging onto that belonged to a reject like her? "What do you want me to steal?" he asked.

"A box, about so big." She held her hands apart, "About the size of a common house brick."

"What's in it?"

"You don't need to know that."

He shrugged. Maybe O'Hanlon had a fancy for the exotic too, and the box was full of dodgy photos. He didn't really care. He could always look inside when he took it. "Okay, big secret – big deal. Where is it?"

"It was at his house, in the safe, up until yesterday when something spooked him and he placed it in the bank."

"*Spooked* him?"

Her lips twitched. "Literally."

"How do you know he moved it?"

"She told me."

"You believe her?"

"Yes."

"Which bank?"

"The one you visited yesterday."

"You're joking. You expect me to go back to the same bank, when my face is all over the media – thanks to you? You didn't think this out, sweetheart."

"Oh I did. I know you can get into the bank. I know you have contacts."

"You do?"

"Like I said, I'm a planner, Jack."

"So, it's a box, this size," he replicated the size with his own hands, "and it's in a bank in the centre of town, a bank currently crawling with police. Where exactly, in a safety deposit box?"

"Yes, along with a whole heap of other valuable stuff, I expect. I only want the box. You can take everything else ... as a bonus."

"Must be something special in this box?"

"Special to me."

He closed his eyes briefly and considered. He needed the girl alive. She was probably the only way he was going to wriggle out of the situation he was in, but going back into the same bank twice was madness. Getting in once was risky enough and that's why he'd always stayed outside. He'd planned every job down to the last detail, but as for getting his own hands dirty, that just wasn't his style.

"Well?" she prompted. "No time for napping. I hear the forecast is for heavy showers, turning to snow and Jazz can't swim or make snowballs with her hands and feet tied, can she?"

He undid his seat belt and studied her a moment longer. He had a sense of being corralled into a very tight corner and didn't like it one bit, but realistically he had no option and the worst of it was, she knew it. She gave him that kooky little smile and snorted softly through her nose, as if it was all cut and dried, and he was almost persuaded to finish it there and then. A hand at her throat, a gun at her head, it would be over in a flash, but that wouldn't solve his problems and it certainly wouldn't save the girl.

"Okay," he sighed "I get the box, you give me Jazz. Deal?" He held out his hand and counted the seconds as she hesitated before placing her hand in his. Four seconds. Fuck. She was still playing with him.

"Deal," she replied sweetly.

"First things first. I need to get into my flat."

"How? You saw the police. They're all over the place."

"You drive. Park in the lane behind the flat, a few doors down, I'll tell you where." He twisted out of his seat and heaved himself into the back of the van, out of sight. His shoulder screamed at him. Pain that had been simmering and almost bearable jagged out from the centre of the wound as far as his elbow and he cursed under his breath.

"Still hurting, Jack?" Spook asked as she slipped in front of the wheel and adjusted the seat forward.

He gave in and popped a pill. "I'm fine, just drive."

She reversed the van into a parking area eight houses down from Miller's flat. Originally a back yard, the owner had knocked down the rear wall and created enough space for four cars, one for each of the converted flats. At just after lunchtime, the property was empty, all the occupants having left for work or university. There was no one to notice the banged up builder's Transit van sitting on the drive.

A lone police officer stood on duty at the rear entrance to Miller's flat, his focus not on the lane or the van, but on a cat making its way along the top of the neighbour's wall with a mouse dangling from its jaws. The remainder of the team were either still inside, searching for anything that might lead them to Miller or his captive, or busy loading the CSI van at the front.

"I need you to create a diversion in the front street, something that will get the police attention away from the rear of the building and the fire escape."

Spook shrugged, "Okay, let's see what toys I have to play with." She climbed over the seats to join him and rummaged around in the builders crap that filled most of the rear space. "Petrol can, oily rag..." she turned to Miller with a grin. "I don't suppose you have a match on you?"

"No."

She pulled on an oversized pair of overalls and rolled up the ankles so she wouldn't trip. "What do you think – Bob the builder?"

Miller shook his head. She looked like a child playing dress-up. "Here," he said as he threw her an old baseball cap that was hanging from a nail hammered into the interior plywood panelling. "You need to cover your hair. It's a dead giveaway."

She reached into the cavernous pockets and with an accompanying smile, produced a lighter, like a rabbit from a hat. "Okay. That's more like it. Give me five minutes."

He caught at her arm as she squeezed past him out of the van. "What are you planning?"

Her eyes sparked with danger. "Something noisy."

He counted her down. Exactly four minutes and fifteen seconds later a huge explosion rocked the van – and sent plumes of smoke so high into the air, Miller could see them from where he stood in the back lane. The cat shot off with a strangled yowl and the police officer gave up any pretence at keeping watch and dashed into the flat, leaving the rear of the building unguarded. Miller took advantage and, despite his handicap, he was up the fire escape and had gained entry to the attic flat above his before the cacophony of car alarms began.

He paused inside the door to catch his breath and turned when he sensed Spook's presence right behind him. He watched distractedly as she shucked out of her disguise. She hadn't broken a sweat. "What the fuck did you do? I said create a diversion. I didn't say blow up the entire street."

"I didn't blow up the entire street. I blew up the CSI van. Oh dear, it had all your stuff in it...oops!"

"Great! Now I'm a ruddy terrorist as well as a bank robber and a kidnapper. Anything else you'd like me to hang for?"

"Oh, stop complaining. Why are we here? Your flat is downstairs."

This time it was Miller's turn for a smug smile. "The flat registered in my name is downstairs. This is the flat where I keep the stuff I don't want blown up."

"Oh! Clever, Jack. Very clever."

He raised a warning finger. "Shhhh ... the sound insulation is shite in these old buildings. They'll hear us from downstairs if we're not careful."

She tiptoed across the kitchen floor and into the living room which was fitted snugly into the eaves.

"This is nice," she said as she flopped into the corner of the sofa. "Very IKEA, not what I would have expected from your average robber-about-town.

"And here's me thinking you'd prefer something more gothic. A dungeon perhaps?"

"Oh, I'm very adaptable, Jack. I carry my weapons of torture with me at all times."

"Yeah? Well, make sure you don't impale yourself. I need to change and grab a few things." He crossed to the dormer window and glanced out between the vertical blinds. The van was well alight. There was a general panic as officers with fire extinguishers attempted to contain the blaze, while others frantically tried to move squad cars out of the way. There was so much additional traffic in the street they were having difficulty and the road was pretty much gridlocked.

"You had fun, I see."

She nudged him out of the way and peered through a gap in the blinds. "Yup, I don't do things by halves, Jack. Remember that."

In the distance Miller could hear the approaching fire engines. It was all a little too reminiscent of the previous night. He sighed and ran his fingers wearily through his hair.

"Tired, Jack?"

"Tired and pretty much fucked." The pill he'd taken was beginning to take effect, he could feel a warm glow descending, cancelling out the pain from his shoulder and dulling the raw edges of comprehension. "We should be safe here for an hour or two," he muttered. "It's the last place they're going to look and I'd say they're going to be far too busy mopping up the mess outside."

"We don't have time to hang about, Jack."

"Look, you want me to break into a bank? then I have to plan it. That takes time. If you have to go see to your guest then you do that, but for the next hour or so I suggest you stay right here."

She glanced again at the commotion in the street. One man stood out from the crowd. Ginger-nut, the copper in the suit.

"Hey, Jack, before you go all trippy on me, do you want to take a look at this guy. He was there when they lifted Jazz's car this morning, and he's here now. Kind of hot on your trail wouldn't you say?"

Miller wriggled halfway out of his autopsy T-shirt and gave up. "What guy?"

Spook yanked the remainder of it over his shoulder and pointed to the man who was holding court vocally in the front street, trying to maintain order within the hastily built cordon. He had his phone at one ear and was gesticulating wildly to the melee while barking commands. "DI Baker, aka Ginger-nut. He's a bit of a moron ... and he can't count."

Miller shrugged. He'd never seen him before. "You know him?"

"No, but I don't like him."

"There's a surprise." He watched as Baker gave an exasperated scowl and retreated back into Miller's flat. Spook opened her mouth to say something and Miller placed his hand firmly over it.

"Shhhh... " he breathed against her ear. "He's downstairs." He cocked his head and tried to listen despite the noise outside. It sounded like DI Baker was going through his cupboards like a man possessed.

Spook knocked his hand away and glowered at him. "He seems a tad too interested in you," she whispered and Miller shrugged his disinterest.

"He can search all he likes, he won't find anything other than what I want him to find. Everything of any importance is up here and anything that could hang me is back at the infirmary." He crossed to the bedroom and paused in the doorway "Make yourself useful, keep watch while I get changed."

He pulled the door closed behind him and sagged wearily against it. Things were unravelling and he needed to stop and rewind. Crossing to the wardrobe, he moved aside hangers to reach the damaged back of the ancient closet which was wedged in place by a folded cardboard chock. The slightest pressure released the panel and Miller was able to slide the wood free and pull out a small canvas holdall from the space behind.

He sat on the edge of the bed, resisted the temptation to just lie down and sleep and unzipped the bag, upending it on the mattress. Inside were a variety of documents, blueprints, a Glock 17, two clips of ammunition and a passport. He picked up the weapon, checked it was loaded and put it to one side. He needed to ditch Frankie's gun. It linked him to the girl's car and he couldn't afford to have any evidence, no matter how circumstantial, connected to him. No matter what it looked like to the press and the police, or even to Otto, he hadn't touched the girl and he needed to keep it that way.

He hurriedly unfolded the first blueprint and spread it out over the mattress. A floor plan of the bank they'd hit the day before, it had merely been used to allow Frankie and Spidey to familiarise themselves with the layout of the main banking hall. There had been no need to consider those restricted areas that required additional authorisation, because they were assured of easy pickings direct from the cashiers. It was all part of the plan – his plan. Miller traced the layout with his finger until he located the safety deposit area. He had limited options to gain entry. One was to open an account, which under the current circumstances he figured would be denied. The other was to have someone open the locks for him.

Miller pulled out his phone and scrolled down the list of contacts. He paused at H, his thumb grazing the single letter. Last time the number was busy, now it failed to connect. He skimmed forward to M. If he wanted back into the bank, he needed the current security protocol. There was no way he was going to risk a Frankie and Spidey special, bursting in through the front door and terrorising the cashiers. No, he needed direct access to the safety deposit area and only McKenzie could get him the clearance.

He checked his watch. Thanks to Spook, the police had his number and were probably waiting for him to use it. He figured he had less than three minutes before they triangulated his location. He smiled, heads would roll when they realised the call was being made from the same building they were currently searching. It was tempting to stretch it to the limit, but he couldn't take the risk. He had to keep his conversation short and to the point.

He punched out the number and waited. It didn't take long for McKenzie to pick up, less time in fact than it had taken Spook to shake on their deal. Perhaps that was significant or maybe he was over thinking. He wasn't sure.

"Finally. I wondered when you would call."

Miller's gut twisted sharply, painkillers on an empty stomach or the sound of McKenzie's arrogant voice? Both were equally irritating. "We need to talk."

"We do indeed. You missed our rendezvous. I await your explanation with interest."

Miller began to gather up the contents of the bag. Blueprints skimmed to the floor as he struggled with one hand. "Not now, they're probably tracing this call. We don't have long."

"Who's tracing the call?"

He crouched and scooped up the papers, wincing as his shoulder caught the bed frame. "Who the fuck do you think?"

"Ah, I see. Best make it sharp then. Usual place?"

Miller shook his head, what was it with people and *usual places?* He hadn't a clue where he meant and didn't have time to play guessing games.

"Where?"

"Don't you remember?"

"No I fucking don't. Come on, where? The clock is ticking here and I've got the Serious Crimes jokers so close I can smell their bloody shite."

"Paddy Freemans, by the boating lake."

"Huh?"

McKenzie chuckled softly. "It's going to snow. I always did like Jesmond Dene in the winter, very picturesque."

"And very cold." Miller glanced at his watch and did a mental reckoning. "Okay give me an hour. And watch your back. I'm dragging a bit of debris in my wake."

"So I hear. Make sure you don't get fouled in the net."

Miller ended the call at 2.45 minutes and slipped the phone into his pocket.

"Who were you calling?" Spook slouched against the doorframe, watching him, her sharp eyes darting from the bag to the last of the papers scattered on the floor.

"I thought that door was shut."

"It was. That's why they have handles so people can open them again. It's a neat trick."

"Funny. We have to move."

"I asked a question. Who were you calling?"

Miller stood and grabbed a shirt from the hanger. "Just a guy who can help us get your box."

"Good. Do you trust him?" She dropped to her knees and gathered up the last of the debris from the bag.

"No, but I don't trust you either."

"You should. I'm very loyal to the deranged and deluded."

He wandered into the bathroom and turned on the tap. "Thanks, that's good to know."

Spook extended her arm and patted the carpet to make sure she hadn't missed anything under the bed. She retrieved the passport and flicked it open at the photo page. "Hey, who's the 007 lookalike?" she smiled. "The name's Miller. Jack Miller," she drawled in a faux Scottish accent. "You look halfway human when you haven't had the weight of a car pummelling the life out of you. And you know, Jack, while we're at it we need to have a little chat about drugs ... you're getting pretty fond of those babies. You need to learn to say no. One friend to another – they're going to effin' kill you."

"You're not my friend," he grunted. "And if I die in the next twenty-four hours, it won't be from painkillers. I can assure you of that." He flexed his arm and kept it steady. "You want me to be able to hit a target don't you?"

She glanced his way as she scrabbled about beneath the bed. "True, but you need to be awake to do that, not skipping off to la la land whenever you get a twinge. Man up, Jack, stop being such a softy." Her fingers wrapped around something small, rectangular and flat, and as she pulled it out, Miller turned.

"What are you doing?"

"Just helping," she said as she lifted the bag onto the bed and zipped it tight. "That's me, Chummy's little helper. Come on, stop dawdling, Jack. We have things to do, reputations to ruin, bad people to kill."

"Jazz O'Hanlon isn't bad."

Spook smirked, "Why, Jack, don't tell me you're going all gooey over cover girl Jazz."

Miller glowered at her.

"I'll let you into a secret, lover boy. You'd have to rob the Royal Mint before you could afford her."

"Oh I don't know. One more bank and she's mine for the taking anyway. Whether she likes it or not. That's the deal isn't it?"

Spook shook her head reprovingly. "*Whether she likes it or not.* Oh, Jack, you do have a bad side don't you." She tossed him the bag. "In fact I'd say there's a whole side of you that you're keeping under wraps." She suppressed a random giggle with a hand across her mouth. "Sorry," she spluttered, "but I do love a multi-faceted personality. They're so much more fun. Don't you think?"

Miller slipped a thin sweater over his head and topped it with a warm coat. "You're crazy."

"So you keep saying. But you know, it takes one to know one."

"Yeah, maybe you're right. I'm crazy to let you tag along. I should have put a bullet in your head while I had the chance."

"No. I'm crazy for letting *you* tag along. I should have left you to burn."

"Yeah, well we all do things we're not proud of, sweetheart."

She cocked her head and twitched her lips smugly. "Don't we just."

Twenty Two

Samuels had declined the opportunity to accompany Baker to Miller's flat. He knew they wouldn't find anything. Miller was a professional. A career criminal, as Davies had rightly said. When the call came in to say the CSI van and all the 'evidence' taken from the flat had suffered a mishap, Samuels risked a wry smile. Baker was a fool, a dangerous one, in that his manner of charging in, guns blazing was going to skew the investigation and probably lose them their key suspect. But a small part of him wished he'd been there to see the look on Baker's face when the van went up.

Instead he'd stayed at his desk and gone back over everything they had. He just couldn't get it to add up. Something was staring him in the face and for the life of him he couldn't see it.

The bag men, Frankie Sutton and Stephen Robson aka Spidey had burst into the bank just before closing time. They'd followed the same pattern that had proved successful on each previous occasion – noise, guns and a clearing of cashier's tills. As with the other jobs, the tills were particularly heavy, but not unusual for the pre-Christmas rush. The shops had been busy and the movement of cash, withdrawals by shoppers and deposits by retailers had been buoyant. Security guards had been silenced and held immobile by Frankie and a loaded weapon while Spidey collected the cash. The automatic shutters that should have locked down at the first sniff of trouble had suffered a malfunction, or been purposely de-activated, again the same pattern as at the previous banks, but as with each of those crimes, subsequent investigation of the mechanisms had proved fruitless, there was nothing awry with any of the systems. Investigation of the bank staff was ongoing.

Both men wore masks, apart from one three-second shot captured by the CCTV where Frankie broke from the usual plan after spotting a customer in the queue. It appeared that he raised his mask just for an instant, for a better look perhaps, and that was sufficient to identify him.

Although the camera was able to capture the moment when Frankie relieved the customer of his intended deposit, the customer himself was obscured from view and to date had not come forward. Samuels sat back in his seat and pondered on that for a moment. He was sure if he'd been at the business end of a loaded weapon and relieved of his hard-earned, then he'd have been ready to shout long and hard, particularly as it was now common knowledge that the perpetrator was dead and could no longer pose a threat. Then again Miller was still out there, which brought Samuels right back to square one – Miller.

Miller and the missing girl, it just didn't add up, any of it and he sensed a disturbing need within the department, driven by Davies and supported by Baker, to tie all the loose ends of both cases neatly in one Miller-shaped package. Samuels was sure it wasn't that straightforward.

Maybe the tech guys could enhance the CCTV image or obtain a shot from a different camera and get him a better image of the guy in the queue? As far as he could see, apart from the rain, that was the only thing that had occurred that was different to the norm – and out of four robberies, this was the only one that had crashed and burned...literally. Samuels didn't like coincidences.

The gun had never been fired during any of the robberies, but from what he could see of it, held firmly in Frankie's outstretched hand, it matched the type that ballistics were saying had been used to shoot out Jasmine O'Hanlon's car window. He knew Frankie hadn't been anywhere near the car, as by that time he was already squashed flat and burnt to a crisp, so that suggested the gun had transferred from Frankie to Miller. Why? Samuels shook his head. There was only one person who could answer his questions – but according to popular belief, and the press lynch-mob, he was currently holed up with the girl listed as most likely to bag a billionaire, not a bank robber.

He pulled out the transcript of the phone call made by Jasmine to the newspaper editor Cameron. Why had she called him instead of the police? Why had Miller allowed her to make the call without making any demands?

It seemed he was no further forward.

He picked up his phone and hesitated briefly before tapping out Miller's number, it was time to get some answers. All he got was a busy tone. He was interrupted by the phone on his desk.

"John, you busy?"

Samuels disconnected the call to Miller with a muttered curse. "Yes, as it happens. We do have a major enquiry or two running at the moment."

The caller chuckled, "It's Stan, I have something that might interest you."

Samuels smiled. Forensics, he'd been waiting for their call. "I'm all ears."

"Okay, first things first. I have a definite ID on the two who were killed in the crash. Both had recent dental work in prison which made our job a whole lot easier."

"Great. I can sign that off and get someone out to break the news officially to their families."

"They have families?"

"Yes, Stan, despite what we might think of them, they're some mother's sons."

"Think you'll get anything from the relatives?"

"Doubtful, they're all as thick as thieves, well, seeing as they *are* all thieves, that's no real surprise. Anyway what else have you got?"

"We ran some tests on the car. It wasn't easy, you saw the state of it, but we did manage to get traces of blood from the driver's side. It matched the blood we sampled from the second car."

"Miller's?"

"Yes."

"So we can take it that he's pretty beat up from the wreck. Head injuries?"

"Quite likely. The car was upturned and although the BMW has a robust safety cage, the roof was crumpled and the windscreen had been smashed prior to the explosion."

"So he went through the windscreen, that's how he got out?"

"No. Different blood group on the samples of glass that didn't melt. What was interesting and what might account for the volume of blood in both cars..."

"Yes?" Samuels prompted impatiently.

Stan laughed. "There was a bullet hole shot clean through the left hand side of the driver's seat. The way I see it, our man Miller took a bullet in the shoulder or the chest and he's been leaking copious amounts of blood ever since."

"Any sign of the shell?"

"Not in the first car, but we did recover a shell from the second car."

Samuels paused to put things into sequence. "There's an altercation in the car, Miller's shot, he crashes the car?"

"That sounds about right."

"So there's the car, upside down, on fire. He struggles out, staggers away, bumps into Miss O'Hanlon and forces her to drive him away."

"On the money, John. As always."

Samuels shook his head. "No. That's not right. Why did he shoot out the window if she was in the car?"

"To scare her? To get her to open the door?"

"Maybe. But why did he need to hotwire it, if she was sitting in the driver's seat with the keys?"

"Can't help you with the whys and wherefores John, just with the facts, and the facts are, Miller was shot in the first car and he travelled as a passenger in the second car. Beyond that, you'll have to ask him."

Samuels cradled the receiver. He was even more confused.

Twenty Three

I do love a secret, but they're tricky things to hang onto. Like hot coals in a frozen palm, once you start to thaw out, the less you treasure the coal – and the more you fear the burn. Oh my, Jack is such a dark horse and a very hot coal indeed. There's no way he's getting out of my sight, not now. The voice is cock-a-hoop and crowing at my discovery, but I haven't time to share the celebration. Maybe later when I finally have what I want.

We're on our way to meet the man who'll help Jack deliver up his end of our bargain. Or at least that's the plan. It seems a little too simple for my liking. I glance at Jack and wonder whether being pain free is all it's cracked up to be. I need him on the ball, ahead of the game. He doesn't look it. I mean, yes, he's smartened up, less desperate and more desperado, but his eyes have that *shit man* glazed look that would be fine chilling out back at the flat, but not on the way to a rendezvous with a guy who can apparently fix things at the drop of a hat. That kind of guy should be treated with respect. I should know. I've been fixed more than once and only lived to tell the tale because ...well... just because. If any hats are going to be dropped today, Jack and me, well we need to be prepared.

"Got a plan?" I ask.

He takes his eye off the road and looks at me as if he'd forgotten I was there. Like he'd just driven the last two miles on his own, in his sleep.

"Sure I have a plan. Meet the guy, get the security codes, steal the box, take the girl. Simple."

"Right, this is the Mr Fixit you don't trust, remember?"

"I remember."

"So, like I said, do you have a plan other than walking straight up to this bloke and saying 'give me the gear'? I mean, call me old fashioned, but that sounds a bit reckless. He could have a gun. He could be a copper. This could be a trap."

He shakes his head and smiles, like I'm the idiot, not him. "Trust me. I do this for a living."

"Oh sure you do, Mr Bank Robber." I shrug. His overconfidence doesn't impress me. "I thought we already established that we don't trust each other."

"Shush, just for once, will you?" He turns back to the traffic and I shush. Not because he tells me to, but because there's nothing more to say. Okay, so he doesn't want my help. Let's just see how he gets on. But I'm prepared if it all goes arse up. I'm always prepared. I snigger softly and the voice joins in.

He drives straight past the meeting place and the almost empty gravelled parking area adjacent to it; pulls into the hospital opposite, and noses that clunky old van around until he finds the last empty parking space. Visiting time, wouldn't you just know it.

"Go get a ticket." He says, like I'm some buzz-boy at the country club. I glower at him and he shrugs back at me. "They're looking for me, not you. The last thing we need is to come back here and find the van being clamped or towed. Apart from the attention it would attract, I'd have to steal something else from someone who's probably in there right now visiting a dying relative. Is that what you want? Does that appeal to your sense of the macabre?"

I glower some more but I get the picture – and the ticket. Pointless wasting time on a skirmish when there's a war still to be won.

When I return he's leaning back against the van *Mr I don't give a toss*, in *my* sun glasses, catching a few winter rays while he waits, and he tucks me under his arm like we're best buddies or worse.

"Come on let's go lurk around the public toilets and pick up a pooch."

"A pooch?"

"Well it's either that or a kid, but I think we'll get less hassle with the dog."

Now I *know* the drugs have got to him and I kind of want to say, *enough is enough, I'll steal my own effin' box*, but the voice whispers furiously in my ear and yes, I agree, I do want to see where this is leading. Curiosity and all those feline genes, *nuff said.* So I snuggle right in there and go with the flow.

The toilets are a nightmare, in a creepy faux Victorian fairy story kind of way. All gingerbread house cuteness on the outside and men in dirty overcoats on the inside. I mean, who in their right mind uses public toilets in a park? Jeez there's weirdos about, take my word for it. But there you go, there's always one mug. A hapless bloke has tied his mangy mongrel to the railings outside. It's an ugly brute, missing one eye, kind of squat and ready for a fight. Not the type you'd choose to steal, if given a choice, which as there's only one, we don't appear to have.

I make a clicking sound with my tongue and the stud against my teeth, and Jack winces like he's just had a déjà vu moment. Not sure what that's about, but the dog pricks up one ear in a lopsided way and smiles, a great bottomless pit of a grin with flapping jowls and froth and teeth. Or maybe it's a snarl. It's a crazy dog that's for sure and because of that I decide we're going to get along fine. I unravel the lead and pass it to Jack.

"What now?"

"We go walkies, you, me and the mutt, while I check out the park and see who should and shouldn't be here."

Oh right, good thinking. Maybe he's not as whacked as I thought he was.

We do a circuit of the lake and the dog grunts half-heartedly at the ducks. I don't blame him. It's far too cold to give energy away for free. Jack spies out the lay of the land as if he's expecting armed response units to pop out from behind every tree. I kind of expect it too. It's a barmy place for a meet. Not enough people, too much empty space. If we're in someone's cross-hairs then we're buggered, plain and simple.

It starts to snow. I like snow, Jack doesn't. I can tell by the way he scowls. And yes, it is a nuisance when you're trying to mastermind a code grab and scan for snipers and all you can see are great white flakes of fluffy stuff. But all the same, I do like snow. I start to hum, *It's beginning to look* ... Jack just glares at me and doesn't say a word. I zip it. Miserable git. He has no spirit of the season. The voice continues in my ear ... *a lot like Christmas* ... what a rebel. I switch channels back and concentrate, narrow my eyes, hawk-like, and bingo! I spot him, Mr Fixit, over by the play equipment, looking both conspicuous and suspicious. Like a great black raven eyeing up the chicks. The mothers are thinking that too, herding their offspring to the other side of the play area like frenzied bantams. *Cluck, Cluck.*

I turn to Jack, discreetly. "I suppose he's new to this cloak and dagger malarkey." It makes me feel a little better, the fact that he's obviously an idiot and I'm obviously not.

Jack pauses while the dog pees against a litter bin. "Not really. He's arrogant. He thinks the rules don't apply to him."

Oh right, an arrogant idiot, doubly stupid, my favourite kind of fool. "There are rules?" I enquire with surprise. I'm thinking Queensberry or WWWF.

"Of course. There has to be rules. Otherwise we'd all go round killing each other and robbing where we shouldn't."

"A progressive society ... cool. Shame you're all villains. You could run for government." I allow a wry smirk at my own clever sarcasm, but it's wasted on Mr Bank Robber. Jack just raises one brow. What the heck, rules are for fools.

"Do you see anyone else?" He huddles up even closer and I don't think it's because he's suddenly seen me in a new light. He's cold, grey with it in fact, and he really shouldn't be. He's got more layers on than I have and I'm fizzing with heat, adrenalin, anticipation, whatever. He should be too. He should be lapping up all this secret rendezvous stuff, it's bread and butter to an arch villain like him. But he's not, he's actually leaning quite heavily on me and that's a worry. I think about the crash, about the injuries I can't see and Micro couldn't fix. No point in pandering to him now though. He just needs to keep it together long enough to get my box.

I shrug. "Anyone else?" sure, I see plenty. "Kids, mothers, ducks."

He squeezes my arm hard and I snarl my response. The dog looks sideways at me with his one eye. Hurray! I speak dog. A new skill.

"Be serious," he mutters. "I'm doing this for you, remember?"

"No you're not. You're doing this so you can get yourself off the hook."

"The hook you put me on."

I sigh. Jeez, so hung up on the little details. He should stand back and see the bigger picture. The voice sniggers. Yeah maybe not, in my case the bigger picture would scare the shit out of him.

"Okay. We have a couple of cars in the car park. There are two guys in one of them. That seems a bit strange, unless it's a weirdo convention and they're waiting to join the man in the toilets."

Jack nods. "I see them. Come on let's get this over with."

We take a seat by the lake, and the ducks all waddle our way, quacking loudly, ever hopeful. The dog licks its chops, hopeful too. When idiot Mr Fixit, leaves the shelter of the play park and begins to make his way towards us, Jack hands me the lead.

"Take your new friend through the gate and into the dene, not far, keep me in sight. If we need to run we can lose them in the trees and double back to the van."

"Run? No one mentioned running."

"Hey, I'm the one with a gaping wound. Stop complaining."

"Fine, just don't expect me to carry you." I'm joking but he's not laughing and, oddly, neither am I.

So despite the fact that this is my show and I'm still in charge, I do as he asks, reluctantly. If truth be told I'd much rather be ear-wigging into any conversation that concerns me, and for a few heartbeats I try to think of a reason why my presence might be crucial to any negotiation. But, though it pains me to admit it, Jack's right, better not to be linked to a master criminal, not in public anyway. I shoot a quick glance across the boating lake to the toilets and discover another reason not to hang about. The weirdo with the bladder problem has discovered old One-Eye is missing and is hop-skipping it our way. I tug the fat lump along with the lead and he grunts at me. "Don't worry, pal," I say fondly. "Forget the weirdo. You're mine now. We speak the same language and everything."

Which is more than can be said for Jack.

Twenty Four

McKenzie took the opposite end of the bench, cleared the slight accumulation of snow with a gloved hand and sat, crossing his feet at the ankles and pulling his black woollen coat around him. "You missed our appointment yesterday," he said.

Hands in his pockets, shoulders hunched against the cold. Miller ignored him and stared out across the lake. The men were still in the car. Whether they were perverts or police, he wanted them to stay there. "I guess you know why?"

"Yes. Word of your exploits has reached my ears. A bit of a fiasco all round. Can't say I'm happy about it. What happened?"

Miller flicked a cautious glance around the perimeter of the park. The children continued to play, oblivious to the cold, the mothers pushed swings, chatting and relaxed now that McKenzie had moved on. Miller was less relaxed. His hand tightened around the Glock in his coat pocket. Beneath his many layers, cold sweat coated his skin and he wasn't sure whether it was the result of tension or fever. He turned to McKenzie and considered his reply.

"It was an accident. I'm not particularly happy about it either."

"Tragic."

"Yeah."

The dog owner was making steady progress, trudging around the western perimeter of the lake in their direction. Miller watched him distractedly. He looked just like his dog, pug-ugly and ready for a fight. It seemed everyone had a bone to pick with him today.

"You dropped off the bag with Otto?"

"What?" he dragged his attention back to a scowling McKenzie.

"Pay attention. The bag, you left it with Otto?"

"Yes. This morning."

McKenzie nodded. "This morning? So where have you been?"

"Here and there. Laying low." Miller smiled wryly. "You know how it is when infamy catches up with you. Your life's just not your own any more."

"There was an explosion in Jesmond. I suppose that had nothing to do with you?"

"Nope."

"I heard you were hit. Nothing serious I hope?"

"Just a scratch."

"Really?"

Despite his layers, Miller's shoulder throbbed with the cold like an angry tooth.

McKenzie smiled as if he knew it, and Miller smiled right back at him.

"So what can I do for you, Jack?"

Jack? McKenzie never called him anything other than Miller. He flicked a glance across the lake. The parked car was empty, the men nowhere to be seen. He had a sense of a noose being tightened and accepted an urgent need to move things along, before he froze to the spot or the aggrieved dog owner arrived to pick that bone.

"I need an out. A guarantee. I thought you were the man to help me out with that."

"If everything had gone to plan yesterday, you would have had the closure you wanted, Jack. As it is..."

"When have I ever let you down? I delivered ... eventually."

"A day late. That changes things."

Miller inhaled slowly, rationing the icy air. He knew it was pointless to argue. McKenzie was an arrogant bastard. Well connected, but a bastard nonetheless. He believed that he had Miller on the end of a very long chain and wasn't averse to giving it a nasty jerk when he felt it justified. Miller empathised with the one eyed dog. He shot another glance at the owner's progress. He'd been waylaid by a child's bouncing football and although obviously disinclined to play kick-about, a wailing child was sufficient for him to delay his pursuit for a moment or two.

"What do you want?" he asked McKenzie as it appeared quite obvious that the man was waiting to deal.

"What do you have to trade?"

"I have the girl, O'Hanlon's daughter."

"Good, I'm glad to hear it, Jack. Otto will be pleased. I believe he has plans for her." He turned toward Miller, rested his arm against the back of the bench and smiled. "The thing is, Jack, that's not enough."

"Huh?" What else could he want apart from the girl? According to Otto, she was worth her weight in gold, or coke, or whatever Otto was currently coveting. He shook his head, confused, and as he turned away, the men from the car slid back into his line of vision. They were to the east, rounding the lake. In a moment they would be obscured behind overhanging willows, once they cleared the trees there would be nothing between him and them but a wide expanse of grass. McKenzie was biding his time, waiting for them to draw closer. Miller figured he was wasting his time asking for security codes.

"Frankie? Tell me about Frankie?"

Miller pulled himself off the bench and made a show of stamping his feet to combat the cold while he did a slow three-sixty degree turn. His heart rate was climbing. He'd just offered up the girl on a plate and all McKenzie wanted to talk about was Frankie?

"Frankie's dead. A car fell on his head."

"Yes, messy, and rather unfortunate. You see Frankie was running a message for me and his sudden demise has left me in a pickle and you in a very tricky position."

"I have no idea what you're talking about."

"Oh I think you do, Jack, you end up with the bag and the girl and no Frankie. Convenient, wouldn't you say?"

Miller shrugged. "Funny. That's what Otto said."

"Hilarious, Jack, and that was before he checked the bag."

"I told him I had expenses. You expect me to take all the risks and end up out of pocket?"

"That's not what I'm talking about."

Miller frowned. "Then perhaps you should get to the fucking point."

"The point? Okay, where is it, Jack?"

"What?"

McKenzie shook his head slowly and his mouth twisted into a less than friendly grimace. "Don't mess about, Jack. Frankie was delivering something special and it seems it got lost in the post. Now how do you imagine that happened?"

Miller risked a glance toward the narrow gate where Spook stood, shrouded by the dense woodland beyond. He knew where she was waiting but he couldn't see her. That was good. One less thing to think about, his mind was overloaded as it was. *'You're a dead man, Jacky. Dead and buried.'* He tried hard to remember, to pull the garbled conversation from the part of his brain that was still half-set. Frankie was bragging, sounding off in the car, that's what started everything, what had ultimately caused the crash, fucking Frankie and his big mouth. *'Wait 'til you see what I got, Jacky lad. We're gonna be the talk of this town.'*

"Is it coming back to you, Jack? All that stuff you've conveniently forgotten?"

Miller exhaled slowly, his breath pluming in the icy air. He gripped the Glock in his pocket a little tighter. The two men in suits had cleared the trees and their gentle stroll had quickened into a brisk walk. On his other side, the dog-man had rid himself of a gaggle of excited kids and was on a mission, head down, puffing like a steam train. He turned back to McKenzie.

"I don't know what you're talking about. Frankie had the bag. I gave the bag to Otto. Took my cut off the top," he shrugged painfully, "I was owed, for my trouble."

"And the bag, it never left your sight?"

This time he resisted the urge to glance Spook's way. "No."

"Then we have a problem, Jack. A big problem. I need what's in the bag. Otto says he doesn't have it. You say you don't have it. Somebody's lying... unless."

Miller tried very hard to concentrate. To the east the men were so close he could see their faces – Baker, the fucking ginger bastard from earlier. *Hot on his trail*, Spook had said and she wasn't far from the truth. He edged away, found the heel of his boot on the concrete edge of the boating lake. Only the noisy outrage of the resident ducks saved him from taking a step too far.

"Unless what?"

"Otto tells me you have a new *pet*, someone a little different to your usual type, someone who might be receptive to my powers of persuasion. Maybe that's who I should be talking to? Is that what you want me to do, Jack, talk to your friends?"

The two detectives were less than twenty feet away. Miller glanced over his shoulder, across the expanse of the lake. The car park had filled up. Blue lights glimmered eerily amid the falling snow. *Fuck!*

"I thought we had an arrangement."

"We did, you fucked it up, Jack."

"What about our deal?"

"Deal? What deal? Jack, you're an armed robber, a kidnapper, hey, I could probably stretch it to killer as well if need be. Do you really think you've got anything to deal with?"

"I have the girl."

"Is she still alive?"

He prayed she was. He shot a glance at the gate. Twenty yards of open grass. "Of course she is. What do you take me for?"

"Where is she?"

He smiled, took a casual step forward, kicking randomly at the snow flurries, like it wasn't a big deal and his heart wasn't banging. He stepped around the bench, took some measure of comfort from the fact that he now had something solid between him and McKenzie, but Baker was a step closer too and he could see the look of eager anticipation on his face.

"Where is she? Do I look stupid? I tell you where she is and what happens? You give the nod, the armed response officers, over there by the pavilion, put a bullet in my head and I go down and take all your dirty little secrets with me."

McKenzie nodded, "That's one possible outcome. Hardened criminal shot by police, innocent victim saved, I don't think the public at large would lose sleep over that, do you?"

"You shoot me, she dies and you'll never get back what it is that Frankie was meant to deliver."

"So you do know where it is?"

Three feet from the bench and he kept stepping backwards towards the dene. It was a futile hope. Every step he took was matched by Baker, all polite and low key. The marksmen, almost hidden from view, had their weapons trained on him and were simply awaiting a nod from McKenzie or a command in their ear. He could almost hear Spook in his own ear nagging, '*What's the plan, Mr Bank Robber?'* He didn't have a plan any more. McKenzie had scotched the only one he had. For a planner, that wasn't good, and a pretty good indication that there was something seriously amiss with him. He took another step and glanced toward the play area, the kids and mums were oblivious to the drama. He clung to the hope that no one, not even McKenzie, would sanction an order to shoot while there were innocent civilians underfoot. But he wasn't sure. He wasn't sure about anything.

"Jack, concentrate. Do you have the package or not?"

And whether he did or he didn't, he was damn well sure he knew exactly where it was, as far as McKenzie was concerned.

"I can get it."

"Sure you can." McKenzie shook his head at Miller's prevarication.

"No, seriously, I can get you the package and the girl, just call off your men."

"I don't think I can do that, Jack." He gestured vaguely with one hand. "All of these witnesses, all of this expense, I have a responsibility to the law-abiding taxpaying public. How's it going to look if I let you walk away?"

"Hey, you're the one who brought the posse."

McKenzie smiled. "Back-up, Jack. Always have a back-up plan, particularly when you're playing the kind of games we are. You should know that."

Miller smiled right back at him. "How do you know I haven't?"

"Have you?"

Miller shifted his weight and tried to zone out everything other than McKenzie. He tossed a throwaway glance at the marksmen. "I could just hold up my hands and give up. Throw myself on the mercy of the courts ... find myself a sympathetic judge."

"You could, but without my protection you may struggle to survive the arrest and interrogation, and I hear the current suicide rates on remand are quite shocking." McKenzie brushed a light covering of snow from his coat and continued. "I understand you had a hard time inside, last time around, Jack, spent a lot of time in solitary. Why was that, I wonder?"

"Wouldn't you like to know?"

"Hit a sore spot, Jack?"

Miller scowled. "You want the package, then you need me, and all this shit is just theatre for your own fucking gratification."

McKenzie shrugged. "Need you? Actually I don't. You've served your purpose, Jack, and now you're far too big a liability. Go-between, patsy, snitch or criminal mastermind. We both know exactly what you are, Jack. The public need someone to vilify and I'm afraid you're it. Not Otto, the respectable club owner who donates to charity and helps out at the local food bank, and certainly not me, a highly decorated senior police officer. No one will believe you, Jack, but why should I take the risk when I can finish it here?" He shifted slightly on the seat and began to raise his right hand. Miller braced himself for the sound of gunfire and the force of a collective barrage of shots, but he was saved, not by the bell, but by the arrival of the irate dog owner who blundered straight into the line of fire.

"Hey, you fucking tosser, where's my bloody dog?"

Miller staggered back as the furious dog-man jabbed him hard in the chest repeatedly, blows that served to push him away from the threat of McKenzie and nearer to the safety of the dene. McKenzie dropped his hand, and Baker, momentarily stunned, soon recovered and began to run, his cohort a few paces behind. In the confusion, Miller took his one and only chance and grabbed his aggressor's wrist as he came in for a hefty punch. He swung him viciously around and forced his arm so far up his back that the man's tirade was hiked a few decibels into an outraged squeal. Using the man's bulk as a shield, he pulled the gun from his pocket and jammed it hard against his assailant's ear.

"Jack! Put the gun down," called McKenzie. "You can't get away. You're just making things worse."

Miller ignored him, shot a desperate glance around the park and zeroed in on Baker, who stopped dead with his hands in the air, his partner skidding to a halt behind him.

"Everyone just back off!" he yelled. He yanked the guy backwards, awkwardly, his excessive height and weight, although an ideal protection from the snipers across the lake, added an additional strain as Miller's shoulder took the brunt of the exertion.

"I'm not going to shoot you," he hissed in the man's ear, "unless *they* make me, or *you* make me." The man gave a token struggle and Miller increased the pressure on his wrist. His shoulder was screaming at him louder than his captive and Miller could feel the sutures tearing, one stitch at a time. He dragged in a great gulping breath and staggered back, pulling the man with him. "Don't make me, for God's sake." And then they ran, together, a desperate loping gait, slipping and sliding on the thin covering of snow, Miller dragging his reluctant partner like a felled beast, until they reached the gate and he was able to let him slip to the ground with relief.

He looked desperately for Spook as he burst through the gate, unable to stop even if he'd wanted to, catching a fleeting glimpse of shocking blue-black hair as he barrelled past. She was crouched by the gatepost, knife in hand, and as soon as he was clear she yanked a short length of the dog's extendable lead taut across the opening, a foot from the ground, and then helter-skeltered after him, dragging the dazed dog behind her.

The path, a series of uneven rough log steps cut steeply into the dene, hurtled down through dense undergrowth. Dangerous in summer, they were a death trap in winter, the mud and accumulated leaf debris waited like a festering wound for them to step inside and succumb to infection. Once they were on it, gravity took over as they slid and skittered their descent along increasingly perilous twists and turns. The dog followed, carried downwards by virtue of its own weight alone.

"We need to get off the path," yelled Miller as he reached out a hand, grabbed Spook by the wrist and stumbled off to one side, dragging both girl and dog through a mass of tangled rhododendron and onward down to the base of the dene, where the river and the road hugged the valley bottom.

"Go right," shouted Spook. And she helped him on his way with a hefty dig in the kidneys.

The path narrowed until it became a track frequented only by wildlife and it was necessary to force their way through matted undergrowth and lethal briars.

"Where?" he gasped, "Where are we headed? We need to get back to the van. We'll never get there at this rate."

"Yes and whose fault is that?" she snapped back. "This is your plan remember. Jeez! One smart-arse bank robber and a senile dog, hardly *The A Team*." She yanked at the dog's collar and he baulked, setting his back legs obstinately into the mud and his bottom firmly on the ground.

Miller took advantage of the forced stop to drag in a much needed breath. His chest was heaving, his whole body shaking with the exertion. He leaned heavily against a tree and tried to get his bearings. He could hear, from far above, the sound of crashing undergrowth as officers ill-equipped for the terrain discovered Spook's trap and attempted the same rapid descent, head first. He hoped McKenzie had led the charge, but somehow doubted the man had hung around. That wasn't his style and it appeared he had a new boy to do his dirty work for him. He turned back to Spook. She stood, feet splayed, hands on hips, shaking her head at him. She hadn't even raised a sweat. Behind her, the dog deflated like a leaky tyre, dropping its chin onto its front paws wearily, while the tip of its tail twitched in response to her voice.

"Leave the bloody dog here, then," he snapped back.

Spook rounded on him. "The dog's with me!"

"For fuck's sake!" He'd had enough. He swung his arm and aimed the gun at the dog. Spook responded by pulling out her knife. She gripped it tightly, arm extended threateningly.

"I said – the dog stays!" She stepped around the flagging beast and forced herself up against Miller until his gun no longer sighted the dog but rested against her heaving chest instead.

"Get out of the way," he hissed. "There are armed police out there. This is serious, it's not one of your kooky *let's get weird* games. We don't have time for this and we don't have time for a fucking dog. Do you understand?"

She narrowed her eyes, and dropped her voice to a low feral growl. "Do you want the girl or not?" Ignoring the gun, she slammed one hand hard against his chest, pushing him, goading him, the knife, glinting dangerously, mere inches from his face.

He glared straight back at her. "The girl will die waiting if we don't lose the police."

"Then stop bloody complaining and pick up the effin' dog."

Behind them, the sound of raised voices and the thrashing of undergrowth broke the tense silence.

"Fuck!" He lowered his gun, knocked the knife out of his face and picked up the dog. "Later," he hissed. "If there is a later, I'll explain the odds to you."

"Odds?"

"Glock versus butter knife."

Her lips twitched into a massive grin. "Rock, paper, scissors. Ah, the fun we'll have."

Miller lugged the dog awkwardly under his good arm. Its hind paws trailed the ground and with every jarring step it grunted its disapproval. Miller contented himself with thoughts of what he would do to Spook once the O'Hanlon girl was in the bag, and what he would do to McKenzie when he eventually got the chance.

Spook led the way sure-footedly, Miller followed, head down, dogged determination alone powering him through a pain barrier that was so barbed it threatened to rip him to shreds. When they reached the entrance to a dark, stone vaulted tunnel cutting through the hillside, he didn't stop to think, just put one foot after the other until they emerged in a small heavily wooded ravine quarried out of the rock. There was evidence the spot had been used recently as a drinking den, with a scattering of empty cans and bottles strewn around a blackened fire-circle. Graffiti marred the rock escarpment; some of it so high and precariously positioned that only someone totally lacking in fear, or sense, could have placed it there.

"You come here often?" Miller wheezed as he dropped the dog and sank to the ground, exhausted.

"Hey don't knock it, Chummy. My superior sense of direction is going to get us out of here. Listen..."

He turned his head. Now that has own rapid breathing had slowed and the dog had stopped grumbling, he could hear the noise of traffic up above the edge of the rock wall. By the volume, he figured she'd led him to very tip of the dene, adjacent to the road that led right past the hospital car park.

"Great. If I was a bird I'd be shaking your hand with my wing right now." He rolled his neck and slipped his hand under the lapel of his coat in an attempt to ease the pain in his shoulder, his fingers came away wet and sticky.

"You're bleeding again."

She said it like, *Oh no not again*, as if the altercation in the park, the scramble down the dene and the weight of the dog had bugger all to do with the state of his wound and it was somehow all his fault.

"You don't say." He wiped his hand on his jeans and assessed the steep cliff. He wouldn't give her the satisfaction of knowing he was about ready to put the gun to his own head and put himself out of his own misery, but he knew for a fact he couldn't climb up the cliff. "Blame the dog," he muttered.

She reached out a hand and patted the animal's scarred head. "For heaven's sake, he's not that heavy."

"No, but try lugging around the guy who owns him."

"*Owned* him." She dropped down onto the ground next to him, crossed her legs beneath her and looped one arm around the ugly dog. All around them the snow fell softly. Miller was happy to let it. He didn't have the energy to move or a plan of where to move to. They were safe in that limbo-land between shit and creek, and while they waited for the police tracker dogs to sniff them out, all three took advantage of the chance to re-charge.

"So, after all that drama, did you get what you came for?" Spook asked.

He turned to look at her. "Are you serious? Did you see what just happened up there?"

"I did suggest that it might be a trap. I guess you weren't listening. Right?"

He closed his eyes to shut her out, while he struggled to recall what McKenzie had actually said.

"Jack!"

"What?" Her sharp tone jerked him back and he took a few seconds to fast forward and re-orientate himself. He was chilled to the bone. He forced his eyes wide open, and scrubbed one hand against his face in an attempt to stay focused.

"This is no time for napping. We have to get the box. *You* have to get the box. That was the deal."

"The box? The fucking box? Never mind the box, tell me about the bag instead."

"What bag?"

"The bag with the cash. What did you take out of it?"

She frowned as if she didn't quite get what he meant, or was too busy thinking up a plausible story.

"I took some money to pay Micro for your effin' shoulder. Lot of good it did. Don't expect me to help you out this time around. You can plug your own damned orifices, natural or otherwise." She snorted her indignation and scrambled to her feet, dusting off the snow in his direction.

"What else did you take? McKenzie said there was something in the bag in addition to the cash. A package. He wants it back."

"Hey, your bag, your responsibility."

"He thinks you might have it."

"Me? He doesn't even know me."

"Your reputation precedes you. That's what comes of trying to be a clever shite."

"Trying? Hey, Chummy, I'm a lot cleverer than you'll ever be." She raised her hand as if she was going to accompany her words with a jab at his chest for emphasis, but she stopped short, and he watched the whole re-figuring shit playing out on her face, nose wrinkled, brows drawn together, teeth chewing at her black lips. When she'd arrived at whatever conclusion she'd drawn, instead of an angry jab with her talons, she merely smiled slyly and patted him gently instead.

"You don't want McKenzie on your case, believe me." He shrugged her off and flexed his arm to encourage the circulation. It was time to make a move. He glanced at his watch and tried to do a mental reckoning.

Spook snorted and the dog joined in with a conspiratorial grunt. "You ready for another squeeze already?"

"Did I say that?"

"Oh come on. Look at you. A gentle stroll in the woods and you're ready to reach for the jelly beans. What did I tell you about saying, no? Tough it out, Jack. You have a bad guy reputation to maintain. Give me the keys, I'll go get the van and meet you on the main road."

"The bag?"

"We don't have time to chit-chat, Jack. You said it yourself – we don't want to mess with McKenzie, not while Jazz has her pretty little face in the water. You want to talk about bags and cash and secret stuff? Fine, we'll do it in the van. Deal?"

Miller cocked his head. He raised a hand to shush her. He could hear something other than the thrashing of bushes or the muttered curses of thwarted police officers. A low thud repeated over and over, with no real sense of direction, until it became clear that it wasn't coming from those trailing them on foot but from the air. He grabbed Spook by the sleeve of her jacket and dragged her beneath the cover of the stone outcrop.

"Looks like McKenzie *does* mean business," said Spook as the police helicopter passed overhead, its search beam flooding the quarry with white light. "What's the deal with you and him anyway?"

"The bag?"

"Don't you think we should vamoose?"

"The bag?" he repeated.

"Er, Jack. There's a great big eye in the sky and any minute now it's going to zero in on us, and bingo! Nobody's going to give a shit about the bag or the package then."

"They can't see us beneath the trees."

"They can track body heat," she replied smugly "surely you know that."

"Body heat?" Miller snorted. "Sweetheart, I'm so bloody cold ..."

"Oh for goodness sake, man up, Jack. A little bit of snow, a little hole in the shoulder and it's whinge, whinge, whinge ... You want to know about the bag? I'll tell you about the bag. I took it out of *your* crashed car. I dropped it on the floor while I took care of *your* effin' scratches and when Micro was finished saving *your* ungrateful arse, I paid him one hundred and fifty quid off the top of *your* stolen cash. That's it, the story of the bag from start to bloody finish. I should have kept the sodding money and left you to burn!" She jabbed him hard where the blood stain was beginning to seep through the fabric of his coat. He swayed but stayed on his feet. "Now are you coming? Or do I leave you to play truth or dare with Mr Fixit?"

Getting out of the quarry was a blur of secret pathways winding this way and that through a maze of thick undergrowth.

Spook had no problems ducking beneath the low hanging branches, while for him every trip and stumble seemed to follow the same jagged neuro-path to his shoulder. It was the easy way out, she'd assured him, the other way was straight up the escarpment and although he had no doubt she would have expected him to climb it with one dead arm, she accepted reluctantly that old one-eye just didn't have the correct physique.

He was fuelled entirely by his burning desire to get even, not with McKenzie his nemesis, but with her, Spook, his chief tormentor and by the time they emerged from the dene under the comforting blanket of dusk he was about ready to put a bullet in her head and leave the O'Hanlon girl to her fate.

Twenty Five

Samuels topped up his coffee and returned to his desk. He was keeping his head down following the failed attempt to apprehend Miller. The whole station was in uproar, with various hypotheses being offered as to how one man could continue to evade capture quite so successfully despite the authorisation of an armed response unit and helicopter support. They'd scaled down the search of the park and dene when nightfall had made the terrain too perilous, and would resume at first light with dogs. Meanwhile the area was in lockdown, with road blocks at every main exit from the city.

Baker was underplaying his role. Considering he'd been at the front end, and according to reports, a mere hair's breadth from grabbing Miller, his modesty was surprising. Samuels studied him from across the rim of his coffee mug.

"That was a close thing," he commented. "How did you know he'd be there?"

Baker shrugged. "Tip-off, from a reliable source."

"Anyone I know?"

"I doubt it."

Samuels doubted it too. It appeared he didn't frequent the same circles as his colleague. "I thought you didn't rate tip-offs, what was it you said? A waste of time..."

"Depends on who's doing the tipping."

"Still couldn't catch him though, eh?" Samuels couldn't help the smug edge to his voice.

Baker merely shrugged, oblivious to the undertone. "He's a slippery bugger."

"So where does your *source* reckon he'll spring up next? I'm sure Davies will be keen to get there first. That's if he survives the roasting he's getting from the top-brass."

Baker rose from his desk and headed for the door. "You'll be the first to know. Got to get on, crooks to catch."

Baker's sudden enthusiasm for the job was intriguing if nothing else. Samuels narrowed his eyes and tried to figure him out. Maybe he was headed for an expensive divorce and thought a promotion would pay his bills. Whatever the reason, Samuels didn't have time to ponder further. "Where are you off to?" he shot a glance at Davies' office, where raised voices indicated the blame game had begun. "The boss will want to hear your version of events – sooner rather than later, I'd hang fire if I were you."

Pausing with his coat over one arm and a hand on the door, Baker turned. "I'm off to shake Otto Braun's tree, I'd ask you to ride shotgun but it looks like you have plenty of paperwork to keep you busy?"

Samuels declined the offer with a shake of the head. Strong-arming local mobsters wasn't his style. "No, Martin, you go play chicken with Otto, see if you can get anything new out of him, but don't blame me if you're locking horns with Davies when you get back."

"The boss needs results, not pen-pushing, John."

"What he needs is a case that will stand up in court. Procedures followed to the letter and officers who know how to behave."

"I know how to behave, John. I always have, it's you that's stuck in the dark ages, so tied up with rules and regulations you're too scared to make a decision off your own bat without running it by the boss first. Okay, so Miller got away this time, but I nearly got him, almost had my hand on his fucking collar and I only got that far because I took a risk. So don't sit there and lecture me about behaviour."

A risk? Samuels held his tongue. If Baker wanted to dig a hole and throw himself headlong into it, he would happily stand by with an extra shovel, but just now he had some Ts to cross and Is to dot and thanks to some diligence in that area he might just have the last laugh.

The call for witnesses to the latest robbery had paid off and Samuels now had the identity of the customer Frankie had rolled from the queue at the bank. Leonard Parkins had been waiting to deposit the takings from his model aircraft shop. He'd had a particularly good day, it being so close to Christmas, and he'd given a full statement to the police officer who'd called at his house, so full that Samuels suspected the man enjoyed being part of the ongoing drama. Experience warned him to read between the lines of embellishment. The man had eagerly agreed to come into the station for further questioning – despite the lateness of the hour, he sat across from Samuels in the interview room with a coffee and a self-important smile. No doubt happy in the knowledge that as a *star witness* he would dine out on the story for some time to come.

"He ran straight in to me," Parkins explained, "I was very lucky that he didn't shoot me, very lucky indeed."

Samuels slid the still photo from the additional CCTV footage across the desk. The shot captured Frankie in the process of stumbling over Parkins. He was looking over his shoulder, away from the cashiers and the exit, his mask held clear of his face by one hand. "Let me get this straight, sir. The man in this photo stood at the door with the security guard while the second cleared the money from the cashier's tills?"

"Yes. His partner was doing all the work, stuffing the loot into a sports bag."

Samuels checked his notes. The witness statements had been cross checked and the lime green sports bag had been mentioned more than once. There was no evidence of it in the wreckage of the car.

"And the man with the gun ..." he laid a much clearer mug shot of Frankie in front of Parkins, "... this man, according to you, then left his post and threatened you with a weapon before taking your deposit and almost knocking you over as he fled?"

"Yes. Like I said, I was lucky. Very lucky. I may develop some sort of post-traumatic stress as a result."

Samuels suspected a claim to the criminal injuries board would be forthcoming but he didn't encourage the man. "Did he say anything to you?"

"Who?"

"The man with the gun," sighed Samuels.

"No. He just grinned."

"When he took the money from you?"

"Well..." Parkins took a sip of coffee. "Not exactly, he was about to, I'm sure, but it flew out of my hands when the other gentleman stepped back into me. The suspect stooped to pick it up."

"The other gentleman?"

"Yes. I did explain. It's all in my statement. The man with the stick. He wasn't in the queue initially, just waiting for an appointment, I expect, but all of us were herded together away from the cashiers and he almost trod on my foot ... or perhaps it was his stick. I don't recall. I was too busy keeping my eye on the robbers."

"So what you're saying is the suspect pushed past this gentleman, who collided with you?"

"No, no, detective. He pushed past *me*. He seemed annoyed that I'd got in his way."

Samuels looked up sharply. "You just said he was grinning. Which was it, grinning or annoyed?"

Parkins gave an exasperated sigh. "He lifted his mask and grinned like he'd just landed a winning lottery ticket, then he scowled as he shoved me aside and smiled when he picked up both our deposits. Is that clear enough for you, detective? Good grief, it's little wonder these criminals have been running wild for so long!"

Samuels gritted his teeth. "Both?"

"Pardon?"

"He picked up both deposits?"

"Yes, detective. Like I said in my statement, I had over seven hundred pounds, a mixture of cash and cheques, all in a brown envelope. A drop in the ocean when you consider the reported value of the haul, but to me, a small businessman, money I can't afford to lose. I shall claim on my insurance naturally."

"Naturally. But you said the suspect picked up *both*. What did the other man drop?"

"A package."

"A package?"

"About this size." He held his hands apart to illustrate the size. "In one of those Jiffy bags. That's why I imagined he was waiting for an appointment rather than a cashier. It didn't look like it was filled with money. It was box shaped and heavy. It clattered as it hit the floor."

Samuels spread out more photos. None of them were particularly clear. "The other gentleman, is he shown on any of these images?"

Parkins adjusted his glasses and studied the images, taking his time, humming and hawing as he stretched Samuels' patience to the limit. "That's him there." He stubbed his finger at the image. "He was a little rude, as I recall. Storming off after the robbers left, without so much as a beg your pardon. I mean, if he hadn't knocked me, I wouldn't have dropped my deposit and I'd be seven hundred pounds richer."

Samuels frowned. He recognised the man leaning heavily on a walking cane. More importantly, he now had the connection that Davies had been looking for. Frankie hadn't singled Parkins out of the queue, he'd been grinning at someone far more interesting.

Curiously, Judge O'Hanlon had neglected to mention his visit to the bank on the day of his daughter's disappearance, or the subsequent theft of his property. Wrong place, wrong time? Somehow, Samuels doubted that.

It was time to have another chat with the judge and he was tempted to get the man out of bed. Perhaps he'd be more inclined to tell the whole truth about his daughter's absence if he was stood on the front step, in his pyjamas. He pulled on his coat and reached for a Dictaphone. He needed to be sure he caught every word the judge said – and everything he didn't. As he palmed the tape machine, the lack of weight indicated that someone had taken the batteries. "Bloody coppers, always thieving something," he grunted. Of course, he knew who the culprit would be and crossed straight to Baker's desk, yanked the top drawer open and rifled through the assorted detritus. Finally his fingers found the cylindrical shape he was looking for, but when he opened his palm, it wasn't a battery in his hand. It was a shell casing.

His phone rang as he reached the car park. He expected a summons from Davies. The meeting had been breaking up as he'd left the building but he wasn't keen to chew the cud with his boss. He was about to take a leaf out of Baker's book and do a little reconnaissance of his own, en route to O'Hanlon's, and he didn't want to explain to Davies why he felt it necessary to question the motives of a fellow officer.

"Hey, John. How's it going? I'm still hanging on for that exclusive. I've got some kid, barely able to shave, eyeing up my desk. He says I should follow him on Twitter. Bugger that. I'll follow him alright, right to the Quayside and give him a push."

"Ralph." Samuels glanced at his watch. It was after eleven. "You're working late."

"Propping up the bar, John. I'll stand you a pint if you're free."

"Sorry, Ralph, busy busy. Anyway, I haven't got anything new. Try me in the morning, I have an inkling things may be coming to a head."

"Good stuff, that's what I like to hear."

Samuels slipped on his seat belt and started the car, letting it idle while the heater kicked in. "I don't suppose you've had your ear to the ground while you've been terrorising the office junior?"

Ralph snorted down the phone. "Aye, as it happens, that's why I called. I heard something today while I was ensconced in the gents doing my crossword."

"Oh yes?"

"Tosspot Cameron was bemoaning the fact that the O'Hanlon girl had contacted him."

"Strange. I'd have thought he would've welcomed the scoop. He's certainly been making his mouth go about her fate at the hands of her kidnapper. The boss had to have a word in his ear, said he was jeopardising the case."

"Aye, I heard he had his wrist slapped, and ordinarily I'd agree about the scoop, but Cameron's suddenly gone all cloak and dagger. There he was, hiding in the khazi, whispering down the phone. Thought it must be a bird he was muttering to, but then he started gabbling about how he didn't want to get on the wrong side of the judge, didn't want to queer his pitch with the hoi-polloi of Newcastle. The funny handshake brigade I guess."

"Masons, or Geordie Mafia?"

"Bit of both. Business associates, of the *you scratch my back, I'll scratch yours* variety."

"Not unlike you and I..."

"Well, aye but we're not huddled behind the bike shed agreeing deals that should have gone out to tender, we're just two mates doing right by each other."

"Okay," continued Samuels "So Cameron is in with the corporate bigwigs, what has that to do with the judge or his daughter?"

"O'Hanlon is still a respected figure, despite his retirement. He has influence. He's on a few boards, guest speaker and so forth."

"And?"

"And..." Ralph dropped his voice, and Samuels imagined him shielding the phone conspiratorially from the other drinkers.

"And ...?"

"And, Cameron shagged his daughter."

"No!"

"Aye. I thought you'd like that."

"When? Are you sure? I mean I know she plays the field but she's just a kid by comparison to him."

"Well," continued Ralph, warming to his subject, "Cameron was saying to whoever was on the other end of the phone, that he only dated her to get in with her father – and once he was in, he dumped her. He said if it all came out, it'd scupper his position and he'd lose the support of those he's been cultivating. Put it this way, he wasn't pleased to get her call."

"Wasn't worried about being a suspect then, just about losing some business connections?"

"Fuck. I never thought of that. You think he took her?"

"Somebody took her, Ralph – and Cameron's the only one who's spoken to her since. Convenient or what?"

"Hey, the man is shite, but kidnap..."

Samuels checked his mirror and pulled out of the car park onto the main road. The street was almost empty. Snow had reduced the traffic to a trickle of night workers and reckless drivers. "Who was he talking to, Ralph?" There was a lengthy pause and Samuels figured Ralph was trying to get his head round the idea of a psycho boss. Personally, he didn't think Cameron was guilty of anything more serious than being a tosser, but it didn't hurt to explore all possibilities. "Ralph?" he prompted.

"Sorry, John, just getting a refill before last orders. Cameron was in the next stall. I was ear-wigging as best as I could, but even I couldn't get the other side of the conversation."

"He didn't mention a name?"

"I don't think so."

"What was the outcome? Did he mention what he planned to do?"

"I guess they were talking about what he should do if she called again. I think the guy on the other end suggested that Cameron delete the call and say nowt."

"You think it was a man?"

"Well, only because Cameron was effing and blinding throughout the conversation."

"How do you know they talked of deleting messages?"

"Because Cameron went quiet, like he was listening or thinking, and then he swore down the phone, said something along the lines of *'you're asking a lot, you bastard. If I delete everything, can they recover it?'*"

"And then what?"

"More silence, then he grunted his agreement and hung up."

"And there was nothing afterwards? He didn't call anyone else?"

Ralph paused. "No... I waited until I heard him banging out of the door. He was still cursing an hour later when I travelled down in the lift with him."

"And when did all this happen?"

"Earlier today. This is the first opportunity I've had to call you. Bloody Cameron had me up at Druridge Bay covering some protest about opencast mining. I ask you, middle of bleedin' winter, Northumberland Coast. That man has got it in for me. Ruddy leathers are frozen to me arse."

Samuels shook his head, both at the image of a Ralph frozen to his bike and the tangled mess the case was turning into. Jasmine O'Hanlon had a string of ex-boyfriends as long as his arm, so the fact that she and Cameron had been an item didn't really shock him. The reality of the situation, however, was that Miller or Jasmine might well have been trying to make contact through Cameron, only to have their messages deleted. "Have you told anyone else, Ralph?"

"No, I'll leave that to you. Just remember my name when it's ready to go global. I'm looking forward to seeing Cameron pick up his own P45."

Twenty Six

Bloody, effin' snow!

We've been driving around in it for over an hour and it's steadily losing its appeal. It's no longer *looking a lot like Christmas* and to my now jaded eye, looks more like a gulag up north – Blyth maybe. Up and down back alleys and suburban streets we go, keeping out of sight while the police post their road blocks and cast their nets and hope for a bumper catch. No chance. We little fishies are headed way upstream and we're far too slippery for the likes of them. Well, to be precise, *I've* been driving. Jack's just been sitting there, slumped against the door, glowering, getting madder by the minute. I think he may have reached that point where common sense goes out the window and blind rage takes over. For some reason his ire is directed at me. I can't imagine why.

We're looking for Micro, that slimy, double-crossing, thieving tosser, and I guess he doesn't want to be found because he's not where I'd expect him to be. We've checked all his usual haunts, the doorways, the squats, the dark places that cease to exist when the sun comes up, but he's disappeared and I know I didn't give him enough cash to turn over a new leaf and join the rest of the human race. So whatever he took while my back was turned is worth more to him than either me, or the consequences of betrayal.

The voice is scolding in my ear, white noise, and I'm trapped between the stations of laughter and malice with no tuning dial to free me. It's getting louder and I need it to stop so I can put everything in order and decide what to do – because so far nothing's working and time's ticking on. I want to yell *shut up*, that usually works, but Jack's watching me, really watching, like he can see what's going on inside my head. That's not good, so I bang my head with the heel of my hand, in a casual, *jeez, silly me,* kind of way, and whisper s*hush* instead. I'm not sure Jack's buying it but I tough it out, now isn't the time for crazy stuff. The voice is right to mock me, though. I've made two glaring mistakes.

Number one – trusting Micro.

Number two – leaving *her* alone for so long.

One mistake is one too many. I know I'll pay for my errors. She's dying, I can feel it. I need to get back. Back to her, before I lose control completely.

And I need to do it without Jack.

There you are, decision made. For good or bad.

"We're wasting time," he says, pulling himself to attention as if he's been listening to my internal monologue and realises that the ball's just gone out of play. "We're not going to find him. If he's got any sense he'll be laying low, and if he's as stupid as you seem to think, he'll have traded the package for another fix, and, like sewage to the sea, it'll find its way back to McKenzie eventually. We need to make the best out of a bad job, forget about him and pick up the girl."

No. I shake my head. He doesn't get it. I can't forget about anything. That's the whole point. That's what they want me to do. What they've wanted me to do all along. But I can't forget what I don't know. And the need to know mocks me constantly, like a weevil burrowed beneath my skin, itch-scratch, itch-scratch, with no relief in sight. Jack thinks he's calling the shots now, that it's his show and he's in control, but he's wrong. This is my game and I'm still in charge. I had it all planned down to the very last detail and now it's slipping away and the voice is hee-hawing and Jack's got that smug *I'm a better villain than you*, look on his face and I can feel my heart starting to batter me from the inside out.

I don't know how long I can keep this up.

This is how it starts, how it always starts, like a virus deep inside growing exponentially. I try to hang on, think happy thoughts, but what makes me happy would make Jack scream, so I don't go there. In my head I visualise the board, the players and the prize, but it's all skewed, no one is where they should be.

"That wasn't our deal," I reply. "You only get Miss Twinkie when I get what I want." I'm gripping the wheel so tightly my knuckles are bone-white and my arms begin to shake. The van kicks out its back end as I overcompensate.

"Be careful," Jack snaps.

Huh! He can talk, the getaway driver who crashed his own car. I stamp the accelerator, imagine it's his face, and the van fights back, lurching forward in a great hulking leap, bald tyres skidding on the accumulated snow. One-Eye slides back against the van doors, clattering paint pots as he goes.

"Slow down for fuck's sake!"

"Fine!" I spit back at him and slam on the brakes. We both test the seatbelts to the limit as the van slides the length of the alley, One-Eye rebounds with a grunt and slams into the back of my seat. The van's progress is only halted by the opportune dumping of a week's worth of refuse and a sofa-bed.

The ensuing silence is broken by the ticking engine and the gentle rhythmic buffeting of fluffy dice against the windshield. I'm hugging the steering wheel, my cheek against the dysfunctional horn, Jack's hands are braced against the dash, and we're both taking heaving breaths as if we've completed a marathon only to discover it was a false start and we have to re-run it. False starts – the story of my life.

He wants to kill me. Squash me flat like a fly. I can see it in his eyes. I have that affect on people. Big deal. Right now, I want to kill *everyone*. Line them up and shoot them down. Doesn't matter who, doesn't matter why, bang-bang they're dead. In my head, the voice begins to croon approval, softly. It's a tune I recognise from before, a tune I dread. It knows it's winning, which by default means I'm not.

"We need to go get the girl first." Jack's words are icy, menace lightly restrained, as if I'm a child to be handled with care. Maybe I am. I can certainly feel one hell of a tantrum building. He doesn't fear me any more and he really should. I'm still not at boiling point, and boy do I burn. But he doesn't understand. No one does. My bottom lip trembles with frustration and I bite it hard enough to draw blood. "Tell me where she is?" he presses, "You said the room was flooded, is she by the river? You don't want her to die, do you?"

I watch him distractedly, his words rolling over me, blah, blah, blah, as I count slowly down from ten. He's stopped bleeding, or at least the brown stain on his coat isn't any bigger and he seems to have forgotten about the pain. Either he's been at the sauce when I wasn't looking, or he's too preoccupied to notice. Anger therapy – works every time.

I shrug at him like I don't give a shit. But I do. I really do. "A deal's a deal. You can't have her yet. She's all I have. I can't get the box without her."

"Fuck the bloody box," he yells, as restraint finally crumbles. He grabs my collar under my chin, twists it tight and I gag at the sudden pressure against my throat. I know he wants to squeeze harder, I can see the battle in his eyes. He's as desperate as I am, and part of me wants him to keep on going and just put me out of my misery, because I *am* miserable, and warped and not right in the head, and all those other things they've been telling me since I was old enough to start asking questions.

You see, despite all his faults, that loser Micro *gets* me. We're cut from the same scheming, lying, damaged cloth. I need to find him and if Jack won't help me, I'll do it myself – as soon as I've seen to her.

Behind us, in the back of the van, old One-Eye growls a warning. Jack ignores him and leans in close.

"Don't you understand? You're in this as deep as I am. After your little stunt at The Scally, they all know what you look like, and they all know you're with me. Otto and his foot soldiers, McKenzie and his acolytes, they're all out there, right now. You think you're so clever, with your theatrics and weird shit, but you're not. I'm telling you now, they'll catch us and kill us, and they won't give a fuck. The only way we can outsmart them is if we're holding all the cards. Jazz O'Hanlon is the important currency here, not you or me or your bloody box."

He's not shouting now, he's pleading, as if both our lives depend on it. He's worn out trying to work *me* out and I don't blame him, I do that to people, grind them down until there's nothing left but dust and desperation.

"And which are you, Jack, soldier or acolyte?"

His grip slackens and he glances at his hand as if he's just realised how close he was to strangling the life out of me. He's shocked, I'm not. I know more about him than I know about myself. And that's the tragedy of our little partnership. He shrugs a confused apology, thinks that'll work. Any other time it probably would. Today it won't. I need what's in the box more than I need him, or her.

It's time to cut him loose.

I slip the nylon bag from my shoulder and throw it at him. It glances off his cheek, skims his shoulder and lands with a soft thud in his lap.

"What now?"

Yup. I'm a crazy girl. Get used to it.

I wrench open the van door and slip out into the snow. "The deal's off, *Mr Bank Robber*, you're free to go. There's your money and your happy pills. Head for the ferry and have a nice effin' life."

And now I'm running and I hear him shouting behind me, banging the van door, swearing, threatening, pleading and calling me all kinds of nasty things, his heavy, skidding footsteps hot on my trail. But he won't catch me, not in his condition.

Hot tears sting my cheeks and I scrub them away furiously. *I'm in charge, I'm in charge.* I repeat it over and over, the beat marking time with my pounding feet. The voice cackles in my ear, tinny, painful – and joyful. I shake my head to be rid of it, jam my hands over my ears, and then I'm running awkwardly, no arms to windmill my balance, slipping, sliding, scrambling away from him ... my so called *opportunity*. I should have known. My life will never change for the better.

I'm back to square one.

Just me and the voice.

And her.

Twenty Seven

Bloody idiot. What the fuck was she playing at?

He couldn't keep up, she was far too quick, but he had to follow if he had any chance of finding Jazz and saving his own neck. When Spook rounded a corner and slipped out of sight he pressed on, doggedly following her footprints in the snow.

In the distance, sirens wailed eerily, the rough edges smoothed out and buffeted by the snow, so he'd no idea which direction they were coming from. He'd been aware of them off and on since the escape from the dene, but only now, when he was alone and growing more desperate, was it easy to become paranoid and assume all police activity was in some way connected to him. The likelihood was that the criminal underbelly was simply going about its business as usual and the police were on extra time. That's what he hoped, anyway.

He crossed a silent car park, snow covered cars appearing as shadowy, indistinct icebergs in a sea of white. He hesitated, one hand clutching the stitch in his side as he balanced his desire to be out of the cold and behind the wheel of a decent car with his need to follow on foot. He kept going, exiting the car park through the same hole in the mesh fence as she had, squeezing through the narrow gap, wincing as the ragged wire caught his cheek. Up ahead, beyond a stretch of wasteland, the bright lights of the main road illuminated the vista and he caught a glimpse of her again as she prepared to duck down another alley.

"Spook!" His voice, deadened by the snow, barely covered the distance but she slowed and turned her head.

She shrugged at him dismissively, a slight dip of the shoulders that barely broke her stride. She wasn't waiting and she certainly wasn't coming back. *Fuck!* He pulled out his gun, raised it and aimed, but even as his finger teased the trigger, he knew he didn't want to hit her and equally couldn't be sure that he could miss accurately enough to scare her. What would it achieve anyway? He had enough money to get far away, and if Jazz O'Hanlon was the forfeit for freedom, so be it. She was nothing to him, an over-indulged society babe who should have had more sense than to talk to strangers. *Shit*. He lowered his gun, kicked at the snow and knew he couldn't just leave it like that. Not when there might yet be a chance to save both her skin and his own.

"Wait!" he yelled. "We'll do it your way..."

She gave him one of her crazy smiles and started to run, skidding and sliding, glancing back over her shoulder at him, rather than where she was going. He raised his gun again, levelled it at the snow just ahead of her." Okay," he shouted, "Maybe we'll do it *my* way." He squeezed the trigger and the snow exploded at her feet. It was close but it still didn't stop her.

He saw the car as it rounded the corner, headlights partially obscured by snow, and although he yelled out a warning she continued to run, directly into its path. Barely doing twenty, it cruised silently, like an orca hunting seals, more than capable of stopping in time, easily avoidable if she'd heeded his warning. Instead, the car speeded up. Spook caught the bumper with her hip, glanced off the bonnet and hit the ground on hands and knees, dazed and vulnerable for the first time since they'd been thrown together. He began to run, heart pounding, frustrated curses fuelling his journey as he covered the dark, uneven ground in stumbling, clumsy steps. He'd almost cleared the wasteland, was almost there, when the car pulled up a few yards from where she crouched, and reversed back. A man he recognised climbed out.

Miller skidded to a halt just shy of the road and stepped back into the shadows, his fingers tightened on the Glock as Spook was manhandled to her feet by Baker. Held tightly by the scruff of her neck, her body hung limp and Baker showed little concern at her condition. After a furtive scan of the area, he cuffed her wrists and flung her into the back of the car. She didn't resist, didn't seem able and Miller couldn't be sure whether he was witnessing another of her games, or whether the stakes had just been raised. He took a hesitant step forward. Anyone else and he wouldn't have missed a beat, but could he shoot a police officer and walk away? Was Spook actually worth the consequences of that? He exhaled slowly, raised his weapon and took aim, but no matter how much was resting on it, he couldn't squeeze the trigger. *Fuck!* He lowered the gun as the car pulled away, and as it passed the shadowy spot where he stood, Spook shot an accusing glance in his direction. The look on her face said it all.

He had fucked up.

And Jazz O'Hanlon was going to die.

The vibrating phone in his pocket eventually drew him back and he realised he'd been standing in the dark for some time, staring at the space where Spook had been. His gun hung from his hand. His gut churned, and deep in his shoulder, pain pulsed with the cold. He checked the display, expecting Otto or McKenzie, keen to crow about their latest acquisition. He psyched himself up to play poker with men who cheated every hand, but instead, the *unknown caller* teased curiosity from the depths of his desperation. He blew warm air into his cupped hands and set off in the general direction Spook had been taking. As he walked he took the call, phone pressed tight against his ear, listening silently for the caller to speak first.

"Jack Miller?"

"Who wants to know?" He reached the kerb where the car had halted, kicked about in the snow as if that would offer up some clue – and when it didn't, he crossed the road and headed for the river.

"My name is DI John Samuels. I'd like to help you if I can."

"Help me?"

"Yes. You're in a bit of a mess, Jack. There are lots of people very anxious to speak with you, and a few more who would happily dispense with conversation and go straight to 'reasonable force', but I thought you might prefer to talk with me."

"Why would I want to do that?"

He ducked down a back alley, sought the cover of a doorway and checked his watch. Samuels wasn't going to catch him out that way.

"I'm a very good listener. I'd like to hear your side of the story."

"Maybe I'm not ready to tell it."

"We have a serious situation, Jack. Only you can prevent it from getting worse."

"I doubt that," muttered Miller.

"I know you're hurt. Do you need medical attention? I can arrange that and ensure your safety in custody."

"Safety?"

"You need to come in, Jack. You'll be shot if you resist arrest. You know that, don't you?"

Miller checked his watch, less than two minutes of chat time left."

"I don't want that to happen," continued Samuels. "What I want is Jasmine O'Hanlon returned safely. We all do. Hand her over and then we can talk about all the other stuff."

"Stuff?"

"The banks, the girl and the judge."

"What about the judge?"

"Come on, Jack. I'm not stupid. I know there's a connection. Why else would you rob the man and take his daughter?"

"Who says I did?"

"Jasmine says you did."

Miller snorted. Bloody Spook.

"I've been looking at your file, Jack. I know you have history with O'Hanlon, but revenge, kidnap, is that really you? I don't think it is. I think you're too clever for that. You're not a ..."

"You have no idea what I am."

"Exactly, and that's why we need to get together. Do the right thing, Jack. The girl is an innocent in all of this."

Do the right thing? Miller ended the call and shoved the phone back into his pocket. Everyone wanted the bloody girl and only Spook knew where she was. And now the police had Spook in the palm of their hands and were too stupid to realise it. Of course, that supposed Baker was doing the job he was paid for and not simply running errands for McKenzie.

He pulled his coat tighter around him and closed his eyes briefly. For once he didn't know what to do or who to trust. Relief came in the unlikely form of an ugly great lump of a dog whose growl had Miller reaching for his gun. The dog hunkered down a few feet from him, panting from exertion, its flapping jowls spraying slobber onto the snow.

"Scat!" Miller emphasised his words with a wave of the gun in the dog's general direction. The dog merely moved closer until it sat by his side, resting its weight against his leg. It pressed its scarred snout into Spook's nylon bag and inhaled noisily, its tail twitching. "You're wasting your time, mate. She's long gone, and you don't want to hang around with me. I'm in the mood to shoot something."

Movement across the alley caught One-Eye's attention before Miller was even aware of it and this time the dog's growl was so low and menacing, Miller placed a restraining hand on his collar. "What's up?" he murmured.

Out of the gloom between a builder's skip and a row of wheelie bins came the hunched figure of a man, a down-and-out, weaving drunkenly from side to side as he favoured one leg over the other. The noxious odour preceding the shuffling wreck teased some equally unpleasant memories. Micro. It had to be. Miller smiled slyly. Good things come to those who wait.

He followed him for a couple of blocks, keeping to the shadows, one hand on his gun, alert to the fact that this seemed far too easy and convenient. His footsteps were muffled by thickening snow, but nevertheless he hung back, biding his time, making sure that Micro wasn't being tailed by McKenzie or Otto or the police.

The call from Samuels had unnerved him, put things into glaring perspective, but it had also offered him an out if he chose to take it. Whichever way he decided to jump, he needed something to trade. He had to get to the girl before someone got to him.

Micro ducked into a doorway, light spilled momentarily onto the street and Miller watched as the man exchanged a few muffled words, while an obvious handshake exchanged his next fix. He needed to grab Micro before he had time to enjoy it. As the door closed and the street was plunged into darkness, Miller stepped forward.

"Going on a trip?"

Micro froze at the sound of Miller's voice. He turned his head slowly and offered up a weak smile. His hands raised in supplication. "Aye, well, that was the idea." He shuffled backwards, his eyes flicking from Miller's grim expression to the dark stain at his shoulder. "Listen, it was all down to her, mate. I was just taking orders, doing as I was told."

"You always do as you're told?" Miller weighed the Glock casually in his hand, turning it this way and that, Micro's eyes protruding as he followed every twist. Not as hammered as Miller had initially thought. Was everyone playing a game? The dog shouldered between them, twisting his jowls into a lopsided snarl. Micro glanced furtively from one to the other. Sweat glistened on his pallid forehead despite the weather. He swallowed nervously.

"So ... er, how's the patient?"

Miller raised one brow. "You really want to remind me how you played keyhole surgery with a fucking Stanley knife? Had fun, did you?"

"Fun? I ... I saved your life, mate," stammered Micro. "Keep that in your head when you're playing vigilante."

Miller supposed he was right, and he should be grateful, but he wasn't. He was pretty much done with manoeuvring between the chicane of hidden agendas and dubious motives. "You have something belonging to me," he said. "I want it back."

"Not me." Micro edged away. "I've got nowt ..."

Miller grabbed an arm and spun him around, ramming him so hard against the wall that his head snapped back against the brickwork with a sickening crack. A whimper weaseled out through pursed lips and Miller prevented any further cries with a forearm across his throat. He jammed the gun viciously at Micro's temple and the flaccid skin depressed into an angry red whorl. "Don't make me shoot you, for fuck's sake. It's not bloody worth it. Apart from anything else, I don't need the extra hassle. I'm done with all the games. I want the package you nicked from the bag. You can hand it over, or I can take it. The choice is yours."

"Games?" spluttered Micro "You don't know the half of it."

Miller cocked his head and studied the man, the bulbous rolling eyes, pungent perspiration and layers of grimy ill-fitting clothes suggested Micro hadn't seen good times in a very long time. He was the kind of loser he'd normally have crossed the street to avoid, but for some reason he and Spook shared a connection that was crucial to current events. He lowered his forearm and leaned away from the stink. "What do you mean?"

"She's playing with you. She plays with everyone."

"Tell me something I don't know?"

Micro shifted awkwardly and Miller shook his head in warning.

"She's barking mad," continued Micro, his words skittering past a quivering bottom lip as if he'd suddenly realised the quicker he spoke the sooner he'd be free – or dead. "You know that, don't you?"

"She's different, I'll give you that."

"Don't go thinking she's stupid though, she knows exactly what she's doing. What she wants, she gets, and bugger anyone who gets in her way."

"Do *you* know what she wants?"

"I'm not her keeper."

"Right, but you go way back. She said as much. How long have you known her?"

Micro snorted, "Long enough."

"Where did you meet her?"

"Where do you think?"

"Shared a padded cell, did you?"

"I wasn't an inmate." Micro's mouth twisted into a sly smile and Miller realised that the man wasn't drunk at all, just a very convincing slob. "I was the one who kept them all sweet. Where do you think I learnt my trade? The nutter's best friend, that's me."

"*All* sweet?"

"Misfits. Butter wouldn't melt – sugar smiles – knife in your back."

Miller thought of Jazz O'Hanlon bound to a chair and left to rot. His stomach sank. God knows what twisted things the pair of them had done to her. She was probably dead, had likely been dead from the very beginning, which meant that he could probably look forward to the same fate, either at the hands of Otto, McKenzie, or a marksman's bullet. But there was always the slim possibility that she was still alive and he had to be sure.

He grabbed Micro's throat and applied just enough pressure to ensure the man's full attention. "Forget crazy town, let's keep it simple. I need the package you took from the bag, and I need the girl you took from the car. And before you think about playing any more games, let me just clarify, I'm fucked either way, so pulling this trigger won't lose me any sleep at all."

Micro swallowed noisily as if he couldn't quite get past the stricture at his throat. His whole body trembled beneath Miller's restraining hand. "I ... I don't have the package."

"Really?" Miller leaned all his weight against the gun.

"...but I can get it."

"Good. And the girl?"

"The girl?"

Miller shook his head reprovingly.

"I don't know anything about a girl. The only reason I was there was because of you. She knew I could get the bullet out and keep you alive. That's all, the limit of my involvement. I did you a favour, mate. You should be fucking thanking me. If it had been left to her, she would have cut her losses and hacked off your bloody arm. Like I said, she likes to play. She collects toys, pulls them apart to see how they work. She rarely puts them back together." He raised one open palm to reveal the small packet of white powder he'd just bought. "She broke me years ago. She's still playing with you."

Miller scowled. "Forget about her. I'm the one with a gun at your head. Where's the package?"

"Back at the farm."

"The farm?"

"The funny farm. Where all this started."

"The infirmary?"

"If that's what you want to call it. It's been many things over the years. Hospital, asylum, dumping ground, was even a slaughter house there at one time. Dumb animals, dumber people. Think of the weirdest, sickest thing your mind can come up with, and it went on there. Why do you think they closed it down? Why do you think *she* hangs out there? She gets a buzz from all the weird shit. She can't get it out of her head."

"Can't get what out of her head?"

"Stuff. What she doesn't know, she makes up."

Wasn't that the truth! Spook's head was so messed up she didn't need any more buzz. All the same, Miller was confused. The hospital, institution, whatever name it went by, had been closed for some time. If Spook was as barmy as she appeared, then care in the community had definitely missed the mark.

"It closed down five years ago. She's too young..."

"Old enough."

"And since then?"

Micro gave a lopsided smile. "That's the thing with being crazy. Really crazy people are so mad they actually seem sane. Go about their daily business, like any old guy in the street or girl next door, but it's just waiting, like a virus ... for an opportunity. You got money you can hide it, if you haven't then you adapt. Like a fucking chameleon, you give people what they expect to see ... until they turn their back and then ..."

"Fuck, you're as bad as she is."

"No one is as bad as she is."

Miller inhaled. He was losing focus. He pulled it back sharply. Time was running out. "Forget the girl. Tell me about the package?"

"It'll cost you."

Miller laughed. The little shit couldn't help himself. He had a hand at his throat and a gun at his head and still thought he could deal. Now that was desperate, or insanely stupid. "Okay. How much is your life worth?"

"It's in the shower room, on the third floor," spat Micro, "behind the fucking cistern. Insurance for when things blow up – and believe me, they will. The plod are everywhere, the streets are crawling with the buggers. Your fucking fault, eh? It's not safe now. You want to risk a visit, go right ahead."

"*Insurance*, what's in it?"

Micro shrugged. "I didn't look."

"Oh sure..."

"No. Seriously. It was locked."

"Locked? What kind of a package is it?"

"It's a box, about so big."

A box, about so big. Miller was staggered by his own stupidity. The crash had evidently knocked sense out of him, rather than in. Spook, on the other hand, had the box right under her nose the whole time she was playing *doctor death,* and had failed to spot it. It would have been funny, if the life of Jazz O'Hanlon wasn't hanging in the balance. But what was so important about the contents that both Spook and McKenzie were willing to go to such lengths to get it?

"Half a million in cash and all you take is a box you can't open. Why?"

"Basic supply and demand, the more people want it, the more valuable it is."

"You in bed with Otto or ... ?"

"With whoever's need is greater."

"You do know this is what she wants, what she's raising hell looking for?"

"So?"

"Loyal shit, aren't you?"

Micro's lip twisted sourly. "Loyalty isn't a word she's familiar with. She'd put a knife to my throat if it suited her."

"Maybe she has good reason." He loosened his grip on Micro's neck and lowered his gun. "This had better not be another game, a trick to get me where you both want me."

Micro shrugged. "I don't want you anywhere. If it's a trap, then she'll have done the setting and there's not a damn thing you or I can do about it. Cogs in the machine, mate. That's all we are. Get used to it."

"I'm not your mate, I'm a wanted man, or didn't you notice. How do I know you won't go running to the police if I let you go?"

"I guess you'll just have to trust me."

Miller and the dog snorted in unison. "One last thing, what's the deal with the judge? Do you know why she's so obsessed with him?"

Micro edged away. "He has the truth, and that's all she's ever wanted."

"The truth about what?"

"Murder."

"Huh?"

"You want details, you'll have to ask her." He smiled slyly, "Just make sure you're armed when you do."

"And that's it?"

"All I know is that whatever it is, *not* knowing has shorted her wires. She isn't always this crazy you know, sometimes she'd even pass for normal. Life's kinked her out of shape and it's going to take a bloody big hammer to straighten her out again."

"And that's all you can tell me?"

"That's all I know."

"Shame..." Miller swung the butt of the gun against Micro's temple. It connected with a dull thud and he crumpled to a heap in the snow. "Well, I guess we're done then."

Twenty Eight

It's all going wrong, inside and out. Jack's gone, Micro has slipped between the cracks in the pavement and buggered off to never-never land, she's gasping her last and I still don't have the box. I take a breath. *Think*. In my head the voice repeats the word over and over until I can't do anything *but* think. It wants me to fail, I get that. There's only one of us can succeed, but this time around it has to be me. Okay, I admit it, I was hasty, a weakness of mine. I should have kept Jack on side until the end, but it's too late now. He's out there, somewhere, trying to save his own skin – my bad – and what he fails to realise is that he can't do that without me. I'm the *vicious* in a circle that just keeps spinning around. I wanted to scare him, teach him a lesson for being such an arrogant, effin' shit, but I didn't mean for him to die, others maybe, but not him – he's growing on me in a sick, Stockholm syndrome way, but that's what's going to happen, as surely as night follows day. If he finds the box – if he opens the box, then all he can look forward to is a bullet.

My leg reminds me that it's folly to fight with a car. I have some sympathy now for Jack and his whining, but a dead leg won't stop me. Not when the cop in a suit thinks he's got one over on me. Effin' Ginger-nut!

"You can't do this!" I spit the words at the back of his neck, but he keeps on driving like an automaton. Mirror – indicate – manoeuvre. Jeez and they think I'm the freak. "Let me go!" I kick my feet at the back of his seat, ignore the pain that shoots into my thigh and pummel for all I'm worth. Ginger-nut just shakes his head and changes up a gear. I catch his eye in the mirror and he's laughing. Big mistake.

Hands cuffed behind my back, I'm at a disadvantage. The doors are locked and even if they weren't, my stunt double is busy elsewhere. I settle back, ignore the mocking laughter in my head, and try another tack.

"You can't arrest me. I haven't done anything wrong."

"You can complain all you like, love, heard it all, seen it all, water off a duck's back. Sit tight, we'll soon be there."

"Where? Where are you taking me?"

"Somewhere nice and quiet. Someone wants a little chat, off the record. You tell him what he wants to know and you're free to go."

"You're a policeman, you can't do *off the record*. There are rules, boxes to tick, forms to fill."

"And you'd know all about rules."

He shoots another glance at the mirror and smirks. I remember how he tried to yank me off the wall. Idiot thinks because I'm kooky on the outside it must run all the way through, like a stick of Blackpool rock. He couldn't be further from the truth. Inside I'm not kooky. Inside I'm pure malice.

"I know about rights. The right to remain silent."

"Good, how about exercising that right and shutting up until we get there."

I think about ways of ensuring that he stays silent forever. I get to number ten and the voice whispers approval in my ear.

Outside, the snow is building. A winter wonderland, but this isn't Narnia. If it was I'd be the Snow Queen and Baker would be stone by now. I know where he's headed, I'm counting down the familiar streets and my heart begins to play an unwelcome rhythm. *Panic, fear, miss-a-beat* it repeats over and over, until the missing beats threaten to shut me down. I close my eyes and focus on why I'm doing this. I don't do fear.

I can't stay silent. It's not in my nature, not when I have a head full of words just bursting to get out. I pluck some at random and throw them Baker's way.

"You're wasting your time. I don't know anything."

"I think you do. Why else are you playing stooge for Miller?"

Stooge! This is *my* bloody game.

"Miller? Who's Miller? Never heard of him."

"Cute."

"So, he robbed a bank, big deal. Nothing to do with me. He's a guy in the street, that's all. Snappy dresser, shit driver. What more can I say. Can I go now, officer?"

"Where is he?"

"Robbing the tills at Tesco for all I know." I lean forward between the seats and lower my voice so that he has to cock his head to listen. "It's an illness you know – kleptomania. I can see it now, a traumatic childhood, lifting sweets at the eight-'til-eight and progressing to banks when he grew out of cola-cubes. A good shrink, a few electrodes, and Bob's-yer-uncle, reformed bank robber. He could be a model citizen with a little work. Tinker, tailor, soldier ..."

"Sit back," he snaps.

"I'm just trying to be helpful. I know about these things." I wriggle my wrists, to no avail. The cuffs are far too tight.

"I'm sure you do. Sit back."

"Then again, if you don't get it right. If you squeeze too hard, you end up with a nutter – and let's be honest, we don't need any more of them, do we?"

"Sit back, shut up ..." He reaches back with one hand, shoves me hard and I land like an upended turtle on the seat with my hands trapped beneath me. "... and save it for him."

"Him?" Not the man upstairs, surely.

I wriggle furiously until I'm more or less upright. My clothes are all in a twist, my hair is hanging over my eyes like a whole bunch of broken icicles and the stud in the side of my nose has come adrift. Blood trickles down my lip. It's not painful, merely irritating because I can't reach to do anything about it. *Effin' Ginger-nut!* I press my face against the misted window and use my cheek to wipe it clear.

The infirmary gates are wide open, chains hanging loose, security guards obviously too busy securing something else, and we glide straight through without a sound.

Lamb to the slaughter. Baa, baa.

But I'm not giving up without a fight. And that's exactly what I do when he parks up and drags me out, kicking and scratching. Despite my feline genes I'm no match for the cop in a suit, and when I dig in my heels he grabs me tight around the waist, upending me, so all I can see is the ground beneath me and all I can hear is his laughter.

"Save your fight for later."

"I thought this was just a chat..." I splutter as the blood rushes to my head.

"It depends on your answers."

Right.

Mr Fixit is in the entrance and I'm handed over like the package I've been chasing. Close up, he doesn't look quite the idiot I had him pegged as. He smiles at me in a condescending *pat-on-the-head* kind of way, like he knows exactly what's in store because he wrote the next page. I don't squeal when he yanks at the cuffs, I simply store up the anger like a wind-up torch, one ratchet at a time. I figure I might need the energy later.

Baker looks relieved to be rid of me, or rid of *him*, as he scurries back to the car. I suspect it might be the latter. That's the thing about foot soldiers, always on the end of someone else's boot. I watch as he leans in to straighten out the mess I left on the back seat. Oops! Silly plod, using an official car for dodgy dealings, that'll get him in a heap of trouble. I must remember to make an official complaint.

He straightens up and throws me a puzzled look, I catch it and lob it straight back. Bull's-eye. Huh, he's every right to look confused. *Keep up, Ginger-nut.* Even Jack's not quite there yet, in the working-it-out stakes, he's close, just not close enough. The cop in a suit is way off course and that's why he's looking like he's just lost a winning lottery ticket – I'm all six numbers, the jackpot, the best case he'll *never* break and he's too dumb to recognise it. Oh well, must get on. All I need is one free hand. I wriggle my wrist experimentally and Mr Fixit tightens his grip.

"Where's your friend?" he asks.

"Friend?"

"Miller."

I shrug. I suppose he is a friend, as opposed to an enemy, and I don't have many of those – don't have *any* if truth be told. Too weird, too unpredictable, too much of an embarrassment. The voice agrees with a derisive snort that pings in my left ear. *Thanks for that.* I mutter silently. I'm not a total saddo. I have acquaintances – sure, hangers on – definitely, sad-sacks who know no better – absolutely, users and abusers one and all, but no one to share my dirty little secrets with – until now, until Jack. It's amazing how a sharp blade and a few happy pills can mark the beginning of a beautiful friendship. Best mates, me and Chummy, whether he likes it or not. My lips twitch into a sly smile and I flash it Fixit's way.

"He's no friend of mine. Effin' robber tried to kill me."

Twenty Nine

Samuels waited patiently in O'Hanlon's marbled hall. At such a late hour, he didn't really expect an invitation to proceed beyond the austere entrance, but he could hope. O'Hanlon, raised from his bed by his housekeeper, descended the stairs in pyjamas and dressing gown, but despite the night attire, he didn't look like he'd been woken abruptly. Samuels supposed that if *his* daughter was missing he wouldn't be sleeping either. He clenched his frozen hands repeatedly to improve the blood flow and hoped that O'Hanlon would remember his manners and move through to the study and the warmth of the hearth. He didn't want to sit and take tea, he wanted O'Hanlon to come clean, and do it quickly, before Miller took a bullet and any chance of finding Jasmine was lost.

O'Hanlon was surprisingly accepting of the late visit, as if he'd been expecting it and preparing for it. He paused on the bottom stair.

"Detective Samuels, do you have news?" Although the predominant inflection in the judge's tone was hope, it was tempered with a misplaced apprehension that immediately drew Samuels' attention. He could understand the man's fear of bad news, but this was something else and Samuels couldn't put his finger on it.

"That rather depends on you, sir. You need to tell me the whole truth about your daughter."

"*The truth?* My daughter is missing, what do you expect me to add to that?" Now there was anger, and with no attempt to disguise it, O'Hanlon ascended the last stair and punctuated his words by jabbing his stick aggressively at the space in front of Samuels.

Samuels stood his ground. "I've spoken to Ned. There is no engagement. Jasmine broke it off over a month ago. I've also been hearing about another of Jasmine's *boyfriends*, James Cameron, the editor of The Gazette. I understand you know him. I haven't spoken to him yet, would you like me to?"

The housekeeper, hovering by the door, flicked a curious glance between the two of them and O'Hanlon dismissed her with scowl. He stepped closer to Samuels, shifted his weight to his stick and dropped his voice to a low rasp. "What do you know about Cameron?"

"I know he's involved in some unprofessional activity. Some might say fraudulent activity, alongside people with whom you're also connected. At this point, I'm less interested in that and more interested in how this may be relevant to your daughter's disappearance."

"It has no relevance whatsoever. This is ridiculous. My daughter has nothing to do with any of that and nothing to do with him. She ... she's a vulnerable young women, easily taken advantage of by those around her. She needs protection – my protection."

Samuels checked his watch, fully aware of the worsening weather and the fact that he was a good thirty-minute drive from the city – on a good day. He didn't have time for further procrastination. "Look, I'm not here to pass judgement on your daughter or her lifestyle. I'm sure she's a wonderful girl, she's certainly very popular, and of course you want to protect her and her reputation, but the fact remains, if she has not absented *herself*, then she's been taken for a reason, and that may be motivated by something to do with *her*, or something to do with *you*. I'm merely trying to focus our resources in the right direction."

O'Hanlon exhaled noisily, as if he'd been about to explode and was releasing the steam reluctantly.

Samuels continued. "I asked you this morning whether you were involved in anything that might impact on Jasmine's safety. I'm asking again. Think, Mr O'Hanlon. This is very important. An old case, or perhaps a business deal?"

This time O'Hanlon faltered as if waging an inner battle, and Samuels jumped straight in. "Has anyone been in touch with you regarding your daughter? Have they demanded anything from you?"

O'Hanlon shook his head in denial, but the action was in direct opposition to the expression on the man's face. Samuels pressed on, confident that he was on to something but uncertain whether he had the ability to breach the wall of a high court judge, retired or not. The cracks were visible. It just needed a little more work. He changed tack in an effort to loosen the mortar.

"Can I ask why you didn't mention your involvement in yesterday's bank robbery?"

"I beg your pardon?"

"You were at the bank. We have the CCTV footage. One of the suspects took something from you. I'm curious as to why you didn't mention it when we spoke this morning."

"I ... I had other things on my mind, detective. My daughter, for one."

"You didn't think the two events might be connected?"

"Of course not. The robbery was pure chance. Wrong place, wrong time."

"Really? I'm sure you're aware, sir, that the only suspect from the robbery who is still at large, Jack Miller, has now been linked to your daughter's disappearance and is currently our main focus."

"That's ridiculous. The man is a bank robber, not a kidnapper. Jack Miller couldn't possibly have taken my daughter."

"You're that certain?"

"I'd stake my judicial reputation on it."

"That's a bold statement, sir. I'd like to know how you qualify that."

"I sentenced the man."

"And..."

"Detective, I'm not at liberty to say anything more. Perhaps I should speak to your superior?"

"I'm sorry, but if you have information that is relevant to ongoing enquiries, then I could insist that you divulge it, and I suspect you know that. I hope I don't have to insist, sir."

O'Hanlon gave a weary shake of the head. "It appears I chose an honest policeman after all."

"You certainly did, sir. I'll do everything I can within the law to locate your daughter and similarly I'll endeavour to protect the confidentiality of any information you choose to give me. Beyond that, I must do my job regardless of whether the outcome is to your satisfaction or not."

O'Hanlon shrugged. "Very well, I'll tell you what I know and you can decide on its value to the case. I came across Miller more recently than you might imagine. He was transferred to HMP Durham to finish up a two-year sentence. He came with a reputation, a hard man, a clever man, a man who needed to be kept in check. My experience of the man backs up that reputation. On arrival at Durham, he ran the gauntlet of inmates who also believed themselves hard, but were perhaps less endowed where grey cells were involved, and as a result Miller spent a considerable amount of time between solitary confinement and the prison infirmary, both locations as a consequence of fighting. In between times he was a cellmate of Frank Sutton, a known petty crook and rising foot soldier of Otto Braun, local gangster and ne'er-do-well."

That was nothing new. Samuels had already acquainted himself with Miller's file. He knew that Miller and Frankie had shared a cell and no doubt planned the robberies while enjoying room and board courtesy of the taxpayer. O'Hanlon was correct, it still didn't give him a motive for kidnapping, but he wanted to know why the judge was so certain. "He served fifteen months in Wandsworth Prison and moved north for the final three, his sentence being adjusted to allow for time served on remand. You're not telling me anything I don't already know and nothing that explains your belief that he isn't involved in your daughter's disappearance."

"The file doesn't tell the whole story, detective."

"Go on."

"Have you spoken to the arresting officer? I forget his name."

Samuels shook his head. He'd tried. The man was unavailable. He'd been passed from pillar to post, left a dozen messages and given up. "Beddows, his name is Beddows. He's playing hard to get."

"I see. You should try harder. He knows more than me about the background to the case. Anyway, in the absence of Beddows,

I can tell you that Miller didn't actually spend any time in custody prior to his committal to Durham. He was persuaded that there was another option."

"Huh?"

"Miller is a police informant, detective. Recruited straight from remand, his sentence commuted in return for his compliance. He was placed in Durham for the specific purpose of linking up with Sutton and getting close to Otto Braun. He exceeded all expectations. I told you he was clever, perhaps too clever, eighteen months on and he's out there running the whole show, and presumably has enough to put Otto and his organisation behind bars for a very long time..."

"But?"

"But, he failed to deliver and now it's hard to know which side he's on."

"The banks, of course, it was all too easy. Did he have help? Has this all been a giant set-up?"

"I honestly don't know. I was never party to the details. I was, of course, apprised of the intent, but that was as far as my involvement went."

"Is there a possibility that Otto found him out? Maybe that's why we can't find him."

"There's always that possibility. I doubt very much that Miller has made any mistakes, but at the end of the day, he's a young man with a lot of stolen cash and no future without it. He's established himself as a key player in a gang that commands respect and once he hands everything over, he may well have his freedom, but little else."

"And knowing all that, knowing what he's capable of and how desperate he is, you still think he has nothing to do with Jasmine's disappearance?"

"I do."

"Why?"

"I've just explained, detective, Miller is clever and he knows exactly what he can get away with and still retain the protection of his handler, McKenzie. Kidnapping is a whole different ball game. He's not stupid."

McKenzie? Samuels had heard the name before, recently.

"And yet he was named by none other than ex-boyfriend James Cameron, an associate of yours."

"Hardly an associate, detective. We may have attended some of the same functions, along with the majority of the local business fraternity, however I can assure you I'm not in cahoots with any of them and similarly I'm not in cahoots with him."

"I'm not comfortable with coincidence, Mr O'Hanlon, and there are rather too many here for my liking. Whether you accept it or not, you have a connection to Miller, and through Miller, a connection to the man who singled you out at the bank. Through your business dealings and your daughter, you are connected to Cameron, the one man who provides evidence to suggest that Jasmine is being held against her will by Miller. It's a confusing picture that currently has you at its centre. Perhaps that explains why I've driven through a snow storm in the middle of the night, to better understand the sequence of events surrounding both the robbery and Jasmine's disappearance."

"Perhaps it would have been more sensible to phone," grunted O'Hanlon.

"True, but I was trying to save you the embarrassment of airing your dirty washing in public, however if you'd rather continue this conversation back at the station ..."

"I think you're overstepping the mark, Detective Samuels. I have been open and honest. I have no secrets to protect, dirty or otherwise. I simply have a missing daughter and a need to find her by whatever means. I still have influence, should I care to use it."

"And that's entirely my point, sir. Have you been using your influence where you shouldn't, and is that why your daughter is missing?"

Samuels expected outrage, or simply more prevarication, but what he got, quite unexpectedly, was the collapse of O'Hanlon's façade – and without the support from the cane, Samuels was sure he would have crumpled to the floor. He reached out and took the man's arm.

"Shall we sit down, sir, and you can tell me all about it? Whatever it is can't be any worse than the situation you now find yourself in – and may result in the return of your daughter."

"There was an attempted break-in here at the house, the night before last," said O'Hanlon when they were both seated in the study.

"Attempted?"

O'Hanlon pointed to the floor-to-ceiling bookcases lining one wall. The shelves were filled with an assortment of books, the majority protected by glazed doors. One door was missing and the books, though present, were not aligned in the same aesthetic order as the remainder of the library.

"I discovered a broken cabinet door and books scattered on the floor."

"Valuable books?"

"Not especially. The books weren't the focus of attention, none were taken. I rather think the safe behind the shelves was the main target."

"I see. Was the safe opened?"

"Fortunately not."

"But you didn't report it?"

"As I said, the safe wasn't opened. Should I have reported the dislodging of a few books, or the broken lock on a cabinet door? No, Detective Samuels, you and your colleagues have enough to do without me causing additional work. I decided instead to move the contents to my safe deposit box at the bank."

Samuels supposed that made sense, but it was another coincidence and he didn't like it. "Who knew the position of the safe apart from yourself, Mr O'Hanlon?"

"Other than the company who fitted it, Mrs Pottager my housekeeper, and my daughter Jasmine."

Samuels sighed. "Was Jasmine aware of the combination?"

O'Hanlon faltered. "She was. Lately I've denied access and changed the number frequently."

"Why did you deny access?"

"As I've said, my daughter is vulnerable to manipulation by stronger personalities, as can be witnessed by her frequent partners. She sees the world through rose-coloured spectacles, I'm afraid the reality rarely lives up to her expectations. In the past there have been instances where she has been *persuaded*, by others."

"Others? Do you think your daughter may have been persuaded to gain access to the safe?"

He paused and Samuels watched indecision ripple across the man's features. "It's possible."

"But you don't think so?"

"I'm not certain. She has certainly been distracted of late and I worry that she may have new *friends*. I didn't see her before she left, so I have no idea as to her frame of mind."

"And yet, you told me that you saw her on the morning of her disappearance, before she left for the salon. Did you challenge her about the break-in? Did you argue about this or anything else for that matter?"

"I... I may have expressed an opinion. She may have disagreed. I wouldn't call it an argument."

Samuels was confident that it had been far more than a disagreement, but he was confused. If Jasmine had attempted to open the safe, why had O'Hanlon felt it necessary to move the contents, when he could simply change the combination?"

"Would she have damaged the bookcase door?"

"Definitely not, and in any event, the key to the cabinet was still in the door."

Samuels frowned. It was possible that Jasmine had revealed the location of the safe to another, persuasive individual, perhaps under duress. He made a mental note to have the safe and surrounding area dusted for prints. "It would have helped in our investigation if you'd told me about the break-in earlier, sir."

"I see that now ..."

"When did you last change the combination?"

"When I discovered the attempt."

"Okay, so to recap, you discovered the damage, checked the contents, changed the combination and then thought, *what the heck, forget the safe, I'll pop everything in the bank*. Why did you do that Mr O'Hanlon?"

"It seemed the pertinent thing to do, in case whoever made the first attempt decided to return."

"You must keep something very important or very valuable in that safe, sir."

"That's what a safe is for, detective. There's nothing unusual or overtly suspicious in keeping the things you deem valuable under lock and key."

Samuels didn't entirely agree. There was something undoubtedly suspicious about the whole set up, but he couldn't work out what it was. "Okay, moving on to the bank, and more specifically the robbery. Why do you imagine a bank robber, who already has a million in the bag, would delay his escape and risk capture to single *you* out of the queue?"

"I ... I have no idea."

Samuels pulled a face. "I'm sorry, Mr O'Hanlon, but we're back to coincidence again. Who knew that you were headed to the bank?"

"No one."

"Not Jasmine?"

"No. I didn't discuss it with her."

"And yet you were awaiting an appointment when the robbery occurred. When did you make the appointment?"

O'Hanlon's face changed with sudden understanding. "Of course, I phoned to make an appointment with the bank."

An appointment with the very same staff that subsequently stood by and allowed the theft of a million pounds, Samuels could understand if they'd been given word from above to allow the robbery to go ahead, so a trap could be sprung, but what he didn't understand was the significance of the box that had been taken, at great risk to the taker. "It seems to me that the contents of your safe has suddenly become very valuable indeed. Why would that be, sir?"

"I really couldn't say."

Couldn't or wouldn't. Samuels blew out his frustration through pursed lips. "Mr O'Hanlon, your daughter's life may be at stake here. I think it's time you told me exactly what's in the box."

Thirty

Miller needed to sleep. His body ached for a warm bed, a safe, dark place where he could bolt the door and forget that the entire Northumbria Constabulary was on his tail and McKenzie was after his blood. He hugged the shadows, collar pulled up against the weather as he made his way back to the infirmary.

Of course the girl would be there, where else could she be? He wasn't sure why he hadn't thought of it before and blamed his diminishing cognition both on lack of sleep and the alarming sequence of preceding events. Regardless of the mitigating circumstances and the delay, he was here now, but the challenge to locate her was only just beginning. The place was a vast, crumbling wreck, the heart of the main building held up by scaffolding and Acrow props, while the spreading tendrils of ancillary buildings were in varying degrees of demolition. Dislocated wings which had housed specialties such as psychiatry and immunology emerged from the dim moonlight, scaffolding shrouded in plastic sheeting, all dusted with snow.

Jazz could be anywhere.

Spook had indicated that the girl was beneath ground level and, supposing he could trust anything she said, he was acutely aware of the need to locate her before his ability to do so diminished to critical level and before the worsening weather and risk of flooding removed the need for him to try.

Micro had hinted at the building's murky history and Spook's weird connection to it, but Miller didn't care. His bruised brain was already at capacity and he was way past trying to work her out. He had to keep things simple. Find the box, because it was important to McKenzie and therefore to him, and find the girl to save his own skin.

He passed through the unlocked gates unchallenged, but fresh tyre tracks in the snow alerted Miller to the fact that he may have competition in his quest. He stepped into the deep ruts of compressed snow to avoid leaving footprints of his own and followed the tracks to the main entrance doors which now stood ajar. The chains had been severed with a bolt cutter, the padlock hung useless. At his feet, One-Eye heaved an exhausted sigh and collapsed like a bag of wet sand. "Fuck, are you still here?" Miller muttered to the recumbent beast, but the dog's single eye was already closed and all he got in response was a guttural snore.

He hesitated before entering the main building and pulled out his phone. When the number he needed still proved unobtainable, he punched out his only other option and stepped back into the shadows. "You said you wanted to talk," he murmured. "Can I trust you?"

"You can," replied Samuels. Although his delay in answering, and obvious confusion at receiving the call, alerted Miller to the fact that perhaps he shouldn't.

"I need you to do something for me. Get a message to someone urgently?"

"Where are you, Jack? You need to come in and sort this out before things get any worse."

"Get any worse? You have no idea how much worse they're likely to get. Don't mess me about. I really don't have time for it and neither do you."

"I'm not messing about, I'm trying to help you. I know all about you, Jack."

"You do?"

"I've spoken with Judge O'Hanlon, he told me about Durham."

"Right." Miller's gut twisted. He didn't have time to explain, it was far too complicated. He didn't understand it himself. All he knew was the failsafe, the opt-out, the ticket to freedom, was playing hard to get and he was almost at the point of slamming his cards on the table and yelling *I'm out*.

"But there's more to this than you imagine," continued Samuels. "Yes, we need your testimony, but more than that, we need you to hand over the girl."

The girl. Everyone wanted the girl. "Look, if you want the girl alive you need to do as I say..."

"Whoa, Jack, slow down there. You need to keep calm. Jasmine O'Hanlon is an innocent in all of this. Please don't make your situation worse by using her as a bargaining tool."

"My situation? For fuck's sake, what do you think I'm doing here?"

"I don't know *what* you're doing, Jack, that's the whole point. I know what you *should* be doing and it starts and ends with ten million pounds and man named Otto Braun. But you're way off the radar, doing things that at the very least will put you back inside and at the worst will end with a marksman's bullet. You should be sticking to whatever was agreed with McKenzie."

"*McKenzie?*" Miller snorted. "You know McKenzie?"

"I know *of* him."

"Then you don't know shit. Look, do yourself a favour, just listen. Get a message to Harry, Harry Beddows, he's not answering. He needs to fucking answer. He has my number. He knows what to do."

"Harry Beddows?"

"At the Met, go speak to Harry. I can't do this alone."

"Jack, what do you mean? What are you trying to do alone? I need more than that ..."

"For fuck's sake, just speak to Harry."

Miller ended the call. Inside his head, bells were ringing and all manner of alerts were flashing. His world was shrinking, the game taking precedence, and he had no alternative but to roll another die. He glared at the dog. He couldn't risk old One-Eye waddling in and announcing his presence to all and sundry so he tucked Spook's bag beneath its flapping jowls. "Stay – guard – whatever." The dog twitched its tail half-heartedly and Miller pocketed the phone, withdrew his gun and stepped into the darkened reception hall.

He was aware of voices far off down one of the corridors that branched out like spider legs from the central reception hub. He cocked his head and tried to work out the direction. The noise bounced around the empty place deceptively and he swung left to right in an effort to locate and avoid it. He didn't have the time or inclination for a showdown.

He headed for the third floor shower room, reversing the path he'd taken that morning. This time the route was plunged in darkness and as the exposed cabling showered sparks on his head he resisted the urge to test the electricity. Instead he used the light from his phone, sparingly. One quick charge of the battery at his flat was barely sufficient and his ability to maintain contact by phone was now more important than his need to see where he was going. He stumbled along, one hand on the damp wall, his eyes gradually adjusting until he located the stairwell and began the arduous climb up three flights. His body protested but this time he resisted the chemical lure. Above all else, he needed to keep a clear head.

When he reached the shower room he flashed his light and briefly illuminated the space. It wasn't any less eerie than before, in fact the half-light and shifting shadows caused him to hesitate in the doorway, but not for long. The incoherent garble of voices seemed closer now and he wasn't sure whether the sound was transmitting from elsewhere in the building via the spaghetti-junction of pipe-work overhead, or whether he was about to come face to face with someone who wanted the box, or the girl, more than he did.

He scanned the gloomy interior, showers, urinals, basins and in the far corner, a row of closed cubicles. Above each one, a cistern provided water for the flush. There were six in total and he had no alternative than to check each one in turn. He pocketed the phone, stuffed his gun into his belt and dropped the seat on the first. Balancing precariously, he reached up, lifted the cistern lid and felt above the rim. The stench of stale water and dead things hit him about the same time as the icy water washed over the edge of the cistern. He ignored both as he fished about with his hand. The first was empty. *Fuck*. Five more to go.

As he heaved himself up to check the penultimate cistern, he was interrupted by the sound of footsteps in the corridor outside. He braced a hand awkwardly against the lavatory wall and eased out his gun. His shoulder screamed at him, his hand trembled with the exertion, but despite that, he extended his foot and gently pushed the door closed. The creaking hinge mocked his attempt at stealth. He waited for the footsteps to alter course and investigate the noise and after the briefest pause they did just that. A flashlight swept the room, lingering in the corners.

"See anything?"

Miller recognised the voice that barked from the doorway. He took a breath and shifted all his weight to the leg braced against the door.

"It's empty."

"Make sure," snapped McKenzie. "I don't want any mistakes."

The light swept the floor, leaking under the closed door before moving on. When the first cubicle door slammed back against the partition Miller almost lost his footing, by the second, he had recovered his poise and consolidated his position.

"Jeez, big bad gangsters frightened of the dark. What is the world coming to?"

Spook. Miller smiled. So Baker *was* on the wrong side of the line. He should have known by the way he'd thrown her into the back of his car. It was a mistake he'd live to regret. Let McKenzie try to work her out. He would naturally think having Spook in his possession gave him the advantage. He couldn't be further from the truth. Spook was a poison administered by inhalation; how deadly was entirely at her discretion.

"I'd be quiet if I were you," replied McKenzie.

"Why? You're not thinking of shutting me up, are you? I mean, that would rather negate my presence, don't you think?"

"I said be quiet." Miller heard the scuffle as McKenzie emphasized his words with some rough handling and, quite naturally, Spook fought back. He imagined the look on her face, the sly smile and taunting raised brow and he pictured the response she'd get from McKenzie. Regardless of Spook's gaming skills, McKenzie wasn't a man to play with. *Just go*, he muttered silently as his muscles began to quiver with exertion, *Just fucking go*. The next door slammed back against the partition wall and the whole bank of cubicles shuddered. Inside his pocket, his phone vibrated angrily. He tightened his hold on the cistern pipe-work and took aim at the centre of the door.

"Look behind you!" squealed Spook. The gopher dropped his torch. It skittered across the wet floor, and straight under Miller's door where it collided with the toilet pan, shutting off the light. The room was plunged into darkness and Spook dissolved into a fit of manic laughter.

"Fuck!" The gopher's single expletive was echoed silently by Miller. He couldn't hang on much longer.

"Leave it," shouted McKenzie. "Come on, we have work to do."

"Busy bees," mocked Spook, as she was dragged away, her voice fading and distorting with the weird acoustics, "Can't believe it takes two of you to squeeze a little scrap like me. I should take that as a compliment, but I won't, because you're wrong. It'll take a heck of a lot more than you two."

Miller found the box in the last cistern. It was, as both Spook and Micro had described, the size of a house brick and about half the weight. He didn't stop to open it. Shoving it inside his zipped jacket, he clambered down, picked up the torch and headed down to the basement. Spook would have to look out for herself for just a little longer.

Thirty One

Miller couldn't find her, even with the benefit of the torch. He'd scoured the entire basement of the main building, some of it knee deep in icy water, most of it piled high with rat-infested junk, the detritus of archaic medical procedures, or instruments of undeniable torture? Miller wasn't sure, just relieved that Spook hadn't discovered them before she'd played doctors and nurses without his consent. There was, however, no sign of Jazz O'Hanlon and he was losing both the will and energy to continue. She was his ticket out of the mess he was in and he had to find her.

He checked his watch, just gone 4am, a mere thirty-six hours since the crash, yet it felt like he'd been on the lash for a whole week. His entire body was on emergency battery and running so low he could barely put one foot in front of the other. His phone had no signal down in the bowels of the building and his need to make contact with Beddows was becoming more urgent by the hour. Somewhere above him, in the maze of corridors, McKenzie was holding Spook and he was torn between finding Jazz, digging Spook out of a hole of her own making and his own desperate need for fresh air and open space. He was almost ready to head back up the stairs when a movement off to his right had him reaching for his weapon. He approached warily, expelling a relieved breath when a rat disappeared through an open cupboard door. Rats! The place was teeming with the things and the smell they left in their scuttling wake was enough to turn his stomach. He reached out and yanked the door open, ready to expend some bullets and diffuse some frustration, but it wasn't a cupboard, it was the door to a small room. In the centre of the floor was a hatch – and protruding from it were the top three rungs of a ladder.

He shone the torch down into the dark void, but all he could see from the surface were the legs of an upturned wooden chair and a length of nylon rope.

When there was no response to his hushed calls, he stowed the gun and descended the ladder.

Miller didn't need the flickering torchlight to tell him how small the tiny subterranean room was, his own phobia reminded him slyly that he didn't need to see the walls and ceiling to feel each one pressing in on him. *Fuck*. He closed his eyes and tried to calm his escalating heart rate. *Get a grip*. Stepping off the bottom of the ladder, he took a shallow breath. The smell of bad drains, rat urine and chemicals was intense. He prayed that was all it was. He opened his eyes and turned.

He was too late.

There was no one tied to the chair, no one lying face down in the shallow water that lapped at his feet. But as he swept the small room with weak torchlight, the full horror of what the space contained became apparent.

Spook was more than crazy.

Spook was stark raving mad.

Jazz stared back at him from every wall. Vivid images, photographs, sketches and paintings, covered every inch of plaster, from floor to ceiling, many overlapping, possibly a thousand or more, all vying for space and attention. *Look at me*, they screamed en masse, and he looked, because he couldn't drag his eyes away.

The photographs charted her confinement from day one, to day zero, via a mismatched collection of time-slip images and wobbly hand-held footage. Some, blown up to life-size, were so life-like he edged away from the spectacle, while small Polaroid images enticed him closer. A tripod stood in the corner, the camera pointed at the centre of the tiny room, where the chair would have stood, centre stage, when occupied.

The paintings told a far more chilling narrative, with bold splashes of red that Miller suspected might be blood. The pictures were fear and anger encapsulated, pure horror in roll-up and take-away slices. Stuck haphazardly to the wall, some were displayed upside down, some face to the wall so the colour leaching through the paper gave a weird negative image of the girl, trapped behind. Back to front and inside out, just like Spook. He stepped back, took a breath of rancid air and tried to view them again, more calmly, without the edge of his initial shock, but his horror merely hiked a level as he realised they told a chilling story. From the first painting of a howling, bloodstained newborn ripped from its mother's arms, to the last, a screaming young woman bound hand and foot. He didn't recognise this terrified young woman, she was so far removed from the media image, but he did recognise the feral eyes and the scars of self-mutilation.

He took a further step back, hit the wall behind with his shoulder and swung around, panicked, gun arm extended, his hand trembling. The ceiling seemed closer, darker, the floor shifted beneath his feet and he shut his eyes tight and drew another breath. *Jeez,* he murmured as he tried to regulate his banging heart.

On the final wall, the monochrome photographic images were in stark contrast to the violence of the first three. Calm by comparison, they were the hushed silence before the final ghastly scene, the last gasped breath of the drowning man and they showed Miller himself, unconscious and vulnerable, spreadeagled like a human sacrifice, his wounds delicately hand-coloured with red acrylic. The final photo showed Spook, curled at his side, like a faithful dog, eyes closed, knife in one hand, her fingers stained with blood. There was one space remaining on the wall. One final image to take. As he stepped toward it, the camera whirred into action and the flash scoured the room with unnatural light. *Fuck!*

He righted the chair and sank wearily onto it. His head was a mess and his stomach churned with confusion and dread. He had no idea what game she'd been playing. All he knew for certain was the answer to the madness must be in the box.

Thirty Two

Samuels pulled away from O'Hanlon's in a state of confusion. Frustration at the case and his inability to solve it simmered beneath the surface. Unable to vent his spleen at the judge, he took it out on the car – which reacted to his heavy hand by slewing on the compacted snow. He steered into the skid and took a breath. He wasn't convinced he had the whole truth from O'Hanlon, or that he would ever get it without a court order, but for now his priority was Miller.

Miller had the girl and Miller was desperate. Samuels had to ensure his desperation didn't reach critical mass and lead to anything reckless – *more reckless*. He had to admit it couldn't get a whole lot worse than kidnap. Well – it could, but he didn't want to think about how far Miller might go if pushed far enough. He wasn't sure how he was meant to manage a situation where it seemed everyone was working to their own agenda.

O'Hanlon was mixed up in something rotten, whether by design or bad luck was immaterial, and he was coveting his secrets in a box that was last seen in the hands of Miller's dead associate, Frankie Sutton. Samuels believed the good judge was being blackmailed, by whom and for what purpose wasn't yet clear, though as Miller and Sutton were Otto Braun's boys, he was sure the Newcastle gangster would have his finger, or indeed his whole paw in the proverbial pie. As DI Baker had visited the man that very day, he thought it prudent to speak to Baker. Off the record or on, he didn't much care. The fact that he was considering there might be need of an *off* was telling in itself.

His call went straight to Baker's answer phone. Samuels grunted his frustration. If *he* was working night and day, it was only right that Baker should too. "Martin, pick up this bloody phone!" he hissed. He wasn't convinced that Baker was simply too busy with his latest lady to come to the phone – and his suspicion was fuelled not only by Baker's strange behaviour of late but by the shell casing he'd found in his drawer. If, as Samuels suspected, Baker had strayed across the line, there was nothing he could do to help him, but if he was simply wavering then maybe there was time to pull him back. "Martin, we need to talk. This is important, stop pissing about. Phone me back."

He needed to know more about McKenzie. O'Hanlon had said he was Miller's handler, his go-to contact but Miller hadn't asked him to call McKenzie, in fact he had the distinct impression that McKenzie was the last person Miller would choose to go to. Maybe eighteen months of living the gangster life had corrupted Miller beyond the point of redemption, or maybe the reverse was true and McKenzie was cosying up to the men he was supposed to be snaring with his Miller-sized net. He didn't know, because he didn't know the man. But he had a feeling Baker did.

As he pulled up at the station, he tried again to contact Beddows. At four in the morning, he doubted he'd be available either – and he was right, the phone rang out until the answering service picked up. He left a message, stressed the urgency and after sucking in few lungfuls of cold night air, he headed across the snowy car park into the station. He shunned the lift and chose the stairs, simply because he couldn't think of another way to trick his body into staying awake. Two flights, and his heart thanked him for the exercise by adding a few extra beats.

Baker was at his desk when Samuels entered the office. Head in his hands, shoulders slumped. Samuels scanned the room quickly, empty desks and blank computer screens, anyone with any sense was home in bed. There was only one person who had resisted the lure of the duvet, Detective Constable Spears, newly promoted and diligent as ever. He looked up and Samuels caught his eye.

"Sir," Spears acknowledged him with an enthusiasm incongruous for such an ungodly hour. If he'd a tail, it would have been wagging furiously. "I've been pulling together that information you asked for on Jasmine O'Hanlon."

"Information?" Samuels was distracted, Baker hadn't moved. Either his wife had finally caught him out, or something else was troubling him. Samuels suspected the latter. "Ruddy hell, it's four in the morning, Rob. Don't you have a home to go to?"

"You said it was important..."

Samuels crossed to the coffee machine. "Yes... good, thanks, Rob. Leave the file on my desk and get yourself away off home. It'll be time to get up before your head hits the pillow."

"I don't mind. I can hang about if you need anything else."

The lad was keen, there was no getting away from it. Samuels smiled. "No, Rob, you go and catch a few hours' kip. Tomorrow is going to be a long one, I can feel it in my water." He glanced again at Baker, and Spears took the hint and with some obvious reluctance gathered up his coat from the back of his seat.

"Still snowing, sir?"

Samuels took a second coffee from the dispenser. "Bleaching, Rob. Watch how you go, the roads are shite."

He waited until the DC had left, then settled himself wearily at his desk, opened the file and scanned it briefly, his attention wholly on Baker.

"Bit late for you, Martin..." he glanced at his watch, squinting when his eyes refused to focus, "...or early. Anyway, whichever way you look at it, we don't usually see you before breakfast. Has the wife finally caught up with you, or haven't you been home either?" He slid Baker's coffee across the desk, then picked up his own and took a sip.

Baker finally raised his head. He was anguishing over something, for sure. His face was grey, his eyes bloodshot. His usual cock-sure countenance had been hijacked by a nervous tic that drew Samuels' attention to his left eye. Baker acknowledged the coffee, tried unsuccessfully for a smile and settled on a halfhearted grimace instead.

"I've been calling you."

Baker shrugged his indifference.

"You may as well tell me what's up?" said Samuels.

"You don't want to know."

"Try me."

Baker shook his head, wrapped his hands around the plastic cup and paused as he studied the un-dissolved grains of coffee floating scum-like on the surface. Samuels watched as his colleague stirred the coffee with the end of a biro while he gathered his thoughts. When he was done, he took a gulp of hot coffee and glanced up. "I'm in the shite, John. That should please you."

Samuels sighed. "It doesn't please me at all, Martin. I have to admit it doesn't surprise me, but if you're in trouble, maybe I can help."

Baker opened his mouth to reply, hesitating momentarily, as if the words were stuck somewhere inside or he'd been thrown by Samuel's magnanimous gesture. "I...I don't want to pull you into this."

"Into what?"

"Shit, John, I can't tell you, even if I wanted to." He pushed the coffee cup away across the desk as if concerned he might spill it, or throw it. "I've stuffed up big time, took a risk and it's backfired. This is serious, really serious and I can't stop it. Believe me, I want to, but I can't."

"Right." Samuels turned his attention back to the file and made a big deal of scanning the first two pages while Baker sweated a little more. DC Spears had located another image of Jasmine. She looked different, as if she'd dressed down for the day and left her socialite skin at home on the bedroom floor. No designer clothes or photo-shopping on this one. She was alone and she wasn't smiling. The photo was stamped on the back, Bellevue 2013. He tried to remember where he'd heard the name before.

"This trouble you're in," he said when he finally lifted his head, "Anything to do with McKenzie?"

Baker shot him a glance. Eyes suddenly alert, suspicious, hopeful. "What do you know about McKenzie?"

"Not a lot, but I'm curious to know more."

He turned another page. Spears had done a good job. He'd listed and spoken to all of Jasmine's close contacts, the boutique owner who hadn't seen Jasmine for months, the doctor who, quite naturally, declined to break doctor/patient confidentiality but had hinted at a longstanding condition that would deteriorate the longer Jasmine was without care and medication. O'Hanlon had said she wasn't strong, but he hadn't elaborated nor had he mentioned medication. Samuels recalled the shocking images of Jasmine, bound hand and foot, and any hope of a happy outcome to the case began to wane. He doubted Miller had trotted off to the local chemist to pick up her prescription.

He turned the page and read on. Spears had also managed to have a long chat with the footballer, man to man. He wasn't much of a gentleman and he'd a lot to say about his ex. Samuels scowled, the testimony of an embittered ex-lover had to be viewed with caution, but all the same it added a new perspective to the case. He shot a glance at the door, wondering if Spears had left the building yet, he was interested to hear first-hand how the interview had gone. Baker yanked his attention back.

"That's not a good idea, John. The less you know the better."

"Huh?"

"McKenzie, you really don't want to go there."

"Let me be the judge of that."

"I'm not messing about here. I'm not meant to discuss it. *Need to know*, you know how it is."

"I know we're meant to be a team, Martin, and we have a case that's currently arse up." He held up Jasmine's photo, "If you know something that can help us find this young woman or catch Miller, then you need to share – and bugger the consequences."

Baker focused briefly on the image, blinking his confusion, "Who?"

"Jasmine O'Hanlon. Have you forgotten we have an ongoing major enquiry?"

"*Share?* Yeah sure. I'd love to share. I'd love to rip the whole damn thing into shreds and scatter it out the window, so all the bloody gutter press can have a share. But I can't because it's confidential."

"Who told you that – McKenzie?"

Baker scowled.

Samuels eased back in his seat and stretched out his legs beneath the desk. He didn't have time to cajole information from Baker. "I know about Miller," he prompted.

"Do you?"

"Yes. I know about Durham and the deal he made to reduce his sentence. I know McKenzie is his handler."

Baker raked his fingers through his hair. His hand was shaking. "Sorry, John, but you don't know shit."

"Then for God's sake, enlighten me. I can't help you if I don't know what the problem is. I've got Miller in one ear, making it very clear that McKenzie is not his favourite copper and I have you behaving like Newcastle just lost five nil to Sunderland."

Baker's lips twitched into a weak smile. "Hey, don't joke about the football."

"Okay, so tell me what's going on?"

"You've spoken to Miller?"

"We've passed the time of day, yes."

"How?"

Samuels expressed his frustration in a snort. "How do you think? I phoned him."

"Did you run that by Davies?"

"No, Martin. I used my initiative. Weren't you just telling me I should do that more often?"

"And yet you're asking *me* about McKenzie."

Samuels picked up the file and glanced at his watch impatiently. "You know, Martin. I'm a reasonable man, a bloody good copper. I try to give everyone the benefit of the doubt, hear them out, listen to their side of the story, even when I know it's a pile of shite. And it takes a hell of a lot to rile me, you know that, but here's the thing," he pushed his own coffee out of the way and leaned forward over the desk, "There's a vulnerable young woman out there being held against her will and an armed and dangerous bank robber with an agenda of his own, who is so desperate I have no idea what he might do. I don't have time for you to piss me about and neither do they."

Baker blinked his shock at Samuel's outburst. "Right," he muttered, "You want to know what the fuck is going on behind your back, I'll tell you, but I doubt it'll help anyone, least of all Jasmine O'Hanlon. McKenzie's not just Miller's handler, he's the big man, the one who arranged the whole damn show, the reduced sentence deal, the co-operation from the banks. Why do you think we've been allowed to hang onto this case for so long? Didn't you wonder why it wasn't escalated, why help wasn't drafted in from other forces? Why the organised crime boys at the Met didn't elbow us Geordie plods out of the way after the first million disappeared up Otto's arse?"

Samuels shrugged. He had wondered, but he'd been so focused on cracking the case he'd been thankful when they'd been left alone to get on with it. He hadn't wanted the case taken away, but in hindsight it was a glaring oversight on someone's part. "It was obviously all part of the sting, the set-up. Unusual but I expect it was easier to manage, to keep a lid on it when there was only Northumbria involved."

Baker's lip curled. "Oh yeah, it's a set-up alright. McKenzie's been running his boy Miller for the last eighteen months and Miller has been balancing on a very high wire between Otto and McKenzie, while the pair of them twang that wire as hard as they possibly can. Miller's got a head for heights, but they've been pulling him this way and that, and he's been doing whatever he was told so at the end of it all he'll walk away free."

"So, is that not what this is all about, a trap to catch Otto?"

"That's what it was meant to be about, but McKenzie's creaming off the top, has been from the outset. That's why he's keeping it up here away from prying eyes. Miller's been handing over a cut to McKenzie before the money even gets to Otto, but it'll be Otto who takes the fall...and Miller, let's not forget Miller."

Samuels pulled himself out of his seat. No wonder Miller was running. If he couldn't trust his own handler, there was no way he was going to hand himself in.

"Do you have any proof?"

Baker scowled, "What do you think? He has me tied up in knots just like Miller. Money transferred directly into my account, promise of accelerated promotion..."

"And you took it, the money?"

"It's in my account, what more do you want? I told you I was in the shite."

Samuels crossed to the window and took a moment to gaze out at the snow. Baker was a fool, there was no denying that, but the fact that he was talking about it now suggested there might still be time to put things right.

"Does Davies know about Miller and the original deal?"

"No. I don't think so. Like I said, it's confidential. The less people who know the better, that's what McKenzie said – and let's be honest, when you have a snitch you protect your source.

We all have our informants, we don't shout about them, do we? It all seemed perfectly plausible to me. The operation was set up at the Met, no leaks from this end, the perfect situation for McKenzie to play a little double hand. And I walked straight into it."

"How long have you known?"

"Not long. I was leaning on Otto, leaning heavily. Otto is a hard nut to crack. I was pulled to one side, asked to ease off in case I compromised the case or buggered McKenzie's scam. McKenzie knew things about me, knew I needed cash, and he squeezed and I let him. Now I'm up to my neck and I'm fucking drowning."

"Martin, there's no two ways about it, you're in the mire, but don't take a dive out of the window just yet. Let's think about this. McKenzie might imagine he's untouchable but he's made a mistake. The money going into your account, it's a trail straight back to him. We may be able to get him on that."

Baker snorted. "If it was that simple."

"What?"

"He's not stupid. It comes from elsewhere, a private security consultancy, payment for services rendered."

"Services rendered?"

"I've been doing some moonlighting..."

"Ruddy hell, Martin, don't you ever learn?"

Baker spread his hands wide. "I told you I was fucked."

"Maybe not. We have people who can track funds back to source, you know that, it's not insurmountable."

"Yeah, perhaps you're right, and if it was just that, I wouldn't be sitting here considering how many floors I'd have to fall before all this went away."

"There's more?"

"Much more."

"Go on."

"Okay, Miller's the go-between, the poor sod caught in the middle. He knows what McKenzie's been up to for the last eighteen months but thinks, *no sweat, it's all in the plan.* Up till now, he's been clever, kept out of the way, left the bag boys to do the dirty work. His job was to wriggle his way into Otto's affections, collect the evidence against him and walk away at the end of it with a clear record. Now all of a sudden his name is out there, McKenzie is rubbing his hands together with glee and Miller knows he's going down alongside Otto. McKenzie can't allow him to be picked up.

"The last job, Miller was meant to deliver direct to McKenzie, that's why he was down by the docks instead of hightailing it down the A1. McKenzie told him that would be it, the final payoff and he'd be off the hook. Bollocks. McKenzie planned to take the cash and put a bullet in his head. But of course it didn't happen, because Miller totalled the car. As far as McKenzie's concerned he's a liability, expendable. McKenzie means to kill him, always meant to kill him, and believe me, he will. Whether he does it himself or armed response do the job for him is matterless."

"And the girl?"

"Which girl?"

"What do you mean, *which* girl?"

"Miller has a weird little Goth bird tagging along, ruddy Bonnie and Clyde wannabes, the pair of them. Maybe he's screwing her, I don't know. Either way she's a conduit to Miller, an Achilles heel, for good or bad, and McKenzie intends to exploit that. He has her now."

"Since when?"

"Since I....I handed her over to him about two hours ago, kicking and screaming..." He shot a haunted look at Samuels, "I know... you don't have to look at me like that. It was a spur of the moment thing, a desperate act. She stepped in front of the car. I didn't think."

"You didn't think?"

"McKenzie expects she'll lead him to Miller and the box. He'll squeeze her until she breaks, but I'm telling you, John, that girl is something else." He tapped at his head for effect, "She won't give in without a fight and neither will he."

Samuels frowned, "The box?"

"McKenzie has something on the judge, but the judge has something even bigger on McKenzie."

"Bigger than murder?"

"A whole lot bigger. They're playing chicken with each other. The evidence is in the box."

Samuels checked his watch again, aware it was becoming a habit. He couldn't help it. It was almost 5am. The world would be waking up soon, alarm clocks buzzing, milkmen trudging through knee-deep snow, metro trains shaking the ice from the overhead lines – and somewhere out there in the Newcastle winter wonderland, Miller was holding one girl to ransom and McKenzie was about to torture another. They were wasting precious time.

"What I don't get is why are you're telling me all this now? Why not just keep quiet and let things run their course? You get your money and your promotion. Miller, the expendable informant, gets a visit from armed response and nobody's any the wiser?"

Baker stood and reached into his pocket. "Because things have changed and although I'd like to say I'd had an attack of conscience, you wouldn't believe that, would you?" Samuels shrugged and Baker continued. "The Goth girl went psycho in the back of the car, she dropped this." He threw a warrant card onto the desk. "Our man Miller's not an informant. He's an undercover police officer."

"Shit."

"Tell me about it."

"Who knows?"

Baker shrugged. "Me, you and the Goth."

"And Beddows."

"Beddows?"

"Miller's real *go-to*." Samuels wondered why Beddows was playing hard to get, wondered whether McKenzie's rot had spread all the way back to the Met. He pulled out his phone, tried the number and got the message service – again. "Don't you see, Martin? Miller's not out to get Otto, he's out to catch McKenzie and anyone else with their fingers in the till." He looked up and caught Baker's pained expression. "You're small fry, Martin. Come on, there's still time to turn this around and put things right. Where are they?"

"The old infirmary."

"Huh?"

"Information received..." Baker shrugged. "One of my snouts suggested that's where the box was hidden."

"Do you trust him?"

"Not entirely, the reliability of his information depends on how long it's been since his last fix, but it doesn't matter whether I do or not, McKenzie's dangerous and he's there now with the girl. If he can't beat the truth out of her, he'll tear that place apart until he finds it."

"Or until Miller finds him."

They grabbed their coats and headed for the lift.

"Hang on," said Samuels, "If Miller's one of us, who the hell took Jasmine O'Hanlon?"

Thirty Three

The box gave up its treasures with very little resistance. By the time Miller had hefted it against the artwork wall, the lock had shattered and half a dozen of the bizarre paintings had succumbed to the attack and fluttered to join it on the wet floor. Miller wasn't sure which was worse, having them watching him from the walls like jeering crowds at a cock-fight, or milling snakelike around his feet. Something ran across his boot and he kicked out and sent a rat flying. *Fuck!* He dragged in another foul breath and tried to slow his heart rate. The confines of the rancid oubliette were playing havoc with his senses. He desperately wanted out. The pain in his shoulder nagged relentlessly and he was sorely tempted to give in and seek oblivion with the last of Spook's cure-alls. Spook – he'd almost forgotten her. That wasn't good. That wasn't good at all.

He returned his attention to the box and stooped to pick up the battered remains. Inside was a whole bunch of stuff contained by an overstretched elastic band, birth certificates, marriage certificates, deeds to various properties and a whole heap of bank statements, presumably from dodgy offshore accounts if recent events were any measure. The usual stuff, the kind of documentation you wouldn't want to lose if your house went up in smoke, hence the metal box, but nothing that screamed conspiracy or murderous intent. Miller snapped the band and flicked through them quickly, disappointed, unsure what he'd been expecting to find and what, if anything, was so important to Spook that she'd felt obliged to throw off her straitjacket and sharpen her knife.

The torch flickered and he shook it impatiently. At the bottom of the box were two envelopes. The newer of the two, brown and business-like, had McKenzie's name scrawled on the front, the other was addressed to Jasmine O'Hanlon. Both were sealed.

Miller didn't need to open McKenzie's to know what it contained. Judge O'Hanlon was already on his list, right at the top next to McKenzie. He hadn't retired from the bench, he'd bid a hasty retreat before the extent of his disgrace had become known. Perhaps that explained McKenzie's interest in getting his hands on the box. He'd assumed O'Hanlon was the only one with the evidence to put him away. Miller smiled. He was wrong.

He reached for the second envelope and held it up to the failing torch. The paper was old, pink, a remnant from a special occasion perhaps. On the back, printed in blue ink across the seal, was a date, September 1st 1989, Jasmine's date of birth, he guessed. A ripple of caution chided him against going any further and opening the door to something which, he assumed by the lengths O'Hanlon had gone to keep it under wraps, was best left shut. But despite the twist in his gut, he hesitated only briefly before tearing open the envelope.

Inside was a single sheet of paper and a photo of a young woman who, in the half light, looked very like Jasmine. The same gamine figure, beautiful, but strangely vulnerable. O'Hanlon had said the same about Jasmine, that she wasn't strong. Maybe they shared an affliction, mother and daughter, a wonky gene that made them susceptible to anything – or anyone. Miller shrugged, if they did, then Jasmine was doing marginally better than her mother, who had died at the age of twenty three, shortly after giving birth. He knew, because he'd made it his business to know all there was to know about O'Hanlon and McKenzie and all the others who threatened his very existence. Or at least he thought he knew everything. Now, he wasn't so sure. The story relayed to the public at the time was that Mrs O'Hanlon had died during childbirth. Very sad, poor judge, poor Jasmine. But Miller knew that she hadn't and suspected O'Hanlon had suppressed the fact that Sophia had taken her own life, to safeguard his own career and avoid the pointed fingers and accusatory stares, or perhaps to protect his vulnerable daughter? O'Hanlon had lots of secrets to protect.

He laid the photo to one side and unfolded the paper. A letter headed invoice, it detailed the receipt of a consignment transferred, on September 28th, 1989, from an undisclosed location. It provided the account details where payment could be levied and a monthly payment schedule which indicated that back in '89 the good judge was shelling out a great deal of money for something. The address at the head of the page confused him. What was O'Hanlon's connection with the Riverdale Alternative Therapy Unit? And why was he keeping it a secret?

Miller looked from Sophia's photo to the horrific images that screamed at him from the wall and shook his head in disbelief as realisation dawned. He was dealing with some seriously fucked up people, he knew that, but right now there was no one as messed up as him. He heaved himself up, stuffed both envelopes into his pocket and as the torch light finally flickered out he picked up the box, reached for the ladder and began to climb.

He found her, eventually, but he was too late, far too late. Jasmine may have been reported missing less than two days before, but Miller suspected she'd been absent for much longer. Gradually slipping away, vulnerable, impressionable, fragile Jasmine, desperately clinging to normality, to life, like mother like daughter, while Spook fought tooth and nail to be heard.

He'd followed her feral growl as it echoed through the empty corridors, cautiously hugging the shadows, gun at the ready as he neared the operating theatre where McKenzie had taken her, or she had lured him. He suspected the latter. Spook knew the place intimately and this was her game. It had always been her game.

All the same, he was shocked when he saw her, battered and bloody, cowering – or waiting to pounce, he couldn't be sure, but inside his gut tightened. He'd wished her gone repeatedly and even wished her dead once or twice, but that didn't mean she was fair game for anyone else.

Otto's barman, Benny, stood over her, open cuffs dangling from his hand, the lure of the exotic colouring his sweating cheeks with anticipation. Only she didn't look exotic now, her weird persona had slipped and what remained was some strange hybrid, part girl next door, part wild child. Her white makeup mask was a muddied mess, black lipstick smeared across her cheek, mascara teared beneath eyes that were red rimmed and furious. Vulnerable wasn't the word he'd use to describe her, but by removing her cuffs, Benny had placed himself in a very vulnerable position indeed.

"Tell me where it is." McKenzie paced the room, pausing to inspect the various pieces of abandoned equipment. Spook glared her response and McKenzie leaned back casually against the operating table and studied her as if he had all the time in the world. "Or you can tell Benny, I'm easy either way."

Thirty Four

So, here we are – all three.

The voice and her – and me.

The rhymes are back but I don't care now, because it's all too late and I'm losing control. The voice is laughing, shrill and cruel, in my head or out-loud, it's hard to know, but by the look on Benny's pockmarked face I guess my inner demon has come out to play. He steps back, a little less keen now to play truth or dare with a bona-fide psycho.

"Where ... is ... the ... box?" repeats McKenzie in a slow drawl as if I'm an idiot, or a refugee who speaks English as a second language, *Parlez-vouz Anglais*. What is it with men in effin' suits? If I knew where Pandora was, it wouldn't be *there* any more, it'd be in my hot little hands, and I wouldn't be *here* now, allowing myself to be used and abused by a couple of no brainers who haven't got a clue what this is all about.

I flex my muscles and attempt to stand but Benny's boot, hard against the small of my back, prevents me. He's keeping his hands to himself this time, just in case my madness is catching, like chicken pox or impetigo. It's one of his better decisions, me being so exotic and all. I imagine what I'll do to him when the boot is on the other foot.

"So," I say with perfect diction – just to prove a point, "Is this the latest interrogation technique? Ask the same question repeatedly until I fall asleep from boredom...?" I yawn theatrically "or until I lose patience and cut out your tongue?" I wrestle a sly smile onto my face, the voice wants more – always the drama queen, *she* wants less and I'm stuck in the middle – as usual. *Do this, do that, blah blah.* But while I'm still here and my heart is still banging, I'll give it a go. I'm not a defeatist. If I was, I wouldn't be here at all. *I'm in charge, I'm in charge.* I repeat the words under my breath like a Buddhist chant and in my head I hear the tinkle of accompanying bells. *Omm...* It's all a game. But it's *my* game and I'm not done playing.

McKenzie blinks his surprise. He doesn't get me, no one does. He doesn't quite understand what he's caught in his nasty little trap. And the more he wonders, the stronger I get. Confusion – the panacea to all my ills. Now my smile is wide and I'm focused, the internal nagging has stopped. The other two who rent rooms in my head are holding their breath – in anticipation and dread. Rhymes...what did I tell you?

"You want another question?" he spits at me, "I can do that. Here's an easy one – Where's Miller?"

Where indeed? Like I said, I was hasty. If he's got any sense, he's probably halfway to Costa del Crook by now, with two hundred grand in his back pocket. And who would blame him? I'd have done the same – but only after I'd finished off McKenzie. The voice sniggers and way back in the darkest recesses something pings. Of course, Jack's no different from me. What he wants he'll get, no matter the consequences. I shift my gaze from McKenzie's mug and search the shadows for Newcastle's most-wanted. He's not here – yet.

"I have no idea," I stall. "Google, *Bank Robber Inc* or try the local Payday-Loan shop, or the nearest A&E. Last time I saw Mr Bank Robber he was looking slightly anaemic. I guess you've been working him too hard, eh? All that secret meeting and dodging police marksmen stuff – jeez but it's tiring."

McKenzie shoots a glance at his gopher and his mouth slides into an ugly grimace. I see the *will I – won't I* calculation in the narrowing eyes. He wants to shut me up for good, but not yet. For now I'm still useful.

I get another nudge from Benny's size elevens and I stumble forward onto all fours. Benny sniggers behind me, a snotty, nervous laugh that echoes around the big room and bounces right back at him. Big brave man, throwing stones at the three legged dog, I know his type. Big mistake. I shuffle back onto my haunches and wrap my arms tightly around my grazed knees. I'm freezing, so cold my joints are stiff and my fingers scream painfully at me. They took my jacket, my boots and plan to take more, and what they left me isn't enough. The cold is seeping into my bones but I'm buggered if I'll give them the satisfaction of knowing it. I rock back and forth, not because I'm a raving loony, but because it eases my calf muscles and I have to be ready to spring into action, or spring at someone's throat. Then again there are advantages to being deemed a nutter, so I cock my head and flash him a manic grin.

"Fucking weirdo," mutters Benny.

McKenzie shoots him another of those *shut up* glances and risks the safety of his tongue by stepping closer to me. "I'm surprised you find the situation so funny. It appears your lover-boy has dumped you and run for the hills."

Lover? My lips twitch. Not quite how I'd describe him. A quick grope outside The Scally barely counts as anything but a taster by anyone's stretch of the imagination. To be fair, there are things that I *do* love about Jack-the-lad, and things that I don't. His ability to get back up after all manner of dastardly things have knocked him down and stamped on him is certainly one to admire, even if he does have a tendency to labour the point. And I reckon, after yours truly, he takes the prize for keeping secrets. *Sneaky Jack*, so that's got to be another thumbs up from me. But perhaps what I love most about Chummy is that despite his *armed and dangerous, fuck-you-all* persona, he's as predictable as I am not, left to my right, up to my down, and it's that whole plus and minus shit that's going to fettle Mr Fixit sooner rather than later. Genetics, chemistry, physics, call it what you will, but two wrongs always make a right in my book.

"I dumped *him*," I explain patiently, "Effin' loser couldn't keep up."

"Well, let's not waste time debating who's penning the *Dear John* letter, the fact of the matter is you've strayed into something you shouldn't and I'm offering you an easy way out. Tell me what I want to know and you can crawl back to whatever squat or weirdo nest you hatched from."

"And Jack?"

"Don't worry your freaky little head over that waster, leave him to me. You've been screwed, sweetheart. Jack Miller isn't who you think he is. Jack Miller is a dirty little snitch."

I narrow my eyes, partly so I can see him more clearly in the dim light and partly so I appear more convincing in my bewilderment. Of course he's not who he says he is, and he's definitely not who Mr Fixit thinks he is, but who am I to enlighten *he who knows everything*? I roll the dice and watch them tumble.

"I know he's a crap getaway driver."

"That's very true."

"But hey, that's eff all to do with me. You're a copper, yes? So tell me, why are we here, playing truth or dare in the death house with the hired guns, instead of down at the station with all the other shiny plods?"

"You really don't know when to be quiet, do you?"

I curl my lip at him, a threat if he had the sense to realise it, but I know the effect is diluted by the fact that I'm crouched at his feet like a beaten child. "You don't have a lot of options here," I taunt recklessly, "Either arrest me or let me go."

"You forget the third option." He raises his weapon and points it at my head. "At the risk of sending you to sleep permanently, where's the box? We know it's here somewhere.

We're back to the box, which is only right, since that's what this is all about and why *she* won't survive the night. The voice hisses a warning in my ear but I don't listen. I've come this far without any help apart from Chummy – and just now, with a gun at my head, I'm not sure whether he's on the help or hindrance list. Time will tell.

No one could want the box as much as me. I know *I* don't have it and that only leaves Micro. Effin' two faced, double crossing Micro. He took it, he hid it, he blabbed about it. I told him what happens to tittle-tattles, he obviously wasn't listening. I glance around, expecting him to shuffle into view at any moment with his slack jaw and piggy eyes. But it's not Micro who appears from the shadows.

My stomach rolls, a quick sensation that floods my senses in a way that's so alien, my antibodies issue a call to arms and my heart struggles to keep up with a drum-roll of additional beats. Chocolate, puppies, fat ponies and skinny latte, things that are far too nice for a freak like me, fill my head to the tune of *My Favourite Things*. I'm slap bang in the middle of an *I am Spartacus* moment. My first. No one has ever stepped up for me, or come back for me. I'm the weirdo you cross the street to avoid, or pay others to hide. But my sudden euphoric, triumphant *Yes!* shrivels and dies before the word makes it past my lips.

Jack doesn't look like the cavalry.

Jack looks like someone dug him up and left him for the crows.

"You're wasting your time. She doesn't have it," he says as he stumbles into the light.

He's talking to McKenzie, but he's looking at me, all weird, and I know that look. My heart sinks. I know where he's been. I know what he's seen. A little bit of me shrinks inside, that feeling when you catch someone reading your diary and no matter how hard you try you can't remember whether you *wrote* all that evil shit or just thought it. I catch his eye and hold it, and my answer is reflected back at me. Oh yeah, I *wrote* it. The voice whoops with delight at my dismay. Jack just shakes his head, a warning, a dismissal, a disappointment, it's hard to read and I don't know why I'm bothered anyway – but I am. I'm not Spartacus and neither is he. He turns away and focuses instead on McKenzie.

"Jack. I thought you might drop by to join the party. Your little friend doesn't seem to realise how serious this is. She says she doesn't have the box. You say she doesn't have the box. You know how much is riding on this, so perhaps you can tell me who does?"

Jack shrugs and stumbles closer. There's something not right about him and I can't work out what. He throws Benny a look that suggests they have unfinished business and I expect they do, or will by the time the sun comes up – if I don't get to him first. I will Jack to look my way and hate myself for being so needy. But I need him to understand and I don't think he ever will, not now. There's a sheen of perspiration on his face, a slight tremor in the hand hung casually by his side. I wonder, not for the first time, about the things Micro couldn't fix.

He glances down at me briefly before turning to McKenzie with a sly smile. "She's no fucking friend of mine. Little weirdo tried to kill me."

What? Bloody cheek.

"Looks like she's not the only one, what the heck happened, Jack?"

"Shit happened."

He looks my way again and I wonder what he's going to say, whether he'll say anything at all, about me – and her.

"The box, where is it?"

"Where's Otto?" Jack scans the room. He's nervous. I can read the signs even if the others can't. It's not what he's been popping. I can tell when he's juiced and he's bone dry.

"Don't worry about Otto. He's been paid, he's happy, he'll keep his mouth shut."

"And your armed response pals?"

"Stood down, Jack. After the trick you pulled at the dene, I figured we'd best sort this out ourselves. But they're only a call away if I need them. I'm not stupid."

"And neither am I. What about these two jokers?"

He means Benny, who it has to be said, is worthy of a joke or two – and me. And I don't joke about anything.

"Be nice, Jack, we're all friends here. You want the Goth? you can have her. You want to make sure she doesn't blab? you can have that too." McKenzie swings his aim back to me, "There's even an extra grand in it for you, but I need to know who has the box."

Jack looks at me like he's debating whether I'm better dead or alive.

"Twenty grand and I get to kill her."

Effin' twisted turncoat. He's no better than Micro. Huh, *Spartacus* – I'll nail the bugger to the cross myself.

McKenzie's laughter resonates around the tiled room. "Jack, you've grown a pair. Shame it's taken so long, we could have made a good team."

"Sure we could."

"Be my guest. Shoot her now and get it over with."

"Too easy. She's led me on a fucking wild goose chase all over this city. It's time she did the running."

"You want to play hunt the freak?"

Jack shoots me a smile and I throw a snarl back.

"Fine," agrees McKenzie. "Twenty grand and you get to claim the fox's tail. But you do it in your own time. Okay?"

"Okay."

"So, Jack, tell me, who has the box?"

Jack reaches into his jacket, pulls out a battered tin and holds it aloft. "I do."

"Noooooo!" I launch myself forward, the first dog out of the trap, the first runner off the blocks – always ahead of the pack, and Benny, caught off guard ogling my arse, does a double take and rugby-tackles me from behind. Effin' loser catches my ankles as I scoot across the tiled floor. His full weight slams into the back of my thighs as he scrabbles to get a decent grip and keep it. "It's mine," I scream at Jack, as I pedal furiously, wriggling, twisting, kicking until my scatter gun attack catches Benny square in the face. He howls his protest and suddenly his punctured eye is the centre of his universe and I'm free.

Never underestimate a three legged dog.

But I'm not. Free that is. Now it's Jack who has me by the throat and I'm still fighting, jumping, reaching for the box like some pathetic urchin begging for scraps. I'm sobbing my frustration inside, and screaming my fury right at his face. I hate myself for my feeble desperation and I hate him even more. I reel it in and take a breath.

He throws the box at McKenzie and I watch impotently as it tumbles through the air, broken lid flying open, papers fluttering free like confetti at a bizarre marriage of inconvenience. "Noooooo...," I repeat softly, helplessly, the word stillborn, barely able to squeeze its way around the giant boulder of disappointment and betrayal that threatens to choke me. Even the voice is speechless with disbelief. McKenzie lowers his weapon and dives like a rabid dog frantically scrabbling for the prize. Jack steps back, tightens his grip at my throat and shakes me sharply. My teeth rattle, stars cloud my vision. I jam my eyes shut tight and howl my dismay, and there in the blackness, the moment repeats in slow motion. Pause replay, pause replay and I see what I'm meant to see.

The box is broken.

The box has already been opened.

Jack leans down until his mouth is at my ear, his breath hot and urgent. He's breathing heavily, like he's the one who's just done a workout, whose world is about to explode and I know it's adrenalin and drugs and all kinds of weird shit that's been cooking and curdling inside him for the past thirty-six hours. I know that's my fault because I've been playing with him, prodding and pushing him. But all the same, he's Chummy – my Chummy, or at least I thought he was ...

I feel the barrel of his gun at my temple and his breath in my ear.

"Run," he whispers.

And I run.

Thirty Five

Davies' face was puce. Dragged out of bed at stupid o'clock was reason enough to sour his milk, but when apprised of the situation, and Baker's complicity, he'd rattled into action in an effort to prevent the whole sorry show from going tits up. Now at 6am, the derelict hospital was surrounded by officers, with all possible exits blocked, while inside the grounds armed response kept a more discreet vigil. Still dark, the snow had finally stopped and the whole site lay shrouded in white.

"Are you sure they're in here?" He pinned Baker with a look bitter enough to make a lemon wince.

"This is where I dropped the girl off, sir."

"Dropped her off? I'll drop you off, you bloody idiot – right off the top of the Tyne Bridge. You can ruddy well swim home. See how that clears your sinuses. Where was your fucking brain when all this conniving was going on, eh?"

"I didn't know that Miller was one of us, sir."

Davies shot an incredulous look at Samuels. "And you reckon that makes a difference? Bent is bent. Murder is murder, doesn't matter whether it's an undercover officer, a crackhead, or a poxy snitch from the Scrubs."

"Yes, sir."

"Aye well now's not the time for post mortems, there'll be plenty time for that when Internal Affairs get their teeth into you. Now's the time for making ruddy silk purses out of sow's ears."

Baker shrugged his confusion and Davies stepped close, jabbing a fat finger into his stab vest.

"We know who Miller is now, and it's up to us to make sure he gets out of there in one piece with Jasmine O'Hanlon and the girl you so kindly handed over. You know what you have to do, Baker, and you'd better not stuff up this time – or so help me,

I'll shoot you myself." He turned to Samuels. "Any luck with Beddows?"

Samuels shook his head. "The man is either on an extended sabbatical or a figment of someone's imagination."

"Or dead at the bottom of The Thames." Davies scowled his annoyance at the whole situation. "Who knows what that scroat McKenzie has been up to? Twisted southern tosser, thinks he can come up here, corrupt my officers and play stick-'em-up on my patch. I always knew there was something different about Miller. I never fancied him for the kidnap..."

Samuels' raised brow was lost on Davies.

"Why in God's name would anybody want to hide out here, tell me that?" continued Davies "You know what this place is – what it was?"

"I understand it was originally a psychiatric hospital, sir," replied Samuels as they made their way to the main building, just as Miller had done earlier, following the barely visible tyre tracks.

"Aye a bloody nut house, I suppose that explains a few things, but before that, back in the days before processed food and e-numbers were rotting our bairns' noggins, this whole site was an auction yard and slaughter house. You name it, all manner of beasts were legally traded, illegally baited and topped and tailed on this very spot." Davies flashed a grimace at his men. "Makes you think, doesn't it? All that blood has to end up somewhere. Good for the gardens I suppose."

"Thanks for that, boss," muttered Samuels. "I'll never eat another burger." The place was eerie enough without a freebie ghost tour courtesy of Davies. "What happened to it?" They were nearing the entrance to the building and Samuels dropped his voice to a gruff whisper.

"The abattoir or the asylum?"

"Both."

"Economics, John. Price of land I expect. Sides of beef and pork sausages made way for society's misfits, who made way for your run-of-the-mill sick people, who in turn were shoved aside by developers. The way of the world, dog eat dog. Can't imagine who'd want to live here now though, with the ruddy motorway rattling the crockery."

"I wonder who was on the planning committee?" Samuels mused aloud.

"O'Hanlon and Cameron."

Samuels turned to Baker, "So that's the connection between those two."

Baker shrugged, "Tip of the iceberg, John."

"Write it all down, son," muttered Davies "you're going to need all that and more if you want to wash off the stink."

"Where did they go?" Samuels paused in the entrance lobby, waiting until all those with them were in position. One–Eye, disturbed from slumber, issued a menacing growl and the detectives stepped warily around him.

"Bloody dog," muttered Davies. "Someone see to the ugly great lump. We can't have a ruddy mutt nipping our ankles. Sorry, John, where did who go?"

"The patients...the misfits?"

Davies shrugged. "Shipped out. Care in the community. We don't lock them up any more, John. We just fill them full of drugs and convince them they're sane." He turned to Baker. "Okay, lad, let's see if I'm right in sticking my neck on the block for you. On you go, we'll be right behind you."

Thirty Six

Mother went crazy the day I was born. Put a gun to her temple and blew out her brains, right there in front of my crib. Not the best start in life, I'm sure you'll agree. That's what the voice told me when I was old enough to listen and that's what it's been telling me ever since. Me, I think she was crazy from the get-go – and I should know, I'm my mother's daughter, after all. But I don't believe she pulled the trigger. And that's what this is all about and why I'm here, to find out who did.

They call it the death house, a place of lost souls and broken dreams. A decrepit mausoleum that reeks of fear and decay. First a slaughter house, second a mad house. Now a giant empty vessel of man's inhumanity, a reminder to the civilised that we're only ever one step away from chaos. I can still see the hoof marks pounded into the concrete floor. The velvet nosed, sad eyed, beasts are long gone but the memory lives on in the bones of the building. If I close my eyes I can see them, packed together, crazed cattle and crazier people. In my head they all run in together. One seething mass of injustice – and right at the front, prodded and poked by faceless, white-coated monsters, is mother, all serene and trusting. A lamb to the slaughter. She was crazy alright. But not half as mad as me.

I'm not here to protest the slaughter of dumb animals, worthy cause or not. I'm here to prevent the slaughter of a man who knows what really happened and more importantly, why. And he's here somewhere in the maze of wet concrete and graffiti daubed walls. He's here to hide the truth he thinks I shouldn't hear. I'm here to persuade him otherwise, before we both catch a bullet.

I've been running. Not flat out, but in that stealthy, hold your breath and peep round corners kind of way. All the same, my heart is pounding and my limbs are trembling, a combination of adrenalin and anticipation. I take a breath. I can hear them up ahead. Or are they behind? The acoustics taunt me. Noises ricochet in the concrete shell, swimming pool confusion threatens to overwhelm me. But it isn't chlorine stinging my nostrils. They call it the death house for a reason. Bile floods my mouth and I swallow it down and follow the sounds of collusion and deceit.

He gave me a head start, sixty seconds. I'm counting it down in my head. Fifty-two, fifty-three... They could have just killed me there and then. He wanted to, Mr Fixit, in fact he wanted to do far more, him and his acolyte Benny, and they would have if it wasn't for Jack. Bloody Jack! I should be grateful but I'm not. Another few minutes and I'd have had that slimy, corrupt excuse for a cop on the back foot but Jack had to interfere. Okay, so I was on my knees and headed for a meat hook like the poor sad cows before me, but I had it in hand... like I said, I'm crazy but I'm not stupid. Now, instead, it's a sick game, hunt the psycho girl, and they're one step behind, or one step ahead and I can hear their laughter as they echo the count ...fifty-four, fifty-five.

Jack whispered "Run," in my ear. He meant, *escape*. No chance. They think they're chasing me – wrong! I'm chasing them, right back to their dirty little lair. Jack thinks he's protecting me. He's not. He's just pushing me nearer to the truth. Someone killed my mother and I'm not leaving until I know why.

When I get to fifty nine, silence hangs ominously in the air. I pause, mid-step and strain my ears, desperate for the slightest sound that might indicate their position.

"Sixty. Coming to get you!"

They're ahead, just around the corner and I'm running, bare feet slapping on cold, wet concrete, arms flailing for balance as I skid through a doorway and helter-skelter down a steep flight of stairs. I'm following the sound of their laughter and cat-calls and trying to get my bearings. I'm beneath the old slaughter hall, light fractures through grates above my head like faulty fluorescent bulbs, off and on. I blink, gulp a breath of rancid air and push on. I'm not scared, I'm never scared. Fear is for losers.

I round a corner and there they are. McKenzie and Jack and both have weapons – pointed at me. Shit. Jack shrugs in a *told you so* way, like this is how it was always meant to end. But he's wrong. It's not over yet. I'm not my mother.

"I warned you," he says, in a soft voice that masks the threat beneath. I cock my head and clench my fists. I shouldn't be disappointed but I am. I thought he was on my side.

McKenzie scowls, his eyes flicking back and forth between Jack and me. He's wondering about us, and all the things that don't add up. That's not good. The papers are stuffed in his pocket. He hasn't read them, hasn't had time, but it doesn't matter, he didn't need them – he knows. I shoot a glance at Jack. He wouldn't tell him. He couldn't tell him. Maybe McKenzie followed him down the ladder. Maybe he saw what I did.

"On your knees!" he orders, closing the gap with a shambling gait as if the chase has taken its toll. He aborts my response with a gun at my temple and leans in with a sneer. "Like mother, like daughter."

"What are you saying? Tell me the truth?" I can't help it. I need to know and I don't care any more if I hear it from the man who pulled the trigger or the man who loaded the gun. They're all guilty. *They all have to pay.* The voice yells in my ear, drowning me out. Inside my head, doors are slamming as my unwelcome guests prepare to man the lifeboats and flee the sinking ship. Sirens wail their warning and blue lights flash. And here in the dark of my own personal death house, I wait.

"Stop." Jack stumbles forward, arm extended, gun steady, but he's not. He's swaying. Whatever is cooking inside him is about to boil right over. "She's mine. Twenty grand and I get to pull the trigger. That was the deal."

McKenzie shrugs an apology at me and smiles at Jack, "Sorry, sweetheart, but Jack's right. A deal's a deal."

I drop to my knees as the gun explodes. White light, stars, cordite and deafening noise. But it's not *my* brains all over the ground.

"You want the truth?" Jack hisses as he drops to his knees and his gun clatters to the ground. "You really want the fucking truth?"

In saving my life he's ruined his own and he knows it. McKenzie is sprawled at my feet, his skull a bloody mess. He'll never make the witness stand. I lower my eyes, I can't look at him, I can't look at Jack. Of course I want the truth. It's all I've ever wanted.

"I told you to run. Why couldn't you just run?" His breath is coming in short sharp rasps. As if his lungs have switched off and he's used up all of his oxygen supply. He's drowning right in front of me and all I can think about is me and my sorry life. He drops his head in his hands and sucks in another breath. "Eighteen fucking months and now I can't even hang the bastard."

Now I can see the blood seeping through his jacket and it all makes sense. I should care, but I don't, I can't. I hate myself, but right now all I care about is that he doesn't die before he tells me. I pick up his discarded weapon and turn it right back at him. "I have to know who killed her."

He crouches close, reaches out, and sighs when I flinch away.

"Crazy girl," he whispers. "No one killed your mother. Your mother... isn't dead...."

Thirty Seven

I'm sitting on the steps at Bellevue, like a parcel waiting at left luggage for someone to check me out. Jack sorted out the paperwork. He's the only one I could think of. The only responsible person I know and the only person who gives a fig or a fuck about whether this little nutter ever sees the light of day again. I'm going to try hard this time. I have to. I'm not coming back – ever. I've said that before, I know, but this time things will be different. They have to be.

I've ditched the black, but I've kept the piercings. The scars on my arms go with the territory. They're who I am and I'm proud of the battles I've fought and won. I expect there'll be more. I expect to win them too. Scores to settle – wrongs to put right.

Inside, they gave me the usual spiel, the shrinks, the pedlars in misery, repeated by rote, like call centre staff, in a singy-songy happy-clappy way, telling Jack what they think he wants to hear, that I'm cured, a model citizen, when in truth they expect me back by the end of the month. Breaking news, they can re-let my room – I won't be back. My hand fastens around the bottle of meds in my pocket.

One a day to keep me sane,

Two a day to keep me tame,

Shhhh... I place a finger against my lips. *You promised*, I scold gently.

"Who are you talking to?" asks Jack suspiciously. He narrows his eyes, has that look that says he doesn't believe a word of what the white coated jailers said about me. He's right. Once a nutter, always a nutter.

"No one," I reply. "Just waiting for a ride, hoping some cool getaway driver will get me away from this sorry excuse for a health spa."

He extends his hand and helps me up. A strong grip – warm and welcome. He looks better. Well he'd have to. He was knocking on the pearly gates when I last saw him. Blood poisoning, punctured lung, what a wuss, I told you he liked to whinge. I knew Micro should have worn gloves. Anyway a week on intravenous cure-all, at a hospital where they don't lock you in at night, has put some colour back in his cheeks. Or maybe that's just bruising. Oh well, better out than in.

"You're late," I taunt. "You think I've got all day to hang about in the cold waiting for you?"

He gives me a *what the fuck* look, but he doesn't say it out loud. He's on best behaviour, me being fragile an' all, he doesn't want to rattle my cage and risk a relapse while he's on duty. "Stuff to do," he mutters instead. "Reports to write. Your ass to cover."

I shrug. "He shouldn't have attacked me."

"You shouldn't have put out his eye."

He means Benny who unfortunately learned the hard way about the perils of exotica. "I did more than put out his eye." I smile and ignore the tiny snigger inside."

"I know."

"He attacked me, I shot him."

"With my gun."

"Oops. Why am I not in irons?"

"My gun, my prints. My responsibility. I squared it. He was a scroat, he attacked you when I was down. End of story. If anyone asks, I shot him. Other than that you don't know anything. Have one of your turns, howl at the moon if you like, but you don't say anything. Okay?"

"Ginger-nut saw me. He was first on the scene. I dropped the gun, but he saw."

"I know."

"He'll blab."

"He won't. He has enough crap coming his way. I can make it worse for him or I can make it better. He won't say a thing."

"You did that for me?"

"I guess so."

"Why?"

"You pulled me out of a burning car. I pulled you out of the shit. We're even now."

Okay, that works for me. Once a chummy, always a chummy. Of course he doesn't know about the other gun. Frankie's gun. That's my little secret.

"You ready for this?" he asks as he starts the car. I hunker down in the seat and make a big deal of oohing and ahhing over the futuristic dashboard and flashing lights. *Beam me up, Scotty.* I press a few buttons, fiddle with the radio, anything to avoid his question. I don't know if I'll ever be ready for *this*.

It's a cool car. "You nick it?" I ask by way of deflection. I wrinkle my nose. I recognise that stink. Behind, on the back seat One-Eye thumps his tail and fans *Eau-de-dog* around the interior. "Cool, you brought the pooch. You nick him?"

Jack scowls like he's having second thoughts already. There's dog drool all over the upholstery.

"I made his owner an offer he couldn't refuse. I reckoned you deserved each other."

I grin. I don't know who to squeeze first. "See, you love him really. Admit it."

He glances across at me and I know what he sees, and what he's thinking, a game of two halves; a hybrid, a mutant and still a little weird, but unique and finally complete ... if only. Yeah I look normal, *take me home to meet your mother* normal, but that's just the suit I put on when I go outside. Strip me naked and you see the real me. It's not a pretty sight. Too many years of playing the media whore. I know how to act. I deserve an effin' Oscar.

"Cut it out," he snaps.

"What?"

"You know what I mean. You look fine. You are fine. You just have to believe it. No more weird stuff, no more..."

"Killing?"

He twists his face like he doesn't want to be reminded. "Yeah. The next time you shoot an unarmed, one eyed guy in cold blood, you won't have me to destroy the evidence. You used up your one and only free coupon, sweetheart. You got away with it this time, don't push your luck. I'm not a dirty bank robber any more, I'm a detective, remember? I'm meant to catch killers, not aid and abet them."

He makes me smile. He should know by now I never take advice and there's still a small matter of unfinished business.

Well not so small actually, I have a list. Micro's at the top. I warned him what would happen if he tittle-tattled ... "I owe you one," I reply sweetly.

"Bloody right you do. Keep away from him."

"Who?"

"You know who. If that tosser ends arse up in a skip, I'll know exactly who to come looking for. Do you understand?"

I understand. I turn away, rest my head on the window and listen to Jack's classical music as the world goes by. Every mile takes me further from the past and closer to the future. I should be glad. I *am* glad, but I'm also terrified and I don't do fear.

It's a big place, Riverdale, a beautiful place. High up in the Coquet Valley where the air is clean and the hills join hands and gather round it protectively. It's straight off the top of a Christmas cake complete with snow dusted trees and glitter and good cheer, but for once I can't think of a suitable rhyme, so I file that away for later. I'll never forgive my father, but at least he wasn't a cheapskate.

"You should go see him," Jack says as if he just read my thoughts. I squint at him and wonder whether I was thinking out loud.

"No."

"Promise me you'll think about it. He thought he was doing the right thing."

"He wasn't."

"He knows that now."

I let my silence answer his question. I'm not here to think about my father.

"Are you ready?" Jack asks, as he reaches across and opens my door.

"As ready as I'll ever be."

"You want me to come in with you?"

I do, *so much*. I want him to take my hand and hang on tight, because for the first time ever, I'm vulnerable and need someone other than my own paranoia. A real blood and guts person. A Spartacus. A Jack.

"Nope," I reply with a, *couldn't give a shit*, shrug.

"You want me to wait?"

"Do *you* want to wait?"

His lips twitch his amusement. "I guess I could do that."

"Thank you." My heart is banging. A little cheer erupts in my head. I lean across and plant a wet one on his cheek. Very restrained – polite – I'm learning.

"What will you say to her?"

I take a breath and smile.

"I'll say, 'hi, Mum, I'm Jasmine. My best friends call me Spook'."

Also by B.A. Morton